"*Route 66 Kids,* follows the fortunes of his earlier hero and heroine of *Growing up on Route 66* , Mark Landon and Marcia Terrell, taking them through high school to the eve of Mark's departure for college at Southwest Missouri State College and Marcia's departure for ... but you'll have to read the book to find out where Marcia is headed ... . No matter how often you've heard the phrase/title *You Can't Go Home Again*, Michael Lund's book convinces us that Thomas Wolfe was wrong. You can go home again, and *Route 66 Kids* takes us home wherever home was."

--William Frank, FARMVILLE (VA) HERALD, May 31,2002.

Praise for A Left-Hander on Route 66:

"[*Left-hander*] is a howl with just enough of the serious to add contrast and spice."

--William Hoffman, award-winning author of *Godfires, Tidewater Blood,* and many more

Praise for Route 66 Spring:

"... highly recommended for anyone seeking an absorbing story of life in the Missouri Ozarks, peopled not by the archtypical Hillbilly, but by Lund's characters who bring this fascinating and beautiful part of the country to life."

--ROUTE 66 MAGAZINE, Vol. 12, No. 4 (Fall 2005)

Praise for Route 66 to Vietnam: A Draftee's Story:

--"an engaging tale that flashes back to the narrator's Vietnam War tour.

--THE VVA VETERAN, January/February)

--"able to reach that place so many of us seek within ourselves."

--ROUTE 66 MAGAZINE, Spring 2005 (Volume 12/Number 2)

Praise for Michael Lund's Route 66 Novel series:

"I finished your [first] novel ... and was struck by how perfectly it seemed to encircle (of course) the world of childhood and its heady veering toward adulthood. It's a loving and funny book ... and made me recall with mingled pleasure and embarrassment all the twinges and itches and passions of adolescence. Well done, and thank you for putting it into my hands."

--Carrie Brown, author of *Lamb In Love* and *The Hatbox Baby*

"wonderfully well-wrought [first] novel, set in a place that's still the stuff of myth, about coming of age in a simpler time when sex was giddily mysterious and life was filled with endless possibilities."

--Bernard Edelman, editor of Dear America: Letters Home from Vietnam and Centenarians: The Story of the 20th Century by the Americans Who Lived It

"In *Growing up on Route 66*, Michael Lund gives us a loving look through the telescope of memory, resurrecting forgotten feelings in the idiom of adolescence sharpened by the lens of age and wisdom. He takes us back to a time when the road ahead was a winding one, just right for joyrides, meant to be wandered, with curious roadside attractions and shady stops along the way. Reading [his] book is like returning to a summer night when you were young, when life was full of promise, mystery, and terror, that time at twilight, before your mother called you in to wash up and go to bed, when you were playing a leisurely game of kick-the-can and wished that the game could just go on and on. Fortunately, Lund promises that it will go on, in the second book in his series, *Route 66 Kids*, and, I hope, many more to come."

--Eric Kraft, author of The Personal History, Adventures, Experiences & Observations of Peter Leroy

Route 66 Choir: A Comedy

by

Michael Lund

Copyright

Graphics Credits:

Cover painting by Joy Boettcher Utzinger. Cover design and graphics by John Lund.

Publication date 2010

ISBN 1-59630-058-3 BeachHouse Books Edition

Library of Congress Cataloging-in-Publication Data

Lund, Michael, 1945-

Route 66 choir : a comedy / by Michael Lund. -- BeachHouse Books ed..

    p. cm.

"An excerpt of this novel appeared in Route 66 Federation News (Volume 15, Number 1, Winter 2009) under the title of "Monet's Garden"--T.p. verso.

ISBN 1-59630-058-2 (alk. paper)

1. Retirees--Fiction. 2. United States Highway 66--Fiction. 3. City and town life--Fiction. 4. Choirs (Music)--Fiction. 5. Historic buildings--Fiction. I. Title. II. Title: Route sixty-six choir.

PS3562.U486R6785 2010

813'.54--dc22

2010004419

www.beachhousebooks.com

an Imprint of
Science & Humanities Press
PO Box 7151
Chesterfield, MO 63006-7151
(636) 394-4950
www.beachhousebooks.com

Acknowledgements

My association with BeachHouse Books now stretches back over a decade, and my appreciation for the Press has increased each year. I am especially grateful for the skill and support of Dr. Bud Banis, founder of Science & Humanities Press. I hope we will still be working together another decade from now.

I owe Jim Shifflett thanks again for his wise suggestions on how to revise key aspects of the novel and for his always professional editing.

Without the least understanding how she does it, I admire the art of Joy Boettcher Utzinger, whose painting is featured on the cover. I am equally in the dark about how John Lund designs the cover and graphics, but I can only hope my writing deserves such display.

Finally, I must acknowledge the many generous choir directors and fellow choir members who have tried to make the most of one singer. As always, any errors in fact or inconsistencies of narration in the pages that follow are attributable solely to the author.

. . . yellow leaves, or none, or few, do hang

Upon those boughs which shake against the cold,

Bare ruin'd choirs, where late the sweet birds sang

--William Shakespeare, Sonnet 73

In the architecture of my music I want to demonstrate to the world the architecture of a new and beautiful social commonwealth. The secret of my harmony? I alone know it. Each instrument in counterpoint, and as many contrapuntal parts as there are instruments. It is the enlightened self-discipline of the various parts, each voluntarily imposing on itself the limits of its individual freedom for the well-being of the community. That is my message. Not the autocracy of a single stubborn melody on the one hand, nor the anarchy of unchecked noise on the other. No, a delicate balance between the two; an enlightened freedom. The science of my art. The art of my science. The harmony of the stars in the heavens, the yearning for brotherhood in the heart of man. This is the secret of my music."

– Johann Sebastian Bach

"It was my hope when I came here," said Mr. Micawber, "to have got Wilkins into the Church: or perhaps I shall express my meaning more strictly, if I say the Choir. But there was no vacancy for a tenor in the venerable Pile for which this city is so justly eminent; and he has—in short, he has contracted a habit of singing in public-houses, rather than in sacred edifices."

"But he means well," said Mrs. Micawber, tenderly.

--Charles Dickens, *David Copperfield*

'Why do we got to hang it on God or Jesus? Maybe,' I figgered, 'maybe it's all men an' all women we love; maybe that's the Holy Sperit-the human sperit-the whole shebang. Maybe all men got one big soul ever'body's a part of.' Now I sat there thinkin' it, an' all of a suddent-I knew it. I knew it so deep down that it was true, and I still know it."

--John Steinbeck, *The Grapes of Wrath*

Dedication

For Anne

Prologue: Sweet and Blessed Country

Trick-or-treating nearly half a century ago, Stanley Measure fell over a low fence and lost his childhood. Now he thinks adulthood has slipped away from him the day after his doctor told him more drastic measures were needed to lower his blood pressure.

When he fell that first time, Halloween in 1956, he had the wind knocked out of him--"Woof!" He lay on his side momentarily paralyzed. Nearly five decades later, the new dose of diuretic--at least he hoped that was the cause!--took away his ability to make love. "Woof, indeed!" he thought, momentarily paralyzed, lying next to Felicia.

A stunned eleven-year-old that long ago October day, Stan took stock of his world. Such a review seemed appropriate since he couldn't get up anyway. His diaphragm was frozen, and his mouth gaped while he willed himself to take in air.

His universe--that is, the neighborhood and its motley collection of children--were, backlit by porch lights from across the street, happily parading along thirty feet in front of him.

Halloween was a favorite event in those days for Fairfield, a small Missouri town bisected by legendary Route 66. The annual ritual of demanding and giving treats was especially joyful in Stan's neighborhood, The Circle, because there were so many houses with children and automobile traffic consisted almost exclusively of parents coming to or going from homes. On the western edge of town and bordered by the connecting streets of Linwood, Hill, and Oak, it was a magical kingdom. A magical kingdom for Stanley, that is, until that moment when he decided to take a shortcut from the Barretts' house to the Montgomery's' next door.

The official route established by the moms and dads who sent or accompanied their children in trick-or-treating dictated travel on pavement and up sidewalks to the little stoops at the front doors of the two-bedroom houses built with speed during and after World War II. On most occasions there was to be--out of respect for the principle of private property--no cutting across front lawns. (In regular play such rules did not always apply.)

Still, speed was paramount in the competition to fill a brown paper shopping bag with candy, apples, cookies, and miscellaneous treats. Stan especially wanted to impress his mother (widowed in her second year of marriage) with the size and variety of his take. He knew he was approaching the age where it wouldn't be appropriate to participate in this ancient ritual, so, hoping to set some kind of personal record, he dared the shortcut.

Then he tripped on the low fence beyond a garden plot and, unwisely protecting his haul with both hands, landed flat on his side. Frozen in time and space, he looked toward the street and observed a pantomime. Sharply outlined silhouettes--witches, ghosts, Minne and Mickey Mouses, Lone Rangers and Tontos, armed GI's, a Sherlock Holmes with pipe in mouth, an escort of adults, devils and angels, and half a dozen shapes he could not recognize--danced before him, his world in frenzied motion.

When he recalls that scene now, he notes that it is soundless. Weren't those children excited, calling to each other or parents, announcing the best houses so far, comparing this year's goodies to the last? But the show in Stanley's memory is like a silent movie, eerie and--he now believes--senseless. Even at the time he thought to himself, "Why are they dancing?"

As his boy's head began to clear from the shock of landing and his chest relaxed to let air return, he realized that all these children, even their parents, were going nowhere. Worse, they were going around in a circle--The Circle neighborhood literally but a metaphorical repetition that ended where it began. Years later, a cynical man, he would also conclude that the assorted travelers on nearby Route 66, some headed west to the future and others east to the past, were also going nowhere.

Sure, the children's trick-or-treat bags were full, and there would be pleasure later in the eating. But just as soon after came satiety. Stanley knew from last year--when he'd had one too many rich Mounds bars-- that you could come to hate that bag. While he felt he saw, in the shadowy forms of friends and acquaintances, mouths open with smiles and laughter, he was convinced there was no reason for them to be so happy.

"Fools!" he thought as, gasping, he struggled to his feet. "They have no idea how empty their lives are."

Not only did Stanley Measure never trick-or-treat again, he found little joy in other celebrations, even, to his mother's sorrow, Christmas. "Woof!" Childhood, it seemed, was over.

In 2001 mature adulthood now seemed to be over. "Woof, indeed." The crushing limitations of old age, Stanley felt, would drag him to drooling senility. "If you can't make love any more," he whined to Felicia, "what in the world do you live for?"

Stanley's wife knew he was being melodramatic, but she was also worried. She had heard the story of his last Halloween. And, pulling the sheet up over her, she wondered if she had let him give up too easily. She remembered rescuing him before. An event in their courtship rose in her memory.

After his last year at the University of Missouri, he kept the same summer job he'd had the previous three: watchman in a fire tower west of Fairfield. This meant eight-hour shifts alone in a single room atop a 100-foot-high steel tower.

Constructed in 1948, the tower provided, on clear days, views up to fifty miles in every direction. However, like fabled Route 66, visible for miles, the tower would soon be turned into a relic by the forces of change. Satellite observation doomed the fire tower, and America's passion for speed turned most of that highway of dreams into interstate service roads.

Stan invited Felicia to visit him in the single room with its 360-degree view of Ozark countryside. And she somehow suspected that a confession of feeling might be elicited by that quiet space. There would only be the two of them.

"What do you do up here all day?" she asked, breathing heavily after the climb (a dozen switchbacks with decreasing numbers of stairs from turning to turning). She assumed he would pull out hidden reading matter, a portable radio, decks of cards for solitaire. He just looked puzzled at her question.

"Well, you know, I look for smoke. That's the job."

"But every minute? How do you keep your concentration?"

"There are things you do. Regulations say a warden must change his position at least once every ten

4

minutes--looking east, north, west, south." He pivoted as he spoke, and she copied his revolution. "I have a timer." He pointed to a small hourglass.

"Surely there's a telephone?" Her eyes swept the little room and then saw a unit on a shelf below the north-facing window. "You could call someone? If you were lonely."

Stan and Felicia had not really dated, but they'd grown up near each other. He generally kept apart in The Circle. A war widower's only child, Stan built electronic equipment (walkie talkies, a ham radio, his own primitive security system) in an attic bedroom.

During this summer, though, he'd starting coming by Hillcrest Drugs several evenings a week. Felicia worked at the soda fountain, and, always sociable, she chattered as he nursed a vanilla cream root beer. When she showed an interest in the tower and his job, he invited her to drive up. He said the view was great. She imagined the rich variety of tree species.

Staring through the windows in the east wall of his observatory, Stan admitted, "Maybe it is lonely." He saw the radio he listened to occasionally, the phone he'd never used. "Maybe I should be married. I'd have someone to call and someone to go home to." He turned around, the same hollow feeling in his heart he'd had on that fateful Halloween. "You want to?"

He hadn't planned any such declaration. Luckily, Felicia, knowing his sad family history, had anticipated his question.

"*O sweet and blessed country*," thought Felecia years later, recalling in her mind's eye the view from the fire tower and seeing before her now the naked backside of the man she still loved. "*The home of God's elect! / O*

5

sweet and blessed country," she thought. He'd been a good husband--until now.

Had there been a bright side to Stan's Halloween fall so many years ago? Perhaps, the wisdom gained from experience. He was never again taken in by the myth of an Easter Bunny; he knew his mother left a coin in place of his lost tooth; the sky was not the limit to personal ambition.

But what silver lining could lie beneath a loss of virility now, Stanley lamented, gazing at his failed self in the dresser mirror. Before the next summer he would find out. And then--to his mind, miraculously--his manhood revived. Felicia rejoiced; but, every once in a while--every once in a great while--she saw the restoration of his manhood as a mixed blessing.

Volume I: Advent

Chapter 1: In the Likeness of Fire

On the Sunday after September 11, 2001, Holy Trinity's old rector asked his congregation, "What are your thoughts?" It was the time in the service when he usually gave his sermon.

"Our thoughts!" Stanley Measure whispered to his wife, in his mind's eye seeing frantic crowds fleeing down different Manhattan streets. "He's the one who should have thoughts."

"Shhhh," hushed Felicia, thinking to herself that Stan wouldn't have paid attention to the sermon anyway. She also prayed that he was not thinking again of his own recently fallen tower. She nodded forward. Robin Shure was rising from a front pew.

Father Klein had briefly recounted what was then known about the attacks--the burning towers of the World Trade Center, scarred fields in Pennsylvania, attack on the Pentagon--before inviting comments from the congregation. Like Stan, Felicia thought this a dangerous procedure. "A free-for-all," she said to herself. "That's what we'll have, a regular, stirred up, hornets' next."

"I see Christ," said Robin simply. She was standing below the lecture. "I see Christ rushing into the burning buildings."

As she spoke, her eyes swept across the varied parishioners. But then her gaze gradually rose to the one stained glass window high above the entrance doors.

"All those firemen and policemen," Robin went on, "didn't think of themselves or the danger. It might have been the hot flames of hell, but they just came on straight ahead."

Stan grimaced, never comfortable with expressions of faith. He seldom attended church, especially now that his son was grown and his daughter off to college. But this Sunday he had felt differently. Adrift himself in early retirement, he latched onto the tragic national event as a springboard for the expression of his personal frustrations.

Robin's eyes were riveted on the dove high in the window. "Through the doors, up the stairs, into the smoke and . . . and . . . " She paused, as if unsure what to say next. Then she asked, "Who did they meet? '*In the likeness of fire . . . he whom the Lord foretold suddenly, swiftly descends.*'" She sat down abruptly.

The church was silent. Stan was unexpectedly moved by this simple declaration. Felicia, who knew this woman's strengths, smiled in approval. A local artist, Robin lived with an older husband on a small farm ten miles from town. She positioned life-size sculptures in fields and woods. Dogs, porpoises, llamas, pigs--a lifelike menagerie.

"Well, that could have been worse," Stan thought, confident that the invitation for people to speak would still lead to irrational outpourings. He was not disappointed, as half a dozen parishioners soon offered laments for the lost, anxiety about what might happen text, and vague schemes of retaliation. But, by the time the service ended, his generally negative opinion of humanity was contradicted again, this time by a local dignitary.

Before that, Sharon Rich, the social worker who'd puzzled many when she gave up her yodeling, explained, "My neighbor says we need to tear down those grain elevators east of town. They're landmarks. And the same people can use them to bomb Fairfield."

"We should declare war on someone," insisted Chester Lott, the sawmill operator. "I think Russia's behind it." He was known for deadpan irony, but his friends couldn't tell if this time he was being serious.

"Oh, it's Castro," insisted Maria Fuentes, cake maker and gossip. "He's been waiting since Bay of Pigs to get back at us. Those Twin Towers, they are like giant American cigars to him."

"I blame warmongers right here in the U.S.A.," Sonja Petersen nearly shouted. She hated men and blamed any act of violence on their sexual aggression. "Nuke 'em in their ammo belts," she regularly urged The Anti-War Womb, her women's support group.

Finally, even Father Klein seemed to realize the scene was approaching pandemonium. "One final statement," he ordered, gesturing toward Larry Thornton. A former St. Louis lawyer and judge who'd retired to run a worm farm in the county, he and his wife, a member of town council, represented stability and order.

Larry began with what Stan thought was a complete *non sequitur*. "The movie version," he said, "of *The Last of the Mohicans* leaves out a crucial character." This unexpected statement caused the restless congregation to settle down.

"Early in the story," Larry went on, seizing the opportunity, "Hawkeye and the two Mohicans are leading the Munro sisters toward Fort Henry. The soldiers assigned to escort the girls had already been massacred." Felicia perked up at his words.

Stan couldn't remember if he'd watched some of the movie. He tried to visualize what Larry was describing, but memories from his watch tower days were blurred with images of Hardy Boys' adventures read decades ago.

"The officer in charge before the attack, Major Heyward, is a good battlefield soldier, a, veteran of European campaigns. But he doesn't understand the terrain or the enemy."

"Okay," thought Stan. "There's a military connection here, attack and response. It's a bit late for rescue in New York City today, though!" The estimated death toll would, however, go down in the weeks after the disaster, a rescue in numbers at least.

"When they reach a cave behind a waterfall," Larry went on., "Hawkeye posts Chingachgook and Uncas as guards at the two entrances. It's an odd little group, but they need each other. Men, women, soldiers, backwoodsmen."

Stan imagined himself saving beautiful girls who, grateful, later offered themselves to him without shame. Felicia had read the novel and would know no such thing ever occurred in Cooper.

"Inside the cave, a natural sound studio, Hawkeye tells the two young women they are safe until morning. Because the cave is well known to all who live in the area, though, they must move on before the evil Maqua and his men arrive."

Felicia knew, though Stan did not, that Chingachgook and Uncas are the last of the Mohican tribe. Their deaths would mean the end of a way of life. Members of Holy Trinity feel that 9/11 threatens their own civilization, which they had believed to be unassailable.

"Now comes a moment in James Fenimore Cooper's novel that the moviemakers left out," says Larry, a hand raised. "They sing."

"How does a lawyer know this?" wondered Stan. Unlike Felicia, he'd read only trade magazines and technical books for years.

"They sing," Larry went on, "when a character I haven't mentioned leads them--David Gamut, a choirmaster who'd fled the battle with Hawkeye and the others. Oh, he was an embarrassment to Major Heyward and these frontier fighters, not carrying a gun and barely able to keep up with the women. A misfit, apparently."

Stan winced, fearful now that he is a latter-day David Gamut, not the savior of Alice and Cora. Rather than melt at his touch, they would scorn his embrace. Felicia hears his sigh.

"Instead of a weapon, Gamut carries a worn hymnbook, embodiment of Old World liturgy and belief. The women know the hymns by heart, so, when he opens the book and says it's time to praise God, they join in easily, alto and soprano. Gamut is the tenor, and Hawkeye, surprisingly, adds a rough bass."

The picture is a haunting one for Felicia, four souls in grave danger lifting their voices in prayer: "*His oath, His covenant, His blood, / support me in the whelming flood. / when all around my soul gives way, / He then is all my hope and stay,*" said Larry, repeating words Cooper's characters (but not their movie counterparts) might have sung. He paused.

"After Hawkeye and the Mohicans have preserved the friends' bodies, you see, David Gamut brings the party's spirit together in love and celebration, though music, in harmony. They need that fellowship to survive as much as they need more firepower. Even the hardened Hawkeye, remembering his mother singing to him in childhood, weeps." Larry himself seemed close to tears.

"We've heard calls today for more violence on the body, as if we're soldiers and all we can do is fight. I think we must seek God's mercy and God's peace in the spirit. We need union, not more division. Understanding, not anger."

"A singer!" Stan said to himself, surprised. "That's what I can be. Member of a goodly quartet." He saw himself rushing into some chamber, joining his voice in concert with others.

He little knew how prescient this odd thought was. Within the year he--a country music fan--would create The Route 66 Choir, salvation (so to speak) of the Episcopal Church of the Holy Trinity. Felicia argued that his inspiration also rescued their marriage. Stanley came to believe that he had saved the whole country--Mohicans and all!

Chapter 2: Thy Promises My Hope

"I need a hobby!" Stanley had complained to his wife, before 9/11, on the morning after he felt he'd lost adulthood. He was sitting on the bed they had shared for over thirty years.

"Nonsense," said his soulmate, rolling away from him. In his early retirement and with her relaxed work schedule, they could both sleep late.

"Hmm," he thought. "So much for mature marital love."

Still, he went on. "Felicia, how about I become one of those carnival knife throwers? You know, you stand up against a wall--in a bikini--drum roll--I fling ten-inch hunting knives, one ker-chunking into the wood right by your left breast."

"You ker-chunk anything at me," she said, looking over her shoulder, "and I'll come at you with a kitchen knife." He didn't like where her eyes were aiming, especially after last night.

"Okay, okay, no knife-throwing. But, say, what about I become a professional gambler? Go on the circuit, 'Ace Measure.'"

"Take up the 'grand' piano," she countered. "Again."

Smiling at her little joke, she slid back toward sleep. Stan had studied ("grand") piano for a year when Benjamin, age ten, began lessons. Since he had to drive his son once a week across town to Mrs. Barr, he had argued, why not take lessons himself? "It would be," he said, "a father-son, learning-together thing." He had vague ideas about learning to play country music.

They bought an old upright from an elderly church member, in part because Felicia always regretted not having learned herself. Mr. De Capa, for decades the church treasurer, anticipated moving into a retirement home and was paring down the furniture he would take. His late wife had played, but he was willing to let the old Baldwin go "for a song" (his little joke).

"That's too little," Felicia said to him, running her hand along the ancient keyboard. "It's a great piano." It didn't fit her decor, but, like any mother, she believed in her son's talent.

"Say it's a 'grand' piano," Mr. De Capa chuckled, "and we have a deal."

She couldn't talk the price up, and Stan didn't want to. So the "grand" piano--tuned and its mottled ivory keys refreshed--became a fixture in the Measures' living room.

Ben went on to double-major in music and history at Western University, but his father was politely (firmly) told to "practice the 'grand' piano" or stop coming for lessons. Because he didn't prepare at all, Mrs. Barr was being more than patient.

But now, fantasized Stan, perhaps this former elementary school music teacher's desperate efforts to explain the progression of keys, the crucial differences among time signatures, and the beauty of counterpoint would be rewarded in a late blooming. And so--for different reasons--prayed Felicia.

She loved her husband, but his business success and early retirement had complicated Felicia's life. The sale of his security company gave her the resources to finance a new round of redecorating, but her idle husband was relentlessly in the way. So, when she later overheard him humming "Get Your Kicks on Route 66" and claiming to be another Nat King Cole, she encouraged him to take up singing. Not that any trio would take him, she added silently.

Felicia rose on one elbow and studied her husband as he stepped out of the bathroom. She tried to imagine him actually practicing at the "grand" piano, which, badly out of tune once more, now served mainly as a shelf for an eclectic collection of family portraits. Felicia wondered if his current restlessness would lead to flirtation with other women.

Stan had begun to propose "experiments" in bed recently, but she wouldn't go past wearing a few odd costumes and participating in role-playing situations. The idea of dressing up as Annie Oakley, twin pistols at her hips, didn't excite her. And she couldn't keep a grip on Stan in his latex Spiderman costume.

Her loner lover, an only child, never seemed to need friends anyway, male or female. For so many years he had worked long days and weeks with little desire for vacations.

Still, thought Felicia, there was that Linda who worked at the bank. Divorced and without children, she dressed in the style of someone ten years younger and looked good doing it. She had a vivacious laugh that suggested she knew how to have fun--"ha-HA-ha-ha!" Felicia realized that Stan remarked on her long legs more often than was necessary.

She tried to slow a growing resentment, thinking, *"Lord, be Thy word my rule; / in it may I rejoice . . . / Thine arm my strong support; / Thyself my great reward."*

Their son Benjamin had recently returned to Fairfield in his first teaching position, but that hadn't changed Stan's stay-at-home routine. He was not one of those children who come back after college to live with their parents. Unlike many of his peers, he'd enjoyed growing up in Phipps County and was pleased at being offered a position at his old school. He'd quickly found an apartment on the other side of town from his parents and renewed relationships with friends who'd never left Fairfield.

His sister, Marian, was going to Southeast Missouri State because, according to Stan, she was exhausted by the rigors of correcting her father. Marian's dad wore his pants too high, talked like the boss he was, and had no appreciation of the finer things in life (Pearl Jam, onion rings, *The Simpsons*).

With an empty nest, their father felt there would be room for new ventures in his own life analogous to those his daughter anticipated in Cape Girardeau and his son remembered from four years in Columbia. But that conviction had not yet led to new ventures on his part.

Felicia recalled again their unconventional courtship, Stan's innocence of his own desires. Maybe she was wise to worry about new romantic interests in his middle age. Should she have played out a bit longer the game he'd suggested the other night?

"Let's say you're a war widow," he'd proposed, "maybe twenty-eight . . . twenty-nine years old. You have one child . . . um, a daughter, about eight. And you're worried about security."

"Oh, so I need Wall-All?" She was wearing, at his suggestion, a one-piece swimsuit. Was he thinking of his own mother?

"Well, yes, something like that. The man who runs it, of course . . . the one who installs his own systems, he's come by one evening."

"Well," said, Felicia, "I work, then, don't I? A nurse?

"No, no, not a nurse. You're a . . . a lion tamer." He had no idea why he said that, though her suit did have a leopard skin pattern. The scenario he'd first imagined was naturally all about him, the security system operator.

"In a circus?" Felicia asked.

"A circus?" Again, his fantasy was stalled. "Um, at a zoo. Yeah, a big, metropolitan zoo, where they have shows all day, morning and afternoon. For the children, you know." He has a mental picture of crowds roaming through the reptile house, past elephant parks, under the trees of monkeys. "Your daughter must get home from school an hour before you," he concluded tentatively.

"Okay," Felicia said. "That's why you . . . er, the security man . . . has to come by, for Matilda. (I've always loved the name, Matilda.)"

"You like the name Matilda?"

"Of course not. I was just trying to be interesting, mysterious. As well as beautiful, you know."

Stan paused, trying to incorporate this character into the story line he'd developed with such painstaking effort for the occasion.. He was supposed to find a box of sexy lingerie in the closet where he would install the alarm control panel. The young widow in a lion taming outfit, whip in hand, had no place in this plot.

"Beautiful, yes," he admitted. "She would have to be very good at taming lions, I guess. I wonder how many she works with?"

"Oh, seven at least. Her show is the major event of the day."

Stan rolled onto his back. "What's a bunch of lions?"

"A brood? No, wait, a pride."

"Okay, a pride of lions. They'd be difficult to control, each difficult in his own way. She gets one on a chair, but the other paces around the edge of the ring. And another sneaks around behind her."

He'd forgotten the closet and the erotic underwear. He recalled Mrs. Barr tapping his hand with her baton when he failed to play scales accurately.

Felicia said, "I'm getting cold."

"It's that diuretic!" he concluded to himself, recalling a warning about possible side effects: *"Impotence may occur."*

Chapter 3: Sleepers, wake!

"What am I?" Stan asked Ben, his hand over the mouthpiece.

At first Ben was puzzled, then smiled (as will a son who knows his father's shortcomings), and said, "You're a tenor, Dad."

"Ah!" He uncovered the phone and told Melody, the music director, "I guess I'd better start out as a tenor, and you . . . um . . . you see what you think."

"Ooh, we . . . need tenors," Melody said. If Stan had been listening carefully, he might have heard the hesitation in her response. She'd had to work with such late-life, would-be singers before and cringed in anticipation of his solitary voice standing out in every chord. She was notoriously kind natured and couldn't criticize anyone.

Melody Robinson was filling in while the vestry searched for a permanent music director, and she didn't deserve the headaches this new tenor's limited ability and troubled soul would bring to Wednesday night practices. The pressures of her day job--middle school principal--had already led to some uncharacteristically sharp (if sotto voce) exclamations at rehearsals.

Stanley Measure had asked his son what range his voice fell in because he'd never sung in public. It is, of course, difficult for anyone to know what he or she sounds like to others. We hear our voices traveling through the flesh and bones of our heads as well as through the air in our ears. In some sense, our voices are alien to us, elements of the person perceived by others but unknown to us. Nevertheless, at fifty-five years of age, Stan felt he was ready to make--and hear--a new sound: tenor, baritone, or bass.

Like many in his baby-boomer generation, he had played a musical instrument through late adolescence and might claim some experience. His adventure in music education ended abruptly, though, after he left the clarinet--sopping wet with his own spit--in a damp basement storage closet at the end of his sophomore year in high school. During Missouri's humid summer the horn and its imperfectly closed, felt-lined case grew a cloud of fuzzy mold shaped vaguely like a 1952 Nash Ambassador.

Viewing the grey monstrosity, his mother said unhappily, "Sell it or throw it out." Whispering a phrase she used only when a smaller sadness unexpectedly opened deeper wounds--"Hell's bells"-- she went back to her knitting in the living room:

Stan never knew what his mother meant by this expression. Was it the clashing sounds which tormented devils brought to the worship of Satan? Perhaps it was a tinkling of pied flames dancing on scorched bodies. Maybe the deep dissonant tones of doom.

Stan still doesn't understand what "Hell's bells" refers to, and his mother, having moved on from this world to knit in God's house, is no longer available to parse the term. But Stan (religiously?) avoided the expression when complaining about his own son, Benjamin.

What made Stanley think he could, more than half a century old, bloom as a tenor--and how that was an answer to pent up resentment--was a mystery. He told his wife it was hearing an old recording of "Get Your Kicks on Route 66" that inspired him to conclude he possessed latent talent.

"I'm going to 'motor west,'" he sang off-key. "'Take the highway that's the best.'"

"Route 66?" Felicia asked. "You're just being nostalgic."

One reason for Stan's early retirement was disgust at the current state of speech, dress, and music among the younger generation. He had begun to recast his own growing up in the 1950s as an idyllic pilgrimage embodied in the mythology of Route 66. He embraced ideas of innocence and opportunity--kids riding in family cars (finally available after WW II) down the "Mother Road" to vacations in the American West.

But in responding to Felicia he had insisted on a positive note (so to speak). "No, I'm not trying to bring back the past. I was just humming along, you see, and I thought, now wouldn't it be fun to sing, to be part of a musical group?"

Felicia raised her eyebrows. The largest social organization Stan had ever belonged to was the nuclear family, and she could more easily see him lighting out for California, single rider on a Harley-Davidson, than joining a barbershop quartet in white suit and straw hat. To her surprise, however, Stan followed up on this impulse, incongruously linking the old television show's theme song to the religious life.

He decided that, rather than seek a teacher to awaken his sleeping potential, he'd take advantage of a group. And the post-September 11 church service suggested an easy venue. Since church choir required no audition, he figured this was a comfortable place for instruction. Apparently he saw no discord between his desire to become a pop soloist and the traditional purpose of church music (a community's praising God).

On most Sundays Felicia went to Holy Trinity Episcopal Church alone. Ben had come home from college a Methodist, and in her senior year of high school Marian declared that scientific logic contradicted religious belief. Felicia didn't know what Stan did while she was out, but she doubted that his day had a spiritual component. She wasn't surprised when she learned that the first practice at church choir foreshadowed difficulty.

"Stanley, you sit between Bill and Tom," the interim conductor had told Felicia's husband. The Lynne twins had sung tenor since their voices changed, and they knew every tune in the current (1982) hymnal-- and those in the earlier one. No Sunday passed without their comparing the new (inferior) arrangement to the 1940 (superior) one.

"So, you guys are my voice instructors," said Stan, picking up the blue hymnal and plumping himself down on the metal folding chair. "I've never done this before."

Tom looked at Bill, then the ceiling. This man could well be another disruptive element for a church some saw as in crisis locally after Father Klein's departure and globally because of questions about women's ordination and homosexuality.

The choir met in a basement room of the parish house, a low brick building across the street from the church. A dozen brown folding chairs in two rows arched around an old stand-up piano. At its bass end a black metal stand held Melody's music and the baton she would soon contemplate using on her latest recruit.

"We warm up by singing the hymns," she explained, smiling encouragement. "The processional is Number 61, 'Sleepers, Wake.'"

Stan saw several dozen black robes and white surplices filling the racks of a walk-in closet to his left. (He wondered if there might be a giant Nash Ambassador made of grey mold in there.) Some gowns, he would learn, had sewn into their collars the names of choir members now singing (it was hoped) in a heavenly chorus.

That Sunday he wore a robe so musty his nose ran throughout the service. Never told that he could get to the handkerchief in his pants pocket through a slit along the side of the robe, he used--a horrified Melody saw--one sleeve as a tissue.

Melody thought about *The Book of Common Prayer*. Previous music directors consulted it regularly in hopes of finding a collect for those who could not keep time (why was it so often the altos?) and those too consistently under the pitch (basses). Now she needed a prayer for nasal incontinence.

At rehearsal Karen, the organist, sounded notes for soprano, alto, tenor, bass; and Stanley started to sing the familiar melody with gusto. "At least, they're starting with something I know," he thought. Like many who sing along in a group, he paid little attention to the lyrics, in this case words of instruction urging readiness. With everyone else, he sang "*Your lamps prepare and hasten there.*"

Stan was startled when Bill nudged him with an elbow and nodded at the hymnal. What was he suggesting? Then, on the other side, Tom leaned closer and sang, too loudly, Stan thought, in his ear: "*We follow all and heed your call.*"

Melody was looking at him. What was wrong here? He lowered his voice. His fellow tenors did not seem to be singing what he was singing, though someone was (perhaps the sopranos?). Where was that fabled harmony, a religious blend of song?

Bill nudged him again, holding his own hymnal up close to Stan's face. He pointed to the bass cleft, the top notes. "Here," he said. "Sing *those* notes."

Memories of piano lessons floated up from Stanley's distant past, Mrs. Barr trying to contain her frustration, Ben in the next room pretending he heard nothing. Stan's former self studied the imagined score on the shelf above the piano keys. Although he'd been told not to, he glanced down at his right hand playing the melody, watched his left hand searching for a chord. Right hand, treble; left hand, bass. Oh! Oooh!

Only Karen heard Melody mutter: "Hell's bells." There were tears in her gentle eyes. She never swore.

Chapter 4: The Long Expected

If Stanley Measure was trying to start a new life at this time, perhaps Holy Trinity was too. After five years of decline (caused, most parishioners thought, by the relentlessly negative attitude of the rector), the church was now beginning a search for a new priest. The new rector would hire a new music director.

"Research for Rebirth," Felicia had said in her capacity as committee chair. But then everyone knew she was as steadfastly optimistic as Father Klein had been pessimistic. On the committee only Larry Thornton seemed to share her positive attitude.

The Reverend Archibald D. Klein had surprised the whole parish six months ago by announcing he had "received a call" to a church in Nigeria. But few were unhappy that he was moving on at the end of September.

"Nigeria, that's where exactly?" Stan had asked Felicia later on the Sunday the rector made his announcement. He refused to learn new names for the African countries that, beginning in the 1960s, emerged, broke apart, and combined with others in violation of the papier maché relief map he and his classmates had constructed in sixth grade. It was worse than the emergence of dozens of -stans after the breakup of the Soviet Union. Stan mourned the loss of the Cold War's simplicity. In a way, he almost welcomed a new global enemy of "Islamic Terrorism."

Some church members, unhappy with changes in the national church (they thought them too liberal), were secretly sympathetic to Father Klein's move to Nigeria. Others, like Felicia, hoped his departure would make Holy Trinity more attractive to young people. Right now there were too few children in the appropriate age range to organize separate Sunday School classes, and no nursery.

"Father" Tack (he insisted on that outdated title) was the interim minister, there for a year as the search for a permanent rector proceeded. An inept preacher, he was ridiculously optimistic about the church's future. "After a storm comes the lull," he asserted, unaware of the contradiction between what he said and what he meant. All Stan hoped for from someone new was a priest with a clear sense of purpose and the ability to explain it.

Until recently, Trinity's choir had also seemed on a decline. With seldom more than half a dozen members, they just picked a well-known hymn as anthem. Oddly, though, their number began to grow even as the church struggled to define its mission.

Melody did not take credit for sudden new recruits (especially not Stanley!), but she was pleased that Robin Shure (alto) had begun to come again and that another alto, Sharon Rich (hopeful that her career as a yodeler could be forgotten) was going to give it another try.

Linda Cooper, the long legged divorcée Felicia had worried vaguely about, was a good enough soprano to handle some solos. She was not, though, the object of Stan's romantic eye during the first (or any subsequent) choir rehearsal. If that distinction fell to anyone, it was a woman the would-be tenor thought of as "a thin slip of a girl," Jean Triplet. (Later, when his understanding of music had improved, he would think of this bright college student and experienced alto as "The Perfect Third.")

Stan might not have noticed this thin slip of a soprano on his first Wednesday except that the Lynne twins kept up a steady stream of (to him) disconnected instructions:

"Accent the first beat of each measure." "The bird's eye means we slow down." "Sustain those half notes." "Listen to the altos; they have the B-flat, too." He had no idea what they were talking about.

Retreating from the Lynnes' musical tutoring, he let his eyes roam over the backs of the women in front of him, sopranos directly ahead and altos to the right. Jean's profile, her clear complexion, the slender build caught his eye. Who was this? Perhaps, he fantasized, the "*joy of every longing heart*."

Now that he was retired and Felicia's passion for decoration left him alone many days, he did long for . . .for what? . . . for something.

Just two years earlier, his wife and two of her friends had launched a charity operation. They would critique apartments and houses for a token fee ($25.00) and propose a unique redecoration scheme for a second fee of $100. They seemed to have a gift for grouping disparate pieces of furniture and art into cohesive patterns.

This redecoration/charity effort had been so successful that Felecia and company were busy most days of the week. And that left Stan knocking around the house by himself. He needed something to do and, despite a natural tendency to withdraw, someone with whom to do it.

At that first choir rehearsal he tried to catch Jean's eye, but she was, of course, facing away from him. He would later learn that she viewed church choir as her one recreation in a focused academic life. She knew the hymns and had a strong voice, but beneath her singing, Miss Triplet, the Perfect Third, was really thinking about principles of mechanical engineering.

That man behind the thin slip of a girl, who was he? Stan saw him glance over at the twins, who were still lecturing him: "be sure to count," "anticipate that key change," "there is a difference between double and triple piano!" Chester Lott--that's who it was--exaggerated a yawn in the direction of the Lynnes, then winked at him. Perhaps Stan was enduring an initiation faced by all new tenors?

Melody interrupted his thoughts. "We've done the Processional, the Sequence hymn. Now the Recessional."

"Did you say 'recess'?" asked Chester. "Out to the playground, everyone." Knowing Chester, everyone sat still.

"That reminds me," Melody went on in an obvious *non sequitur*, "Father Tack, um, wants us to work, um, on a special program for the Christmas season. An oratorio, I believe."

"Ah," said the chuckler. "The Christmas Caroler, no doubt."

Chester, a bass, ran a local sawmill. His success as an entrepreneur had made him resistant to authority, but most often humorously so. If he was confronted by an environmentalist, he would explain his operation as "buy, slash, burn, move on." If his listener had no feel for irony, this ended the conversation. When he or she caught on, more jokes would follow.

"As you know," Melody went on. "Father Tack thinks the church should be growing, so programs have to grow." She didn't care for the interim rector, but, characteristically, kept her feelings to herself.

"How many soloists?" asked Linda, the attractive loan officer at First Fairfield. She had that vivacious laugh that suggested she would be fun to work with-- "ha-HA-ha-ha!" Stanley studied her back. Was one shoulder higher than the other?

"I think it's three," said Melody. "Anyone can try out."

As soon as she said that, she regretted the blanket invitation. She would have to have Father Tack's support in turning people down.

Melody did not envy the next permanent choir director, whoever that might be. This baker's dozen (she was counting that new thirteenth member, Measure) were ferocious individuals, each reluctant to conform to the vision of one leader. Even the Lynne twins, identical in looks, were sometimes as different as night and day.

Every choir member, like any parishioner, had his or her own story, but this group was a particularly odd collection of disparate chapters. They were sort of like the disciples before Jesus brought them together. Oh, worse than that! Melody prayed silently, "*Oh, lend me 'Israel's strength and consolation.'*"

Why had she taken on this position? She couldn't quite say, though she had musical experience (playing the piano from early childhood) and perfect pitch (she'd sung soprano for years, but never conducted). It's only temporary, she thought, until they can put someone on the payroll. I guess I must love the church, she concluded.

Could she love the choir, though? Take Stanley Measure, looking blankly at her right now. He added little but volume to their efforts, and his lack of goals in retirement carried over to his participation here. He wanted to be entertained and amused by the others, not subordinate himself to the group's effort.

Stanley, she realized, was the epitome of the challenge faced by Holy Trinity: an individual who wants to be helped by everyone else, but has no particular talent to offer. "At least he's not flirting with any of the women," concluded Melody. Then she noticed his gaze wandering toward Jean Triplet.

"From my fears and sins release me, / Let me find my rest in Thee," Melody prayed. Then she asked herself: "Can I really do this?"

Chapter 5: Mingled Hope and Fear

"Can I really do this?" wondered Felicia, looking at her husband asleep on the den sofa the following Saturday afternoon. His shirt was untucked, he'd not shaved this morning, and--if history was any judge--it was likely he'd sleep until dinner. She was ready to redecorate the room they spent most of their time in, but she needed Stanley gone to think clearly.

Studying the protruding belly of her husband, who was now beginning to snore, Felicia wondered if she should change more than the furniture in her life.

Recently she learned how much she enjoyed the company of women, especially those who, like her, had lived a conventional life as wives and mothers during times of great social change. "*The Spirit of the Highest*," she thought, "*to a Virgin meek came down, / and he burdened her with blessing, / and he pained her with renown.*" The reward for her burden of motherhood and service was to be this new time of accomplishment and recognition.

Her partners in Over-Due, the charity organization that kept her so busy, were a joy to be with. None of the three had children in the house any longer (if you don't count husbands, of course), and they were all comfortable enough financially to take on new ventures. They loved their planning meetings at the Middleman Bakery, the challenges of new situations like fixing up the Road House, and the pleasure of satisfying clients.

Felicia looked at Stanley again, this time more irritably. He ought to start some sort of exercise program. And what, she wondered, was in this man's head? All of a sudden he thinks he's a future Elvis

Presley, headed from church singing to rock and roll fame. It's all so different from the narrow focus of his past life.

Not that she doesn't understand some of the strain he's put himself under. Thirty years maintaining his own company had left him no outside interests. Having sold Wall-All, he had no idea who he was or what he should be doing.

"I'm coming apart, Fel," he'd told her after several weeks of trying to sing at Holy Trinity. He was beginning to realize he was lost for most of the service. "I used to know what each hour of each day meant to me. And the weeks and months and years added up to success. Now . . . " He trailed off. "It's like there's no me. Or a different me every few minutes."

Felicia knew it wouldn't do any good to remind him of all the times she'd urged him to take vacations, or play games with his children, or join a club. For his last birthday she'd bought him an expensive mountain bike, hoping to inspire him.

"You could help us with The Road House, put in an alarm system," she offered. The Road House was a fledgling Route 66 museum near the neighborhood where she and Stan had grown up. "There's not much to safeguard in yet, but there may be one day."

"I've given up Wall-All. I need something new."

That's why she liked her women friends. They had learned early in life to shoulder tasks for others. Having repressed their own desires for so long, it was a surprising pleasure to pursue them on a modest scale later in life. They found it easy to take on new responsibilities while continuing old ones.

The two other company founders, Margaret Reardon and Donna Allen, had gone to high school with Felicia, then moved away for several decades but returned to their hometown anticipating retirement. While Felicia had never left Fairfield, she'd found her domestic role completely satisfying; and the empty nest was an invitation to begin anew.

Unashamedly nostalgic about their childhood, a time of innocence and unambiguous social norms, the three women embraced the movement to preserve artifacts associated with Route 66, the Mother Road. Over-Due had its office in what used to be a highway landmark, Fanny's Dairy Delite, on the north side of town. They'd hoped to recreate the original service counter and locate antique soft-serve ice-cream making equipment to create a tone.

Restoring Fanny's was slow but exciting, and the trio had other dreams. They thought grandly about redoing the store fronts on Main Street to resemble the town in a famous picture taken for National Geographic in 1957. The caption read, "*America's Small Towns, a Vanishing Way of Life?*"

Stanley was no help in either operation, having little aesthetic sense and surprisingly vague memories of growing up in the era of two-lane highway travel. Thank goodness at least, thought Felicia, for his new interest in singing.

The phone rang, and she left her lump of a husband to take the call in the kitchen.

"We've got a new client," said Margaret excitedly. "Are you sitting down?"

"I am," lied Felicia, standing at the island counter turning pages in a design magazine.

"Well, you know that abandoned metal building on Kingshighway, out near our old neighborhood?" All three women now lived in new developments several miles from The Circle.

"The old roller rink. What was it's name--'The Oval?'"

"That's it. The grandson of the man who owned it years ago wants to restore it just the way it was in the '50s."

"It's pretty much a shell, isn't it?" She pictured the domed building, a half-buried egg and then chuckled at her unintended pun. "Been empty for years."

"Yes, but the old wood was saved, the track itself. We'd have something to start with."

Images of an old-fashioned, family-oriented entertainment center for Fairfield rose up in her mind. She recalled skating there herself years ago. There had been birthday parties, school events, church outings. But the key times were with her first boyfriend, Tom Baettner. Where was he now, by the way?

"It might be fun," she concluded. "And we could do something for the community, especially teenagers. Remember how we used to go there on Friday nights?"

"Sure. We had great times--they played all the cool songs--'The Great Pretender,' 'Blueberry Hill,' . . . "

"'Good Golly Miss Molly,' 'Soldier Boy,'--those were such good days!" Tom Baettner had volunteered for overseas duty, she remembered. "So, what does Donna say?"

"Oh, she's already said 'yes.' This is a big project, not just redecorating but almost building from the ground up. Who knows what it could lead to."

Felicia thought about Stanley, still snoring away in the other room. Where would his singing lead? Nowhere. She might as well go her own way. Maybe even suggest they consider separating, perhaps just a trial period.

Why couldn't he take up golf, like Donna's husband? He was out on the course at least half the day with those other retired men. Couldn't he work in his shop or volunteer for Meals on Wheels like Meg's Don? Even seeing to regular household maintenance (the leaky toilet in their bedroom!) would at least keep him busy.

"Okay, I'm in."

"I knew you'd like it. And . . . " Margaret paused. Felicia feared there was a catch.

"And . . . ?" she asked.

"Well, there is one thing, a little thing. But I don't think it will be a problem, for us. You see, it might be that Mr. Mayle, the owner, he may want, when the rink opens, to have young girls there some nights. Pretty girls, to be hostesses, sort of, who'll, um, skate with men, you know, for a dollar or something. Like in the war."

"And handsome young men to skate with the ladies?"

"He didn't say that, but, surely in this day and age . . . "

Felicia thought this over. "Well, The Oval would be fun to recreate. How he runs it is his concern. We can use things from that era for the decorations. You know you can find anything on eBay!"

"Well, sure. Juke boxes, old soda machines, probably even some original signs--'Ladies,' 'Gentlemen,' 'Snacks.'"

When Felicia concluded the conversation, she was tentatively ready to tackle the project; but she suggested the three of them sit down with the owner and clarify details before making the deal official.

Still thinking about the unexpected prospect, she wandered back to the den. She held the magazine open to a page that had inspired her. Stanley still lay flat on his back, his mouth open. Probably, Felicia concluded, he's dreaming of Linda Cooper and her great legs. She studied the front of his trousers. Good Lord, was he getting excited in his dreams?

On the one hand, men his age seemed to be already in their dotage. But on the other hand, they were still just boys. She felt akin to ancient *women praying, / 'Surely, Lord, the day is near.'*

Chapter 6: The Work of an Almighty Hand

"Stan is just like my brother-in-law," Donna told Felicia after Meg had left. "Or the way he used to be. John insisted life be uncomplicated. And my sister-in-law obliged him for far too long." She told a story to demonstrate.

When they were first married, Donna explained, John and Rebecca had lived in a small duplex on a quiet street in Joplin, a wonderful deal for the meager budget of a young family. Although the rent was low, particularly for the rare privacy, one tenant obligation was to mow the small front yard (the back was completely wooded).

Donna and her husband had lived across town, but the couples got together regularly. So Donna was a witness to what happened when her brother-in-law met Big Wheel Guy.

The duplex's power mower broke down one spring, and John did not want to draw the owner's attention by reporting it. Instead, he revived an old reel mower, stored in the basement and intact except for the wooden roller. Its metal parts were rusty but functional.

"I remember those things," Felicia said. "Drove my brothers crazy, they were so hard to push."

A reel mower was the standard grass cutting mechanism before a small gasoline engine was mounted on a chassis to spin a cutting blade horizontally through the grass. The first generation had to be pushed, but soon the engine was also used to power the machine along its path.

The older style reel mower used the wheels turning on an axle--in the same arrangement of a car or wagon's wheels rolling on the ground--to revolve four blades, each sweeping grass across a cutting blade at the back, mounted parallel to the ground. This machine, powered entirely by the person pushing, was stabilized by a wooden roller fixed behind the wheels.

Donna told how John had cleaned up the old mower. He took a section of a recently fallen branch and, removing the bark, made a replacement roller. It had a few dips and bumps, places where twigs and knots had been, but he smoothed it out fairly well with a chisel and coarse sandpaper. He drove the same metal spikes that had been in the old roller into the ends of the log and fitted it in place at the back of the machine.

The refurbished mower limped a bit, its irregular roller now hurrying, now lagging behind, but it worked in the end well enough. Making do with what you have--it was an old virtue John was pleased to find himself exercising.

"See what I mean?" Donna told Felicia. "He never wanted anything to change. If it had worked in his childhood, he saw no reason it wouldn't suffice for the present."

Felicia recognized Stan in this immediately, the man who wanted to sing in the style of the 1940s and '50s. Donna went on with her story.

Striding across the small, flat, front yard, John chuckled to himself at the quiet metallic whir of his machine. As he pushed, the two big wheels of the mower brought the curved blades up and over the grass to sweep it down and across the cutting blade at the bottom. Anything too tall, dandelion heads or tall grasses, could be left standing. But after a moment's work with the grass whip, his lawn matched the manicured expanses of the neighborhood. He considered theirs, however, achieved by shortcuts, his the result of honest human labor in a traditional mode.

He would be another Route 66 man, thought Felicia, taking two-lane roads rather than the Interstate. Stan, too, believed in a regularity based on the patterns of his childhood, which he asserted as universal, divinely modeled: "*The unwearied sun from day to day / does his Creator's power display; / and publishes to every land / the work of an almighty hand.*"

At the end of a sweep across the yard one hot August day, John heard a roar on the sidewalk beside him and turned to see a boy flying by. He was riding a Big Wheel, one of those low-slung, plastic, three-wheeled riding toys that had wiped the old-fashioned, high-wheeled, metal tricycles off the face of the earth in less than a generation.

The hollow, hard plastic wheels made a tremendous racket, particularly on uneven pavement, and high-geared pedals allowed riders to race past terrorized sidewalk strollers. This rider was probably no more than eight years old, but his manner and attitude suggested a veteran racer, survivor of tough circuits. He turned his handlebars sharply, cutting the large front wheel sharply as he came skidding to a stop just beyond the mower.

"'What [*the hell*] is that?'" Donna claimed he asked, looking back contemptuously at the machine. He did not, of course, actually say "the hell." But to Donna, who had been watching with her sister-in-law from the porch, the rhythm of his speech and the way in which he spat out the words, conjured the expletive out of the environment, as if the situation, not he, required it.

John studied him a minute, breathing heavily from his effort. "It's a lawn mower." It was clear the boy had never seen one.

"Yeah. [*And I'm your Fairy Godmother.*]" Again, Donna was embellishing what she heard. But Felicia understood how the tone could suggest the postscript.

A pause as the boy looked it over. "Show me."

"You see," said John, sweeping an arm over the mowed area behind him, again at the path he was on. Donna could tell he had not warmed to this boy.

"What? This did that? [*Shee-it.*]"

"Sure. When I was your age," John began, knowing he shouldn't.

By now, Donna admitted to Felicia, she was thinking she should intervene. But in her hesitation, John proceeded. "This was all we had when I was your age. Hard work."

"Yeah?" The boy looked up the street, down past John. Another pause. "Let me."

John stepped back, even bowed slightly.

Felicia knew what it was like at the boy's age, less than a hundred pounds. She'd seen her younger brothers throwing their weight behind the mower. They could move it, but the slightest hole or tree root making the ground uneven stopped the mower dead. And the poor child impaled himself on the handle, generally finding the wind knocked out of him.

More specifically, he ran up onto the hard square nut that bolted the handle to the mower's wooden shaft, leaving, all boys believed, after so many collisions, the imprint of that nut permanently in their sternums. It was a mark everyone of that generation could show if they were required, for some unimaginable reason, to pull open their shirts for inspection.

"Yes," someone, an official, would note, checking off the name on a clipboard. "Yes. A member of the generation that grew up in the '50's. Move on!"

Having told this story more than once, Donna amplified.

"You remember how each time the machine stopped and a boy threw himself onto the handle, John or Stan or Don or any friend up or down the street cried out 'Hunh!' and crumpled behind the mower. The mark on his breast would be just a little bit deeper."

Progress in the entire neighborhood's chores on a Saturday morning might have been measured in "Hunh's" more easily than by circuits around yards. The portions of lawn to to be mowed shrank less quickly than the combined strength of the entire male youth of America.

Donna knew (and Felicia now did, too) that John was thinking to himself: "now Big Wheel Boy will try his hand." He smiled, anticipating the anguished "Hunh," the figure doubled over, his own wisdom confirmed.

"The Punk" (later so called by John) swaggered up to take the handle. He sighted down the line of uncut grass. He leaned into the mower. Muscles tensed, and strain leapt to his face.

And, of course, nothing happened. He could not move it an inch!

42

The boy straightened up and looked at John with assurance, however, rather than defeat, as if he'd expected exactly this. He knew this was all some crazy adult stunt John had planned. No one could move this monstrosity across the lawn, let alone make it cut grass! What a joke! He loved it.

Big Wheel Boy grinned; he winked. He walked to his more modern vehicle, eyes still on John in friendly collaboration. Slinging himself down into the seat, giving a final wave of understanding, he spun off down the sidewalk.

"Wait!" cried John, leaping to show him, to mow one strip and prove it could be done, to recall the past and to verify his own existence. But he was too late; the boy did not look back.

Donna chuckled. "That was John thirty years ago. Now he's not like that at all."

"What changed him?" Felicia needed to know.

"Valium, sweetie. He's takes two a day and is a different person. He and Rebecca are on a cruise in the Caribbean as we speak. And I bet he's got the biggest riding mower in Joplin! He rolls with the punches these days, let me tell you. And he's round enough to do a lot of rolling!"

Felicia didn't want Stan putting on any more weight, but he--or she, or both of them--were in need of some kind of powerful mood changer.

Chapter 7: Signs of Promise

Then Melody Robinson quit. It took everyone by surprise because she had been so patient with them. It might mean the choir was coming apart.

Technically, though, Melody hadn't been the best director. "Bless her!" Karen, the accompanist, admitted to Father Tack, "she can't ever get organized!"

It didn't occur to the choir, busy with their owns lives, to wonder why she had such trouble. Stanley had seen none of signs of the gracious middle school principal's distress.

He had watched her arriving on Sunday breathless, her arms full of notepads, a purse, black folders; but he'd drawn no conclusion about her emotional state. When things were put away, Melody changed her mind about who would sing what parts and, once, even what anthem they were to sing in an hour. It was as if tiny tornados came through her house and mind at least once a day.

The choir veterans knew about the pressures of her work but assumed she knew how to handle them. They groaned when Melody admitted she had misplaced the music or confessed that her e-mail address list had exploded. They sighed when she wandered off during practice on tangents of musical history or into points of theory. The more responsible, like the Perfect Third, tried to concentrate, but eventually Melody would see the blankness even in her eyes.

How the choir was increasing in number during her time as temporary director was a mystery. Listening to Stan's accounts of how he was doing (and hearing him practice with the piano), Felicia told Ben she feared the newest tenor would be told not to come any more.

Melody worked hard, of course, spending time going through stacks of old music in the church basement. After the service on Sunday, she waited around to hear everyone's opinion about their singing. Eventually, though, she tired of trying to distinguish honest opinions from flip answers, coming to the sad conclusion that most parishioners paid little attention to the anthems she chose.

Still, she scoured catalogs of sheet music for something she'd once heard somewhere that might fit an unscheduled special occasion. She would sadly conclude that a whole afternoon had produced nothing she could use (or the group could handle). She spent hours making practice tapes for soprano-alto-tenor-bass, playing the piano herself as she recorded.

"You did all this . . . for us?" worried Linda. The choir's faces were puzzled at the picture her account created: Melody moving the microphone from one place to another, accidentally erasing a perfect track, forgetting to label the dozen and one, specially prepared cassettes.

Melody even attended a workshop for church choir directors in Kansas City over a long weekend in October. She came back with new ideas about warming up, but the Lynne twins made jokes and the women were impatient. What should have improved their performance degenerated into something like a free-for-all. The practice room was filled, it seemed, with the sound of alley cats on the prowl or something resembling the final collapse of an ancient carnival calliope. She gave up that part of rehearsal.

They felt bad after each of the sessions when she tried something new (they couldn't change; they were Episcopalians!) or when it was too obvious that the sound she'd imagined in her head was far better than what came from their mouths.

Still, they couldn't help themselves. It was just too easy to study her reaction. Whatever they said registered immediately on her face, good or bad, kind or hurtful, intentional or accidental.

After the pig story, though, they knew they had to reform. Unfortunately, that recognition came too late.

She'd been to the State Fair and got to telling them (when they should have been practicing) about the pig races. It was piglets, of course, not the full grown animals, that she had seen tearing down the miniature track.

"You know what they chase?" she asked, her face bright. They suggested the pigs ran after cars ("Like dogs?" offered Stan); ambulances ("Only those piglets who wanted to be lawyers, of course," observed Chester); "Wild geese" (which, Marvin Barnes worried, Melody herself was on the trail of).

"No, no," said Melody, a pained look on her face. "Oreo cookies!" She pictured the little creatures, each a different size and color. The choir expressed surprise, but not satisfaction, to learn about the cookies. Determined, she went on.

"They're fast. You can't believe it. And they try so hard, so . . . so . . . hard." Her smile waned. She could see Stan rolling his eyes. Someone else stifled a yawn. But she rallied. "And one little pig . . . it was so sad. In the hurdles."

This perked the choir up. "They do hurdles?" asked Jean. "Now, that's interesting."

46

But Bob Lynne had to ask, "How about the steeplechase? Water jumps?" The others couldn't repress chuckling.

"The little guy," she lamented, "he must have tripped. He hit the very first hurdle, hard, and fell down into the dirt. He tumbled head-over-heels."

She should have known by this time that there would be "awww's" of mock sympathy. But she couldn't stop.

"Still, you know, he . . . he got back up. He ran the race. He was last of course, but he finished." She wiped one eye. In the weeks that followed they remembered with deepening remorse her narrating the pig race episode.

She stepped down as choir director later--not, she claimed, because she didn't love it or them. Other duties had emerged--both family (aging parent) and professional (there are always crises in middle school). And they did understand to a degree. She promised to sing soprano with them whenever she could. A tiny glimmer of understanding even shined through Stan's self-absorbion.

Perhaps from guilt--and to solidify their view of her, their former director--the choir began, when she wasn't around, to exaggerate her dramatizing the pig races. They imagined her getting down on her hands and knees, in her excitement imitating the fallen piglet. She wanted them, they knew, literally to see the disaster and the refusal to stay down. So they pictured her acting out the scene. In their wishful memory, she had laid a folding chair sideways on the carpet to represent the hurdle, and they watched her bang her head into the chair's seat. "Ow!" they thought involuntarily.

Melody had bounced up, they believed, smiling and confident that this had inspired them as much as it had her. "We all do that, don't we?" she had insisted (or so they recalled). "We get up, and . . . and we keep going."

Now, after she'd stepped down, they could almost feel bumps on their own foreheads. Their eyes watered in sympathy.

They were also convinced that, when she handed out the black choir folders a few minutes after she had concluded the pig race story, each found, tucked in the little pocket inside the back cover, a cookie, home-baked and not store-bought.

She wouldn't have done it, however, Stan vaguely suspected. Even though she would have planned to hide treats, she would have fallen behind as the week advanced. Her good intentions would have been overwhelmed by events. He imagined another scene, this one coming not long after the rehearsal in which she'd told the story.

She would have come home at the end of a day in which one sixth-grader put a toad in another's lunchbox and a parent came to complain about "foul language" in the girls' bathroom. On the piano, which used to serve as a release for tension, were piled the choir's music folders. She suddenly remembered her plan to bake cookies.

Then the phone rang. It was her mother four states away. Melody's father, who had shown signs of Alzheimer's, had been brought home by the police. He was at the mall but couldn't remember why he'd come, where his car was, or how to get to his house.

Hours later, Stan fantasized, while she was talking to her one sibling in California, Melody would have stopped in mid-sentence and exclaimed, "I forgot the cookies!"

She was the kind of person who would always listen. Why hadn't they? Stan heard, in his mind, the lines from one of her favorite hymns: *Watchman, tell us of the night, / what its signs of promise are.* What could he expect now?

Too late, Stan thought of putting in Melody's folder a single Oreo Cookie. It would have been a token of affection, he thought, she would never have to race in order to hold. Though he failed his first choir director, this was a first step in his own reform.

Chapter 8: Straight What Long Was Crooked

Felicia was surprised to find the attractive Linda Cooper waiting with Mr. Mayle at the meeting. Fairfield City Bank had assigned her to coordinate The Oval's investors, agents, clients. Felicia scowled at the sound Linda's stockings made when she crossed those long legs.

"We want a set of central images, a thematic core," Mayle told the three founders of Over-Due. "Something that recalls the old days, when roller rinks were new, but also celebrates today. We believe rinks are poised to make a comeback . . . or," he chuckled, "to come around again."

The group was seated at a conference table in Over-Due's office, the eat-in area of the former Fanny's Dairy Delite. This space was being redone, and old elements of the ice cream shop were mixed with used office furniture, bought at a recent going-out-of-business sale. Felicia had to stand, as there weren't enough chairs.

"Isn't the roller skating industry over a hundred years old?" Donna asked. "It may be hard to combine those two looks."

Mayle went on. "We also want a lot of color, not so much in the floor, which would have a natural finish, but in the furniture, the decoration, the accessories."

"That's no problem," said Felicia, "though you might want to establish a basic pallet, so that everything coordinates." She watched Linda making entries on a small spiral notepad.

"We want our employees visible, standing out against the background, so that customers can spot them for service. They'll have distinctive uniforms." Linda crossed her legs and, again, the sound of her stockings grated on Felicia. She exchanged quick glances with Meg and Donna.

Meg had taught elementary school for twenty-five years and envisioned Mayle's field of skaters as children on a playground. She imagined a team of teachers, highlighted by bright colors, trying to coordinate fourth graders on a jungle gym, fifth graders playing kickball, one third grader who was "it" chasing her classmates--a field of disorder.

"Music is also important," Linda noted, reading off a checklist. "The owners want songs you can skate to, but we have to please the spectators, too. And those taking a break--for refreshments, say--need to be entertained. They don't want anyone left out."

Mayle concurred. "We'll have to be up-to-date for the young without losing their parents coming in to relive their youth. We're reconstituting America the way it used to be."

Linda crossed her legs once more and issued a soft laugh to the room, "Ha-HA-ha-ha!" This was a new assignment for her, and she liked getting experience in different areas.

Donna squirmed in her chair, in part because the old vinyl cover was hot but also because she didn't like the way this job was shaping up. She'd risen from being a family physician's part-time secretary to hospital administrator who hired and fired doctors. She concluded that Mayle was conveying the varying opinions of different parties. They didn't all mesh.

"Make these rough places plain," thought Felicia. *"Let the valleys rise to meet Him, / and the hills bow down to greet Him."*

51

"Why don't we draw up some designs?" proposed Meg. "Donna does the graphics, so, in a couple of weeks, we'll have options."

Mayle glanced to Linda, who nodded. Then he said, "Fine, fine. We've got, um, investors . . . others to talk to in the meantime." He handed Felicia a thick folder. "Here are some old advertisements for rinks of the 1950s. They might inspire you. And some histories of roller skating--as early as 1740."

"The money's there," Linda assured Over-Due. "But we're also looking into the future, expansion, franchises one day. So, the idea is to do this first rink in style, establish a model."

She was viewing Mayle as the first in a number of clients the bank would assign to her, each one distinctive and the variety preparing her for wider ventures. She hoped to be an independent financial consultant one day, working from home on her own schedule with a plush expense allowance.

"The first 'Original' Oval is what this will be one day," Mayle chimed in. "A rink, to be sure, at first. But also a complete entertainment center--contests, celebrations, even conventions if we can work with local lodging--that can be copied elsewhere."

Over-All's founders raised their eyebrows. They imagined their own future in this forecast as well. If their decorating ideas were featured in The Oval, and it inspired rinks in other towns, who knew where it all could lead? A national arena? Felicia's mind raced: would they become part of an effort to unify the country after the shock of 9/11?

Agreeing to meet the next week, they divided up aspects of the project: Donna would develop sketches and animations to portray the tradition of skating;

Meg would consider ways to accentuate the function and relationship of employees; and Felicia would review the literature Mayle had given her to be sure they were including all the necessary features.

Their restoration of Fanny's Dairy Delight as a Route 66 roadside attraction, as well as their work on the Road House, would have to be postponed. But if The Oval proved as lucrative as it seemed, the projects closest to their hearts would have greater resources later on.

Felicia arrived home excited, realizing that she must feel just as Stan had when he'd dreamed up Wall-All thirty years ago and gotten his first business loan. Of course, his had been totally an individual effort, in which he was management and labor, investor and employee combined. She would have to work with her good friends, and who knew how many more people behind the scenes of The Oval. Still, the challenge was exhilarating.

Her first view of Stan at home was not.

She came up behind him on his hands and knees in the den wearing old khakis that were sliding down his backside. Around him on the floor were file folders and manilla envelopes, some with papers spilling out onto the carpet. The drawers of his desk and two tall file cabinets were open.

"What's this?" she asked. To herself she said, "*Comfort those who sit in darkness.*"

"The true end of Wall-All." He didn't get up. "I'm throwing out everything but a few files that we'll need for taxes. It's time for new priorities, different interests."

She'd been urging him to clean out the den for months.

"Good, good. What brought this on? Space for a new project?"

He swung his head around but stayed on all fours. "Exactly. The new me, ready for the new you." He moved his hips like a dog wagging his tail.

After their recent unfortunate experiences in bed Felicia feared this was a prelude to a discussion of his manhood and its revival. Perhaps he was about to announce he'd begun taking Viagra. Or that he'd subscribed to some bizarre exercise program.

"I have good news about Over-Due," she said, "a big time client."

"That's nice, but something I've expected. Here now, right here, you're looking at Holy Trinity's new choir director!"

"Choir . . . director?"

"I know, I know. I'm new to the game, but Melody was just temporary, replacing Whatshername . . . "

"Claire Stevenson."

"Right, Stevenson. Well, they don't have anyone, it seems to me, and I've got some ideas."

Stan hadn't known where the tenor part was written, he had difficulty in any time signature but four/four, sharps and flats seemed irrelevant to him. Holy Trinity's choir director?

"It's really just a matter of picking out the hymns, the anthems and then keeping time. Anyone can do that. There are a lot of my favorites we haven't sung in years."

"Don't you have to have some training, in music and in liturgy. Hymns are chosen based on the progression of the church year. Like Advent, right now, there are special songs for the season. They go together."

"Oh? Well, I can look that stuff up. Or Tack can help me." Stan refused to call him "Father" Tack, though he'd never articulated his reasons. "The thing is, those people are stuck in a rut."

Felicia, who also believed male priests shouldn't play that gender card, thought about reminding Stan he'd been comfortable in his work routine for thirty years.

"What about the Oratorio? Do you know Bach, the Baroque Period?"

"Bach, Smach. The notes are there, you just sing them. Karen walks us through each part; then we sing."

Felicia started to say something, then fell silent. He was recklessly scooping papers into a plastic trash bag.

Then her eyes narrowed. "By the way," she said. "I think the toilet in the master bedroom is running."

Chapter 9: Earth and Sea and Sky

Felicia hoped that, in his retirement, San's restlessness might be put to use. She'd had always been skilled at redirecting his attention toward constructive--or at least benignly irrelevant--jobs around the house.

In the bathroom, Stan leaned close to the commode. "Whssss," said his toilet.

"Ohhhhh," said Stan.

The toilet's whsss announced a leaky drain. His ohhhh underscored a dwindling desire to achieve. He wondered if Fel were making a related sound.

As a security expert, he felt water was the greatest non-human threat to a building, especially in a state famous for its rivers. One reason he'd enjoyed his youthful fire tower days was how high above the earth he was, safe from the floods that plague residents along local rivers--the Little Piney, the Gasconade, the Osage. From his vantage point in the sky he noted the ridges and high hills where, barring another act of retribution by Noah's angry god, the seas could never come. But now he felt water threatened his domestic security.

In response to faulty mechanisms in a variety of apartments they had lived in before they bought their current home, Stan had developed a series of failing toilet repairs. With the current bedroom unit he was near the last in that series of remedies that prevented Felicia's inviting a plumber into the house.

From the bottom of the stairs Felicia called, "Do you want me to get Tony?"

"No need," he replied airily, trying to convey a confidence he did not possess.

He pulled the ceramic top off the tank, peered within, and saw the oblong dark-gray float riding low in the water. Too heavy, he concluded. It must have been taking on water, gradually gaining weight and sinking lower until the incoming flow would no longer lift it high enough to force the intake valve closed.

Studying the tiny ripples made by the water's leaking around the stopper at the bottom of the tank, Stan thought about himself as Route 66 balladeer, Nat King Cole returned via church/gospel crooning. In truth, he was leaking. (Or deflating, if he thought about recent bedroom episodes.) He should schedule a doctor's appointment.

He didn't want to admit to himself that he'd been exaggerating his commitment to a musical life in the church and perhaps beyond. His manic practice sessions helped him think less about what he hoped were only the effects of his blood pressure medicine. In his heart, he feared he was losing track of what was important and what was trivial.

He'd also begun to sense Felicia's irritation at his recent behavior. At times he was sure he deserved more attention from her, but he also knew she took the search for a new rector and the growing business of Over-Due seriously. He was of no help in either venture.

Halfway down the tank a wooden dowel he had earlier wedged from one side to the other--preventing the float's dropping to the very bottom of the tank-- looked swollen and soft. Were the underpinnings of his 30-year marriage swollen and soft?

"Can you fix it?" said Felicia. She'd followed him upstairs.

"Of course I can. Minor adjustment. I'll get to it tomorrow, right after church." He hadn't planned to go to Holy Trinity the next day because Karen was scheduled to play an anthem on the organ. He'd seen no reason to go if he had no bigger role than respectful audience. Now he needed to postpone his water crisis.

He suspected that the flushing mechanism's combined ailments were probably terminal. Additional efforts to save it would only prolong Fel's relentless questions about his efforts. Perhaps it was finally time to call Tony Drinkard.

"Don't make a mess," cautioned Felicia. As she turned around to change from her business clothes, he tried to imagine a plan of attack.

Their plumber, when they could get him, was Tony Drinkard, a stout, red-faced farmer's son who wanted no more of the failed odd crops of his father--Austrian winter peas, rapeseed, oriental persimmons, lingonberries, glyphosate resistant soybeans.

Tony had moved into town thirty years ago and, without training or capital, set up his own, ultimately very successful business. Still wearing the denim overalls of his father's trade, Tony was ready, Stan knew, to stomp into his bathroom and replace the innards of the toilet tank, at great expense and with frequent remarks about what "someone" had done to ruin a perfectly functional unit.

Stan had been good at designing and installing security systems: coordinating their complex wiring, understanding increasingly sophisticated detection devices, devising multiple means of alerting homeowners and police. Shouldn't such skills be transferable to plumbing: the movement of water through pipes, the integration of connections and joints, the appreciation of valves opening and closing? Apparently not. He imagined water flowing over the top of the toilet, out the door, down the stairs, filling the basement. He wished he could retreat to his old office at Wall-All where order was maintained, a scale of value established.

In the kitchen Felicia poured herself a glass of wine to celebrate The Oval. Perhaps this egg signaled the delayed emergence of herself as entrepreneur, designer, manager. Of course, just when Over-Due had its first major client, her husband was threatening to enter a new stage of retirement insanity.

At the same time she was worried about Holy Trinity's search for new rector. As committee chair, she counted on her home as a retreat from the pressures of that delicate task. Could she satisfy the different groups in the church--those who wanted to return to Morning Prayer most Sundays, those who wanted "contemporary" services (whatever that meant!), the surprisingly large number of gays who were speaking out? The social activists were also drawing attention to the way the war in Afghanistan was being carried out--the arrests of "enemy combatants," the special prisons for detainees, an hysterical fear of Islam. The traditionalists were made uneasy.

Stan as choir director could split up the one church entity that seemed to be growing and getting better. She might need help from "*that Mother, in whose shrine / the world's Creator, Lord divine, / whose hand contains the earth and sky, / once deigned, as in his ark, to lie.*"

Felicia knew that Stan's restlessness grew not only from retirement but also from the children's having left the house. While he had always resisted family activities, he liked having Ben and Marian around. Well, Felicia, too, she supposed.

Though their son Ben lived in town, he had his own circle of friends and regular pastimes. Felicia wasn't sure if he'd want to help her with his father, or if he could. She wondered if he'd take Stan on the new rails-to-trails bike route. After all, didn't teachers routinely bring order to chaos? Well, not always. She winced, recalling an unhappy experience from her own school days--dodgeball from hell.

On rainy days when the seventh grade couldn't go out, Fairfield's physical education teachers took sadistic pleasure in making the girls play dodgeball. In the undersized junior high gym, fifty or so adolescents were divided into three teams, each with one captain and one volleyball. The object: eliminate the opposing team members by hitting each with a ball.

The gym was divided lengthwise into sections: the middle and two ends. Being in the middle was difficult because balls were coming from both directions. Those at each end could watch all throwers, but it was unnerving to see and hear a speeding volleyball flatten itself against the wall right beside you--thwapp! And everyone feared Sonja Hill.

Taller, more fit, and mean, Sonja terrorized the rest of the seventh grade, male and female. A decade later she leveled her sometimes abusive common law husband with a two-by-four--thwapp! Local preachers would compare her to Jael, the wife of Heber who drove a stake through Sisera's head.

Somehow Felicia ended up the last player for one end team, Sonja the final of the middle group. Felicia kept dodging along the wall, stopping and starting, ducking and jumping, evading the whistling volleyball that slammed off the wall above, beside, around her. She wanted the game over but feared the force of the blow that would end her suffering.

She saw herself as an electron with its erratic movement creating a cloud, unlike a solid planet in precise orbit around a sun. Sonja threw into the cloud but never hit the particle. Still, Felicia knew she couldn't escape forever and foresaw a red welt rising on her thigh, her shoulder, her backside when Sonja finally made the winning throw.

"Thwapp," went Sonja's volleyball.

Stan's toilet said, "Whssss."

"Ohhhhh," said Stan.

Felicia, taking another, bigger sip of wine, thought, "Aiyee!"

Chapter 10: God all-bounteous, all-creative

Sharon Rich, the one-time yodeler, came to the next choir practice at Holy Trinity, but she left abruptly when she found that Melody would no longer direct.

"Please come back when we get our permanent director," urged Karen, standing by the rehearsal piano. "I'm just filling in until . . . until . . . " Her voice trailed off as Sharon smiled and slipped through the door.

Although most didn't know it, Sharon would have been a fine addition to the group. She had starting winning talent contests at the age of five, belting out gospel favorites like "Farther Along" and "Just a Closer Walk with Thee" she'd learned from her evangelical grandmother. Patience Smith had adopted Sharon when her own widowed daughter ran off with an encyclopedia salesman who had memorized volumes A-Autograph through M-Number.

At the same practice, Stan, warned by Felicia's reaction, did not propose himself right away as interim director. He did believe Karen would find conducting and accompanying too much for one person, and his proposal would therefore be welcome, whenever he made it. But he was also distracted by his toilet troubles, which he had not resolved the previous Sunday.

Robin Shure, the artist whose farm was distinguished by a menagerie of animal sculptures, knew the former yodeler Sharon's history and told herself she'd talk to her friend later about singing with the group. The two had gotten to know each while pedaling on neighboring ellipticals at the Phitness

Phlatterer. There Sharon had confessed her difficult past.

Mrs. Smith had been about to sign a contract for her talented granddaughter with a Nashville recording studio when Sharon suddenly began yodeling. Riding to a revival in the Bootheel, the twelve-year-old heard, on her grandmother's car radio, Linda Ronstadt adding an experimental riff at the end of "Blue Bayou." Overnight Sharon's vocal style was transformed. Her rendition of "Will the Circle Be Unbroken" the next evening included an extended ad lib bridge oscillating from natural to falsetto tones. Grandmother thought the devil had gotten into her.

"God inspired the songs you sing," she instructed her granddaughter sternly as soon as she could get her away from the microphone. In her head she heard the words that had comforted her in her plans for Sharon: *"O the strength of infant weakness, / if eternal is so young!"*

The tent meeting was on the outskirts of Bloomfield, Missouri, on a humid August night. "And each note He gave you should be the single note you sing," Patience insisted. "You're not Ella Fitzgerald."

"Grandmother, I . . . I don't know what happens. I start in the way I always have, and then . . . and then my voice just changes. It bounces right up and down all by itself. All the notes are in the right key, though."

"Child, child, Satan is in you."

She took Sharon back to Cape Girardeau, forbad her ever to sing--not even hymns with the congregation--and abandoned the scheme she'd nurtured for years of making her a musical minister in the Holy Reverence Temple of the Living Savior. The curse of Babel seemed to have claimed her granddaughter.

Sharon adapted to her anonymity as easily as she had earlier accepted fame. In a few years she was just one of 150 graduating seniors in her high school, and she headed off the next fall to John Brown College in Siloam Springs, Arkansas. But in her heart she was always singing--and yodeling.

After college she went into social work, giving exceptional attention to individual cases. While others in her profession knew and adhered to guidelines and policy, she was adept at escaping defined terms and fixed categories to give each client the best chance of success. Her inner manual of a helping profession was an eclectic collection of "what works."

"Most of us," she said, "are neither round pegs nor square pegs, but, with a little flexibility, we can be fit into a unified order." Her colleagues had no idea what she meant when she made such pronouncements.

Sharon had recently come to Fairfield to work with a growing Hispanic community that took on the agricultural and construction jobs locals avoided. With many non-English speakers, this group struggled to be recognized.

About Sharon's departure from choir, Marvin Barnes, shrugging his shoulders to break the sense of surprise, said simply, "Easy come, easy go." The veteran bass was used to helping others through difficult moments. He'd been on the Fairfield police force for three decades and was the first officer superiors chose to handle domestic disputes. "But don't anybody else try to leave!" he said, hoping it was just a joke.

The Lynne twins chuckled, and the Perfect Third smiled as she thumbed through the sheet music in her folder. Karen played an arpeggio to begin their usual warm-up exercises. The altos sat forward in their chairs. The choir would continue to function, but word of Sharon's coming and going would add to the anxiety felt by many in the congregation that more troubles lay ahead for the church as a whole.

Stan as musical director would not have possessed the means to recruit Sharon again. He associated yodeling only with Swiss mountaineers making sure their voices carry to distant listeners. Neither Stan's speech nor his song acknowledged multiple voices or style. And he didn't know yodeling has a rich tradition.

If he'd ever taken time to listen to the music his daughter liked, he would have known that American country and bluegrass stars yodel in many standard tunes. Had the Reverend Klein, their former rector, been reporting from his new Nigerian post, he might have explained to Stan that African pygmies use yodels within their elaborate polyphonic singing.

It was less likely that anything in Stan's experience would have uncovered the fact that yodeling, or tahrir, is common in some Middle Eastern classical music. Nor could it be expected that he would be aware that, with the krimanchuli technique in Georgian music, the high range of three/four part polyphony involves yodeling. To Stan the world contained little variety.

Oblivious to what Sharon's departure meant for the choir, Stan did for a time try to follow Karen's direction and the lead of the twins. Sadly, for much of that night, though, he heard in the back of his head water running in his toilet.

A few months earlier, at the first hint of this leak, he had simply bent the stem by which the float was attached to the valve. When that metal rod, ordinarily reaching horizontally across the length of the tank, was bent downward, the rising water (replacing the water used in flushing) pushed the float up more strongly. That force, translated to the valve by lever action, effectively closed off the leak.

This simple procedure lasted a number of weeks, during which Stan congratulated himself on his own ingenuity and Felicia was prevented from making her clarion call, "The toilet's running. A tornado has been sighted. We're on nuclear alert." Now the alarm had sounded again.

When the happy period of restored toilet function ended, the unsettling sound of "whssss" spoke for Felicia. Someone more attuned to such things might have heard it as a discordant note in the Measures' marital song.

Stan responded to the return of the leak after church that Sunday by partially unscrewing the float from the end of the stem. This lengthened its reach just enough to press the valve closed.

He was aware that the float could, by scraping along the side of the tank in its up-and-down motion, gradually screw itself back to the former place. Pieces of black electricians' tape, then, were wrapped around the end of the stem next to the float so that it could not retreat, spinning back up the stem. Of course, the tape wouldn't necessarily stay in place. Over time it might be pulled loose and eventually be flushed away.

He had looked at the now misshapen apparatus--bent stem, wobbly float, black tape mass--and winced. Still, he was buying time, hoping these odd elements would work together another week to maintain the unit's essential function.

As his fellow choristers at Holy Trinity were preparing to leave at the end of the next rehearsal, he offered, "I . . . I could be, um, I could direct things for a while."

Had Felicia heard him, she would have moaned. Despite her faith that God is *"all-bounteous, all-creative, / whom no ills from good dissuade,"* she could not believe this would be the path taken by *"a native / of the very world he made."*

Karen's mouth fell open, and even the Perfect Third rolled her eyes. No one even wanted to explain how crazy this proposal was. On the other hand, no one wanted to step in as shepherd to this flock either.

Volume Two. Christmas.

Chapter 11: Sky the Roof and Earth the Pillow

One evening during the next week, Felicia looked at the old photographs of The Oval Mr. Mayle had given her and thought about an egg. She was repressing what she'd heard about her husband and the choir. Surely he hadn't done that? Years later, though, she would remember the event as a turning point in her life . . . and in the history of the church.

What better symbol of wholeness was there, she wondered, than the egg? A living being, food, shelter all in one concentrated space. If Over-Due were allowed to be creative in decorating the rink, they could use such symbolism to draw together past, present, and future, just as the investors wanted. But bringing too many things into the scheme could obscure the overall design. The center would not hold.

She also saw The Oval as the globe, a world now divided between "terrorists" and "us." It, too, might explode into a thousand pieces according to a growing number of news reports.

Stan's object of contemplation contradicted the idea of unity. Grimy with age and dented from his past work on the stem, the deteriorating toilet ball float rode low in the tank. It's unsightly appearance was augmented by free-floating strands of electrician tape, rust from metal parts marking the sides of the tank, and smudged fingerprints left everywhere by dirty hands.

The Oval's management wanted all things that meant the 1950s in the rink's decoration--Coca Cola in bottles, plastic hula hoops, rock and roll vinyl records in juke boxes. This is where Donna, Meg, and Felicia's planning for The Road House as fledgling Route 66 museum might serve them well. There the Mother Road drew all travelers to one path. They needed a similar lodestone--or perhaps the same one?--to draw The Oval together.

Stan felt he'd passed the point where he could control the toilet's flushing mechanism, with the damaged float critical in restoration. Cutting off the water to the tank, he emptied it by flushing once. He would see what was happening.

Felicia answered the phone. It was Sonja Petersen, wanting to talk about the search for a new rector, the last thing Fel needed at this moment. The committee was drafting a profile of the congregation. The mixed results of a survey were giving her fits, everyone intent on his or her own idea of a church. "Profiles of eccentricity," thought Felicia.

"We need a woman," Sonja said without preamble. "Look what happened with Klein, gone on a whim, the way of all men."

Sonja had single-handedly brought women's issues to the fore at Holy Trinity thirty years ago when she demanded that the priest make fifty percent of all references to the deity feminine. She was also among the first in Fairfield to condemn the Vietnam war as male ego unchecked by reason or reality. George Bush's "cowboy" invasion of Iraq would give new life to the Anti-War Womb, her women' support group. She could never tolerate "Father" Tack.

"Couldn't this man," she told Felicia when he first came, "understand that to call himself 'Father' in this day and age is an announcement of his insecurity? Why did he need to assume a status to which women could not aspire?" Felicia had to admit that no feminine variation could draw on the paternalistic tradition of the Anglican church, whose *Book of Common Prayer* consistently acknowledged the authority of "God the Father," never "God the Mother."

On the phone, Felicia told Sonja, ""We have to follow the process. When the time comes--and it's still some months away--we'll look at all the candidates without bias."

She knew her caller had grown up the only girl in a family dominated by boys who, she claimed, "ran amuck from the day one could stand on two legs." She rebelled when a collection of uncles, cousins, and brothers took her ice-fishing miles from their Oshgosh, Wisconsin home.

"Whssss" said Stan's toilet. Removing the float from the stem, he shook it and heard water sloshing inside. Must be a hairline break along the seam where its two halves had been sealed at the factory. It looked worse along one side, and when he held the float with that side down, small drops, like beads of perspiration, appeared along the seam.

Stan sighed, recognizing that he was probably in a no-win situation. If he failed to fix the running toilet, there would be plentiful I-told-you-so's. If he succeeded this time, the system was going to fail soon anyway, and he would be charged ultimately with having failed, probably with having made things worse by his tinkering. Then he smiled and said, 'Shoo-Goo!"

One February Sonja Peterson was the only female in a cluster of ice-fishing shanties on Lake Pepin. Her mother and aunts were helping their grandmother move into a nursing home, and they all assumed (incorrectly) that Sonja would be less uncomfortable on the ice than in a home for old folks. True, she'd always been a bit of a tomboy, able to wrestle, ice skate, and climb trees with the most athletic of her contemporaries. But she preferred to play with girls.

"If you let the men on that committee have their way," Sonja told Felicia, "we'll have another control freak. Men can't work with equals."

In her father's shanty decades earlier, she'd had no trouble baiting hooks with minnows (shiners, fatheads, suckers), wax worms, or maggots; and the bluegill, perch, pike, and walleye deposited in buckets elicited no sympathy, even though she seldom ate fish herself.

Shoo-Goo was the rubbery stuff in a tube Stan used to coat worn spots on the bottom of his work shoes so they wouldn't wear out so fast. Although they looked shabby, with patches of dried Shoo Goo covering the heels and toes, he had read that he could prolong their life for six months with this technique. Shoo Goo had other repair uses as well, sealing off a cracked garden hose, coating the bottom of a leaking dog dish--and, he hoped at this moment of inspiration--fixing a sinking toilet tank float.

Sonja was not put off by her uncles' beer-inspired tall tales narrated when they thought she was asleep in a top bunk. Nor did it bother her that one of her cousins tried to pinch her behind when she inspected the ice hole. But the serial story she found in *RoBust Adventures*, a pulp magazine hidden over the shanty rafters, gave her such an ugly picture of violent masculinity that she wept. And, in the years after this weekend, she would find this type confirmed many times. Eventually she "*sought by cloak of darkness / Refuge under foreign skies.*"

Stan placed the float seam-side-down in the sink, where at least some of the water could drain out. Taking a nail, he made a tiny hole in the shell at one end. Then, with a bigger nail, he poked a larger hole at the opposite end. The larger hole was near the place where the stem was attached, screwed into a little socket that poked out from the surface like someone's navel.

He was impressed by the float's underlying sturdiness, even with damage along the seam. Pushing on the ends did not crush it, nor did hammering produce anything but two clean holes.

Washing the float thoroughly, he placed his mouth over the small hole. His head bent forward over the sink, he blew into the hollow bulb. Drops sputtered and dripped into the sink until he could feel that the shell was virtually empty. Then he set it in the window where the sun might dry it. A sudden vision of his body parts spread out for the doctor's inspection chilled him.

He used Felicia's hair dryer to blow hot air on the float while it rested in a little nest of towel. He coated both holes with Shoo Goo, smoothing the patch neatly with a popsicle stick. For a moment, he considered decorating it like an Easter Egg, painting it with alternate gold and red stripes.

Again he set the float in the window. He thought of baking it for a while at a low temperature in the oven but settled for a few more blasts from the hair dryer. Presto, a perfectly functional, rebuilt toilet tank float!

He could not, of course, bend the stem back straight, remove the dowel, or do without electricians tape in the reinstallation. In addition, mineral deposits on the lever arm that pushed closed the intake valve were little by little decreasing the pressure the float could create to cut off the water flow. And the rubber seals around intake and exit holes in the tank had lost their original shape, the precise fit that prevented leaking.

Finally, the nuts and washers that held float stem, drain stopper, and flush handle in place had become locked in position by corrosion, and the system's integration of parts could no longer be adjusted to compensate for changes over time. He would find Tony's card and be ready to call when he next heard "Whssss." At no point in all this did he consider the possibility that he was repressing more serious concerns in his current obsession with toilet repair.

Felicia finally escaped Sonja's tirade by promising, reluctantly, that she would do all she could to insure a woman was one of the final candidates. She didn't tell Sonja that the Lynne twins had told her, if the church chose a woman priest, they would move to St. Patrick's.

"I have '*followed still as duty led*,'" Felicia told herself with a shiver. "And I'm going to end up running from Fairfield with '*Sky my roof and earth my pillow*.'"

Chapter 12: Through the Cloven Skies

Two weeks later Stan burst into the kitchen, breathing hard. His hair was brushed up and his eyes wide. Felicia was at the oven checking on the meatloaf. "What?"

She feared some new doom had dropped from the skies, perhaps because she'd been thinking, whimsically, of Tom Baettner, her long ago beau.

Stan put his music folder on the counter, stood an umbrella into the corner (rain had been forecast), and collapsed on a chair at their little dinette set by the window.

"It was awful, Fel, awful." Since Stan exaggerated only for effect, she knew this was not a crisis. She studied his face as he continued. "I had had a good day. Talked to Marian, about her courses at SEMO." Felicia smiled. "Picked out some music to suggest to the choir." Felicia grimaced. "And I was thinking," he went on, "as I walked home, thinking that life, my life, our life, was not bad."

She was waiting to see where all this might be leading. At the same time, memories of Tom at the original Oval inched forward from the back of her mind. He'd been a good skater.

"Of course, I've had setbacks lately, as you know: household repairs, um, the problem with . . . um." Felicia shrugged.

"Well, anyway, my manhood had been questioned, a stranger called in to take over . . . the toilet." He frowned. "But I was getting over that, after more than a week. And one can recover, one can redeem himself in other conflicts, other battles."

Felicia bowed her head slightly in sympathy. How old had she been when she and Tom had "been an item"? Ninth grade? Tenth? She'd been too young to know what she was feeling.

"So, I was putting all that behind me, believing that I'd become again the man I once was--businessman, father, lover, Route 66 crooner." He leaned across the table and kissed her.

She almost jumped because he so seldom made any kind of romantic gesture. She'd also been remembering the last kiss Tom had given her, in The Oval parking lot.

"I was walking home, up Crestview, looking at the rays of sunshine slanting through the trees across the road. The waning daylight creating long shadows, larger patches of dark beneath bushes, beside houses."

"What in the world?" Felicia wondered to herself. Tom and The Oval disappeared from her inner view. Stan was uncharacteristically eloquent. *Could* he be the choir director?

He went on. "It was an in-between time, Fel-- between day and night, light and dark. I was walking along, feeling pretty good about the world in general, my retirement, the family. A regular sense of the day's work done, a sailor home from the sea."

He paused, then resumed. "I had my umbrella. And I'm swinging it along by my side at every step, tapping the metal point on the pavement: tap, step step, tap, step step, tap."

"Um-hm." She straightened the silverware she'd set out for dinner, glanced at the stove where green beans were steaming, potatoes nearly done. Since I'd moved on from his reflection about the grand scheme of things to a walk home, her anxiety eased. Long ago Tom had told her he was going to enlist in the Navy. He would say goodbye with a kiss.

"And I'm walking along, looking up the hill, hearing the sounds, traffic behind me, quiet ahead. And I tap, step step, tap along. I look up the street, and I see, maybe, a little bump in the road. Kind of a dark spot with something lying in it, a dip or hole. Nothing that unusual, though I can't tell exactly what it is, lying there. Tap, step step, tap."

In the 1960s, of course, all men were subject to the military draft, so someone's announcement that he was joining the Navy usually meant he wanted to choose for himself a branch of service and a specialty. But Tom was a star student, recruited academically and athletically by a dozen schools. And he could have had four years of college deferment.

"Of course, it's getting dark," continued Stan. "And I can't see too well as I keep walking, tap, step step, tap; tap, step step, tap. Maybe it's nothing, just the road itself. But then, I get closer, and, yes, I think there is something there, something on the street. Someone's purse? A child's toy, football, baseball? Perhaps some natural thing, a rock, larger than usual, or a piece of wood. I don't know, I just keep coming, steady pace, tap, step step, tap, step step, tap."

"What already?" asks Felicia, irritated not so much at Stan's melodrama as by other memories swimming back from that earlier time. The Oval parking lot, and after.

Stan is startled. Then he goes on with a bit more purpose.

"I realize what it is up there. I get closer and I start to really see it. Oblong, dark-gray. It's a toilet tank float!"

He jumps up, pointing ahead, reenacting the scene. Felicia gives an exasperated sigh. So that's where all this was heading!

"And, and, I know it's not just a toilet tank float. It's *my* toilet tank float. Yes, I can tell: Shoo-Goo! There, on both ends, I see the tattered and worn patches of Shoo-Goo."

"Of what?"

His voice drops, taking on an ominous tone. "It knew me, Fel," he says. "It had been waiting for me. It crouches down, flattening itself into the road, it's ready for a jump, an attack. It's going to pay me back for what I've done to it, the years of abuse." He shrinks back now from the remembered scene.

"Stan?" The concern is back in Felicia's voice. Rather than a creature from below, roadside toilet tank float, she hoped for rescue from above, angels. *Through the cloven skies they come / with peaceful wings unfurled, / and still their heavenly music floats / o'er all the weary world.*

"It hisses, Fel, a terrible sound, guttural, fierce: 'Gchyssss!' And it leaps at me. It's going for my throat! Argh! I raise my hands, wishing I had a shield to guard the face."

"Oh," she leans forward, reaches out a hand.

"But those things can't jump *that* high, you know." A pause. Her chuckle is a delayed reaction.

"So it doesn't get my throat, it bites . . . it bites my pants leg, just above the shoe." He looks down, pantomimes the situation. "And I jump back, ahh, it's got me!"

What got Tom Baettner? An urge to see the world? Some patriotic call to serve? J.F.K.'s idealistic siren song? The same thing that was drawing young men-- and women--to the current war in Afghanistan. And the government was hinting at more wars to come.

"It's got me by the leg, but I shake my leg, I kick at it, I yell, 'Get back, you thing, you monster.' And I'm able to knock it loose. It falls back onto the street, rolls to the side of the road. And I raise my umbrella, ready to give it a fight."

"Good for you!" She tries to get into the drama. "You have to protect the family!"

"It hisses again, 'Gchyssss,' crouches, ready for another assault. I take a swipe at it. I'm armed, ready to parry and thrust, to stab home." His account reminds her of the Greek hero Odysseus. Larry Thornton was telling her recently about his using a shield to reveal Achilles.

Tom came back, of course, from two tours in Southeast Asia. She would say "Vietnam," but it wasn't clear in the end that's where he'd been. And he wasn't the same afterwards. But, she wonders, who was after those years? Stan, who didn't serve (a congenital eye defect that never restricted his civilian life), was uncomfortable when discussion came up among his peers. And Felicia, though the war never touched her directly, felt her sense of national pride injured.

"It sees me, at the ready, armed, determined, and it hesitates. ('He who hesitates is lost,' you know.) And I feel I've got it, I'm going to win this one."

Stan pauses, wipes his brow. He bites his lower lip, a worried look still.

The phone rings again. Stan doesn't seem to hear it, and Felicia doesn't want to interrupt his story so close to the end. It's probably someone else disgruntled about the search for a new rector. Could she refer whoever it was to Larry? It could be "Father" Tack telling Felicia her husband must leave the choir.

"But once again, I have underestimated my foe, Fel, the Wild Toilet Tank Float. For it is not alone!"

This is not the end, then, only a dramatic pause. Felicia raises a finger, meaning she must answer the phone. His mouth remains open, ready to continue, then shuts abruptly.

She crosses the room, hearing in her head these words: "*warring humankind hears not / the tidings which they bring; / O hush the noise and cease your strife /and hear the angels sing!*"

On the phone she hears her friend and partner in Over-Due, Donna. "Fel?"

"Yes?" She senses strain in Donna's voice.

"We need a meeting. Meg will tell you. Can you be at the Road House tomorrow, 10:00 a.m.?"

Chapter 13: Bleak Midwinter

From the sound of Donna's voice, Felicia knew there was real trouble. She wanted to think long-legged Linda Cooper would be the cause, but she believed her partners in Over-Due could handle that young upstart. What was the problem?

She said to Stan, "Your toilet tank float's not alone? What? A mate?" He concluded the phone call was insignificant.

"I hear it," he told her. "The float turns, looks back over its shoulder, and calls. It calls into the woods, another sound, a bark or call, a signal: 'Gchyoooo!' And immediately, there's an answer. Leaves rustle, twigs snap beneath moving bodies, there are responses: 'Gchyoooo, Gchyoooo!' And that's when I realize, there are more of them out there."

"Oh, no!"

"Yes, other escaped floats, formerly domesticated, once living calm respected lives in Fairfield homes, now wild, running in herds through the woods on the edge of town, making forays into outlying neighborhoods, into parks and large yards."

Felicia wondered how many parts this story had. She thought again of Tom Baettner, then of The Oval.

"They're trying to incite the native population, the home floats, into rebellion. They have created a network all over town, many floats linked together-- grey ones, brown ones, black, large, small, spherical, oval, rectangular solids. They've probably been digging a complex tunnel system, packing in supplies, readying for guerrilla war. Stalking their prey, small dogs, rabbits, even young children not carefully watched by their parents. And now they're coming, all of them, they're coming . . . coming for me!"

"Why don't they come for me?" Felicia wondered silently. "Take me away from this madness." Generously, she produced a look of mock alarm.

"They're coming for me, Fel, and they're too many of them. Even with my umbrella," he gestured to the corner. "My trusty umbrella. I can't take on this violent mob of angry floats, bent on revenge, on blood. So I run, whew! I run up the rest of the hill, whew! Into the house, whew! Into your arms." He rose and came over to her, his arms wide, a wide smile.

"Stan." She sighed, hugged him, turning to go to her desk and the files on The Oval.

But he was not through. "Of course, I wonder, even as I run, how did it get free? Did Tony fail to dispose of it properly? Or was he so innocent that he simply dropped it in our garbage can, and it escaped? Or was it dumped into the garbage truck, hoisted up and dropped into the bin?"

Felicia had come back into the kitchen, summoning, she believed, the patience of Job to hear him out. Something has clearly broken loose in her husband's mind.

"Yes, that must be it. Only when it was about to be compacted, smashed into nothingness by the giant piston of the garbage truck, did it scramble, wheezing and clicking, calling out to his mates, 'Gchyssss, Gchyoooo,' scramble up the wall of the truck, just in time, leap or fall over the edge, rolling itself into the woods, under leaves, propelling itself with an incredible will to survive into the forest, where it would recover from its wounds, heal, find a mate, and breed."

83

His eyes were wide now. "It will bring more of those terrible things into the world! Fel, we must get out while we can!"

Felicia looked at him for perhaps a minute as he seemed finally to have concluded. Then she asked, "Have you made that appointment with Dr. Heady?" Sometimes her sympathy for his lonely childhood gave way to frustration.

In the space where she'd been Stan pictures Jean Triplet, the Perfect Third, surrounded by a splinter group from the army of escaped toilet tank floats. She cowers in the corner of a bathroom, screaming. He sees, in his imagination, that two buttons on her blouse have come loose, and her small, taut breasts are rising and falling. She would be grateful to the man who rescued her, Stanley Measure, the new choir director.

Tom Baettner subscribed to the Domino Theory, the popular principle of the Cold War. If one country fell to Communism, others would inevitably follow, a chain reaction as sure as the process of an atomic explosion.

Felicia had believed it, too, when she was young. It's us against them, good versus evil, the West's freedom pitted against totalitarian East. Now she's concluded individual countries, even regions, are distinctive. Not all will be drawn by a Pied Piper, Communism or "Islamic Fundamentalism," whatever that is. Church life has taught her that many times over.

Here was Sonja demanding a woman priest; ready to resist that at all costs, the Lynne twins. What middle ground could contain them? Robin Shure breathed the pure air of spirit, but practical worm farmer Larry Thornton lived in an earthly realm.

84

She'd like to subscribe to miracles, evidence of a power beyond anything she's known that could translate matters into a new frame, explode old boundaries: *"heaven and earth shall flee away / when He comes to reign."* But it's hard.

She thought again of a skating rink, The Oval of her teenage years. Perhaps seventy-five people circling the building, all moving in one direction on the same track led by recorded organ music. Were they a unified social entity, or a random coming together of eclectic individuals momentarily sharing an orbit? Would any song inspire them to skate to a common drummer?

Right now she has enough trouble trying to coordinate actions with one other person. She and her husband are supposed to be two people bound together in marriage, perhaps the oldest and most fundamental social unit. She remembered Larry telling her recently about Homer's Odysseus and Penelope, a representation of profound union.

One of Larry's ongoing retirement projects was reading the classics. Years of practicing law and serving as a judge had, he said, made him curious about human nature. How far apart on the spectrum of behavior and instinct were criminal and hero? Works like *The Odyssey* were supposed to answer such questions. He wondered how much there is common to men and women of other countries, different times. His conviction that there is an elemental human nature was, like everyone else's, shaken by 9/11.

"Odysseus has been away from home for twenty years," he had reminded Felicia last Sunday at the after-church social hour, neither wanting to talk about the search. "Before he arrives in Ithaca, he learns that other men have courted the Queen."

"Penelope?"

"Yes, but what they want is not just her. They want the kingdom, the rich estate Odysseus had build up with his strength and cunning and which she has held together, heroically, during his long absence."

Larry had explained that Odysseus, disguised as a wandering beggar, was the only one able to draw back the famous bow he'd left at home, and he used it to slay the arrogant suitors who surrounded Penelope. Perhaps Stan's account of his battle with the toilet tank floats made her recall the slaughter of Odysseus' enemies, though the comparison, sadly, was ludicrous.

"Penelope still wasn't sure this was her husband," Larry continued. "After all, he'd been gone two decades, ten years fighting the Trojan War and another ten beset by hardships on the journey home. She been proposed to by dozens."

"Odysseus had been turned into a pig by Circe, right?" she asked. "He had to be bound to the mast to resist the sirens, nearly eaten by the Cyclops."

"Yes, Polyphemus, a bad man indeed! If Penelope had known all Odysseus had endured, she would have welcomed him with open arms. But she had to be suspicious of any man because so many had tried to woo her, to win her hand . . . and her land."

Felicia thought, not for the first time, of how difficult it is, first, to chose a mate, then to remember why you did. Stan's middle- or later-age crisis made it hard for her to recognize the undisguised innocent nature of the fire watcher she'd fallen in love with so many years ago. But to keep the marriage, she must preserve that image.

"Penelope devises one more challenge for the beggar who claims to be her husband: describe their marriage bed."

Odysseus had built their bed out of the trunk of a huge olive tree. Around the bed he constructed a room, a palace, a kingdom. If the marriage was as deep and strong as the tree, Greek society would endure. Penelope and Odysseus inspired a world.

"Odysseus passes his last test," concludes Larry.

Was the bed Felicia shared with Stan a model for any of the social organizations she belonged to: Over-Due, Holy Trinity, Fairfield, Missouri, the United Stages, the global village? Could she still say after thirty years *"what I can I give him / give my heart"*? Perhaps she should try harder, especially as Stan's father never came home from his war.

Chapter 14: And Heal the Hearts of Men

Sitting uneasily in Dr. Heady's waiting room, Stan thumbed through an issue of *Route 66 News*, a year and half out of date. If a plumber had repaired his toilet, he had concluded, perhaps a physician could realign the machinery of his manhood.

Route 66 News featured a variety of new roadside attractions along the Mother Road: a Kansas motel with a garish neon "Va-Kansas-ies" sign; an Arizona cafe with 37 different kinds of hamburgers; a restored drive-in movie theater in Illinois showing foreign art films on alternate Wednesday nights. Stan hummed a few bars of "Get Your Kicks on Route 66."

"Doc," he imagined saying, "I'm not getting my kicks so often, know what I mean?"

Though he watched television irregularly, he'd seen those Viagra commercials. Even some of his trade magazines included pictures of older couples (their wrinkles politely air-brushed away) in obvious romantic situations: reclining on a tropical beach, suntanned and trim; entering a luxurious hotel room where the bed was turned back, chocolates on the pillow; gazing at a mountain sunset, one arm around a shoulder, another sliding purposely down a back.

"Mr. Measure? Stanley Measure?" called the receptionist, holding up a clipboard and scanning the waiting room.

"Here. That would be me." He would have liked to pursue fantasy couplings. These real bodies, he thought, when they age, are not so pretty. Felicia could have told him only one was pure: "*yet unto earth alone was given / His human form to know*."

"Through that door, third room on the right."

Stan wondered what he would be asked to do, once he explained his problem. Of course, he hoped to be given a prescription, no embarrassing questions asked, but . . . would he, for instance, have to provide details? Were there tests of the system, monitors of response? Would he have to explain what had gotten him excited in the past?

"Have a seat," said the receptionist, scanning the room as if she'd never seen it before. She put the clipboard in a box on the outside of the door. "The doctor will be with you shortly."

"Shortly?" Was that an indirect reference to his problem? In making the appointment, he'd only suggested a review of his medication. Would they know what he really meant? Perhaps he should declare himself cured right now and leave.

Was his problem stress related? Retired, he faced no work pressures or, for that matter, money worries. Still, joining the choir at Holy Trinity made him feel uncomfortable at times--the Lynne twins' pithy but opaque instructions, Melody's teary eyes when he'd shrugged his shoulders at her entreaties, the Perfect Third's failure to see he even existed.

The door opened; a lean, young, energetic woman entered. He had assumed he would see Dr. Heady, his regular doctor.

"So," she said, scanning his chart, "there's a problem with what you're taking for blood pressure?" She closed the door behind her, decisively, Stan thought. Her name tag read "Dr. Montgomery."

He did not answer. How young was this person? She couldn't be thirty! Slim, athletic, undeniably attractive. He stared at her stethoscope, just above eye level in his sitting position and warm, he assumed, in its nest.

"Mr. Measure?" She gave a little wave in front of his face and raised her eyebrows, smiling. "Are you feeling a bit light headed in the mornings? Or when you get up from a chair suddenly?" With one foot in a low heeled pump, she pulled a black and chrome stool on wheels over in front of him and sat on it.

"I . . . um, I thought I would be seeing Dr. Heady. I've always seen him." He was stretching the truth, as this was a team practice. But having had no emergencies, he'd generally been able to schedule appointments with one man.

She smiled, folding her arms around the clipboard. "Oh, he's out with a bug, one of those 24-hour things. I'm Dr. Montgomery." She smiled and held out her hand.

"Ah." He understood that he was to shake her hand and did so.

"And I'm new, replacing Dr. Jensen, who retired."

Stan had known that Jensen, who had once been Felicia's doctor, planned to retire. Still, this wasn't fair.

"I could come another day," he offered, leaning forward as if he was rising, "when Martin is here. Uh, no offense, I mean."

She slid closer on her stool. "Mr. Measure, you do have a history of hypertension, which," she turned the chart around toward him, "has gotten more serious in the last year. See these readings?" The chart blocked any escape.

Stan looked around the office at the examining table, the cabinets, the posters explaining a human ear, bone density, the circulatory system. He saw the box of latex gloves, the cue tips, the jar of tongue depressors. Good Lord, what's going to happen?

"Let's see what your pressure is. Which arm do you usually use?" She pulled the stethoscope from her neck up to her ears, rolled closer to him, and took the cuff from a tray.

He searched for something to say while she squeezed the rubber bulb and watched the dial. She had tucked his forearm between her side and her upper arm, supporting it. He felt the warmth of her body and an unexpected firmness in her muscles.

She pursed her lips as the cuff tightened. He willed his body to relax until air hissed through the rubber tube as she released the pressure. Then she pumped the bulb again.

Was this woman married? With children? Was she really an M.D.? From her looks, she could be Jean Triplet's sister.

"It is up today, more than . . . " She studied the chart. " . . . more than recently." She jotted some notes.

"That's not why I came. I mean, I don't think that's usual, it's the surprise of . . . not seeing Dr. Heady. I'm, um, sort of worked up, I guess."

Oh, surely he didn't say that! "Worked up." Why didn't he just say "turned on" She was still holding his arm, her hand cupping his elbow. Was her knee bumping his?

"White coat syndrome. Yes, that can happen." She let go of his arm, scooted back on her stool toward the examining table. "Why don't we chat a few minutes, then take another reading. You're . . . " still studying the chart, "retired? What work were you in, Mr. Measure?"

"Uh, it's Stanley. Anyway, I did alarm systems, Wall-All Securities, 25 years."

He'd decided, without fully conceptualizing it, to stall. If his pressure went back down, he'd say he had only wanted to double check. He'd schedule another appointment in a few weeks, insisting that it be with Dr. Heady.

"You know, I'm sure, that some people--men more than women--have trouble retiring, learning to relax. Do you have hobbies?"

"I sing. Just a church choir right now, but, I want to start my own group. It's," he lied, "kind of a lifetime ambition that got sidetracked when my career went so well."

"Singing is good," she agreed. "There was a study recently that showed people who are in barbershop quartets actually stay healthier and live longer than others." She leaned back and studied his physique. "Do you get regular exercise?"

Stan ignored the question. "I'm actually working toward a solo role, Nat King Cole, 'Get Your Kicks on Route 66.'"

"Route 66?" She was puzzled. Must not be a Midwesterner, he thought. Those people would know the Mother Road. And she's too young for the television series.

"The highway? America's most famous one?"

"Ah." She had taken his arm again, tucked it against her side. He wanted her to understand.

"Steinbeck, *Grapes of Wrath*, the road people took in the Depression to escape the Dust Bowl?" He felt his arm warm from her body heat. Or was he imagining that? He could smell her perfume as he tried to look anywhere but where the stethoscope had been.

She released the air, whssss. "That's better. Not good yet, but not as high as it was."

He could care less what his pressure was.

"Mr. Measure, Stanley. The medication you're on, Lisinipol, can have side effects. Have you experienced diarrhea or nausea in the last few weeks? How about dizziness or rashes? Do you feel you might have had an unusual number of colds or respiratory problems? Have you encountered any erectile dysfunction?"

He wanted to say, quite honestly, "Not right now." Would it be heresy to think, "*How blest was all creation then, when God so gave increase*"? Yes, he thought, sadly, it would.

Chapter 15: The Rose I have in Mind

"They want a jingle? Some sort of slogan for The Oval?" Felicia asked. She was sitting in what had once been a garage along business Route 66. The little building was to be transformed into a Mother Road museum.

"Jin*gles*," answered Meg, emphasizing the second syllable. Donna had called to say she would be a few minutes late. "About a dozen or so to go around the rink, like Burma-Shave signs in the old days. You know, they'll make messages on five or six little electric signboards."

"Oh, yeah: 'Don't take that curve / at sixty per; / We can't afford to lose / a customer. / Burma-Shave.' I'm not sure we do verse, let alone good verses."

Her inner ear heard the words of one of her favorite hymns: "*It came, a floweret bright, / amid the cold of winter, / when half spent was the night.*" Now, that was poetry.

"Exactly," agreed Meg. "And it's worse than that: Miss Cooper says they will need to change every few weeks. They want them to be distinctive, memorable, but also continually new." The Burma-Shave road sign advertising campaign, begun in 1925, ran for over forty years and produced hundreds of verses.

Donna pushed through the door, followed by a blast of cold air. Winter was coming, and all they had at the Road House right now were two small space heaters. She put off her coat and took the third stool at the counter. This would become an information desk for the museum, if they could complete The Oval and use the earned resources for this project.

She asked Meg. "You've told her?"

"Not the worst."

"There's more!" exclaimed Felicia.

"You say," sighed Meg, nodding to Donna.

"They seem to think . . . well, now I might have this wrong, but . . . Oh, I'm afraid this is right. They want the jingles to be a bit, um, provocative."

"Risque? For a 1950s style roller rink! What are they thinking?"

They were meeting at the Road House rather than in their usual places--the Middleman Bakery or the former Fanny's Dairy Delight--so they wouldn't be interrupted. The town had grown around this garage, and the former owner had put a privacy fence to protect it from vandalism before deeding it to the town. It was the place Over-Due sometimes met for crises.

"We agree," said Meg. "But listen to the sample Miss Cooper passed on."

Donna took a letter from an envelope, scanned it, frowned and read. "Don't go too fast; / You'll end up fallin'. / If you clown, / and go down, / It's roller ballin'!"

Felicia took the paper and studied the lines. "'It's roller ballin'.' Well, the skates have wheels, like balls . . . the skaters are . . .

"Do you know the movie, *Roller Ball*?"

"Um, no. That's what they're referring to?"

"Perhaps, but, it's a futuristic movie, not really appropriate, at least to our idea of The Oval." She'd been made to watch it by her son home from college last Christmas. The violence scared her.

"Maybe they just didn't know that. The jingle makes sense, I guess, though . . there are some other phrases."

"Like 'Go down'?" questioned Donna.

Felicia frowned. "The meter's not right anyway. Why don't we find out what we can come up with-- that's clean, of course--and see what they say? Maybe Mr. Mayle hasn't learned . . . you know, all that."

All three women were pleased to know exactly what she meant by "all that.'" Their generation didn't have to spell it out. Felicia was also thinking about Stan. His recent lovemaking suggestions seemed to have come from nowhere--maybe from "all that."

She knew he didn't read those racy titles that appeal to some women's book clubs; he had no circle of poker-playing, beer-drinking male friends; he didn't, so far as she knew, even surf the Internet for . . . for "all that." But, if he knew about such things, Mr. Mayle surely must know, too.

Meg, former elementary school teacher, shrugged. "Fourth graders know as much as we do, but sometimes their grandparents don't."

Donna chuckled. "You know what? I was thinking about it on the way over, and, maybe if we tried, we could come up with jingles that are suggestive, but tasteful. Cute, sort of."

They were all remembering a more innocent youth, when there was a uniform code for public speech. If you had been properly raised, the theory went, you could include a tasteful reference to any part of the body generally not named in public. It was possible to allude indirectly to an act usually acknowledged only when barnyard animals were involved. Emotional outbursts could be contained in powerful but acceptable expressions.

Now, every age, ethic group, gender, sexual preference, and political interest group had its special vocabulary, its precise standards for what could and could not be said. Society as a whole didn't agree on common meanings or shared syntactical structure--a tower of Babel indeed, thought Felicia.

"Being suggestive but not out of line, that's a tall order," Meg said; but Donna agreed to experiment and report back in a few days. She claimed her years of overhearing doctors' locker room discussion of patients' conditions just might have prepared her for the task.

Felicia explained that she would be traveling some in the future in connection with the search for a new rector, so her work on The Oval would be limited. "And," she admitted, "Holy Trinity needs a choir director."

When she said it, her face fell. Donna noticed and asked, "But that's not your problem, is it?"

"No, that's the vestry's job. But, Stan, my Stan, has talked about volunteering."

"Didn't he just start singing this year? Is he that good?"

"No . . . no, he's not. He's learning, really. I think he's restless and needs something to do. I'm so busy. He's at home alone a lot . . . " Her voice trailed off.

"Here's an idea," volunteered Donna. "He uses a computer, right?"

"Yes, to a degree, mostly e-mail and playing games online, solitaire and things like that." She was worried they would think he wasn't even capable of surfing for sites that showed beautiful women, movie stars and female athletes.

"Here's what you do," explained Donna. "Get him to join Double-I/Double-You, the virtual community. My brother, after his divorce, loved it." She admired the site's quirky, if inconsistent, abbreviation: "ii/w."

"I don't know what that is, though I think I've heard something about it."

"You create an alternative self, completely fictional, and interact with other made-up people--double 'I,' double 'you.' Bill didn't want to date after he and Sarah separated, but he needed folks to talk with. And it's safe. You never see or meet the people behind the masks." She paused. "At least you're not supposed to."

Felicia remembered Stan wearing a Spider-man suit, pretending to be Nat King Cole, escaping an imaginary army of toilet tank floats. He's hard enough to deal with as himself, she thought: her retired security expert, generally kind-hearted if absentminded father, too often self-absorbed husband. Could she survive if there were more of him?

They agreed to meet in a week and hear Donna's report. Meg said she wanted to see if she could find out more about Mr. Mayle. All they knew, really, was that his grandfather had lived in Fairfield and run the original roller rink. Had he grown up in his grandfather's house? Or only visited there at various times?

Noone at Over-Due could remember any children named Mayle in their generation. What could they find on the Internet, that vast, geometrically expanding compendium of miscellaneous information? Learning some things might allow them to shape their design more effectively, anticipating the clients' needs and thus giving themselves more control of the project and their own professional future.

Driving home, Felicia tried to compose a jingle: "Don't take that curve / At breakneck speed; / You'll slip or slide / And find you've peed!" No, no.

Again she heard the beautiful words: *"This Flower, whose fragrance tender / with sweetness fills the air, \ dispels with glorious splendor / the darkness everywhere."* What have she and her friends gotten themselves into?

Chapter 16: Amid the Winter's Snow

Larry Thornton--retired judge, sometimes pro bono lawyer, active worm farmer--was waiting for Felicia in her living room. Stan had told him she'd be home shortly and retired to the den. "A perfect host," Felicia muttered, hanging her coat in the closet.

Because Larry was on the search committee, seeing him in her living room told Felicia that she was bouncing from one set of problems at The Oval to another at Holy Trinity.

"We have the results of the questionnaire," he told her.

The diocesan consultant had insisted the committee survey the congregation. He wanted to develop a church profile and, indirectly, a picture of the rector they hoped to find. Dropping a manilla folder on the coffee table, Larry concluded, "Just what I'd predicted."

Felicia sighed, knowing he'd opposed the whole process. Ever since Larry's comments the Sunday after 9/11, though, she'd paid a lot of attention to his opinions. She was encouraged when he'd cited *The Last of the Mohicans* to suggest adversity brings out the best in all of us.

Unfortunately, she also knew his references to Hawkeye and his companions singing hymns in a wilderness cave had inspired Stan to think he could ride Bobby Troup's classic to stardom.

"Let's talk in the kitchen," she said to Larry.

Larry had heard too many legal arguments in his twenty years on the bench not to predict that gathering the views of 75 or more parishioners would produce 75--or more!--ideas about each issue. And, as a trial lawyer, he had learned that conflicting eye-witness accounts were the norm. His wife's experience on town council had also reinforced his understanding that consensus is a rare event in human affairs.

"You mean the survey doesn't give us much clear direction?" Felicia asked. She set a bottle of Pinot Grigio and two glasses on the kitchen table.

"Well, it concludes that we need to be 'socially active' and concentrate on our own 'corporate worship.' We have to raise money through the every member canvass and reduce expenses. We should explore new liturgy and music while retaining the ancient traditions of the church. Perhaps you don't think that's direction?" He snorted and filled both wine glasses.

Felicia laughed, too. "I suspect we also have to rely on a literal interpretation of the Bible and keep up-to-date on the latest church doctrine, retain our ties to the larger Anglican communion while stoutly maintaining our independence, be more spiritual and put new fixtures in the rest rooms. Our new priest will have to be all things to all people!"

"Perhaps we should hire a committee for our priest."

"Oh, spare us that! I wish Chris Moore would . . . I don't know--decide he had too many other things to attend to."

Chris was on the search committee. He and his wife Betty were accountants, and they ran their own business in Fairfield. Felicia felt he was in love with PowerPoint, his ability to make electronic spreadsheets, graphs, pie charts. He'd spearheaded the survey.

"He should work more with worms," mused Larry.

"Computer worms?" She'd read about malicious invasion by such rogue software and how honey pots could repel them. Relying on younger friends for help with changing technology, she couldn't distinguish worms from Trojan horses or viruses, but knew there were many kinds constantly evolving into yet more forms.

"No, real worms, earthy fellows."

She laughed. "We're not that bad, are we?" thinking at first he was referred to the congregation. Like the Lynne twins and Sonja Peterson, many parishioners continued to press for their own preferences in a new priest. But then she realized he was talking about the earthworms he raised for local fisherman and organic gardeners.

"No, but they teach you humility about calculation. You think you can predict what they'll do--eat, crawl, contract and expand--but you're too often surprised even with such simple creatures."

Larry's wife Susan could never share his enthusiasm for worm farming and had resisted for years returning to Fairfield, where they had both grown up. A contestant in the teenage Miss Route 66 pageant years ago, she'd soured on local politics and small town gossip when she finished high school. But something had changed a few years back, and she agreed to retire to her old home town.

"Earthworms," Larry explained," are one of the few living things I'm willing to put into a single group, but even there, every once in a while you'll find an outlier." He had read recently about a giant albino earthworm, reported to smell like a lily. One study suggested it could spit when threatened.

Felicia thought of Stan as the consistent outlier (if, she added to herself, that phrase "consistent outlier" makes any sense). 'Don't try this at home,' she imagined an announcer saying in a future television commercial. It showed her husband as regular odd man out in Holy Trinity choir. 'He's a trained professional.'

"I like eclectic grouping," she admitted. "Modesty aside, I think that's how Over-Due is succeeding, bringing harmony from disparate units."

"If we can do it with this," Larry thumped the folder with a large forefinger, "we're magicians . . . or class action lawyers."

She realized she should change the subject quickly. For years Larry had battled class action attorneys on behalf of insurance companies, and Felicia had heard his arguments about "classes" more than once.

Before becoming a judge, Larry had encountered too many attorneys who created rather than identified an injured group. Finding one individual--an elderly man who slipped on a banana peel at a Kroger's--they would seek out anyone who'd been injured in any store and claim they were part of a group that had been wronged. Gullible people were easy to recruit to the cause, feeling they deserved reparation if anyone else did. And soon a suit was on.

Larry's counter attack was always the same: to expose the vast range of differences among individuals in the so-called "class." He would argue that the original plaintiff, at age 80, fell because he was unstable; so, he would tell the judge, only white males over six feet tall and older than 80 living alone in an urban environment could be included in this action.

Especially when the suing lawyers were stretching their argument, Larry could convince a judge or a jury that 99% of those included in the suit were not hurt because the store was at fault--let along the chain, the stores in similar chains, the parent corporations that contained a variety of different businesses.

"Just about everyone in Holy Trinity is an outlier," Larry told Felicia. "And this survey proves it. A single example: to question #47, 'What should be the new rector's top priority?,' we have 32 different answers. And that's if you're generous in putting loosely related answers together."

"So, what do we do? Ask to shorten the questionnaire, make it be multiple choice?"

Larry chuckled, and Felicia imagined she was on the defense team hearing him propose a surprise strategy. "Have another glass," he said, pouring one for himself.

She hesitated, then poured. "You sound conspiratorial."

"Only to those who think we have to follow the book in every detail."

"Go on."

"Okay. I'm going to write up a one-page summary of the survey results. We'll say it's been checked carefully with the individual forms. Then we'll conveniently forget where we put the forms."

She thought about what he was saying for a moment, then concluded. "You mean you're going to collate responses in such a way that a clear vision of who we are and what we want will be the result?"

"Exactly."

She thought this would be a sin of monumental proportions . . . or, paradoxically, a miracle. "*Lo, within a manger lies*," she thought. "*He who built the starry skies; / He who, thronèd in height sublime, / Sits amid the cherubim.*"

"Hmm. And who is the 'we' that does this?"

He looked around the room, as if expecting to find the rest of their committee arranged on the sofa and some dining room chairs that had been brought in. "I think everyone here should be fully informed."

"Sweet mother of God," Felicia exclaimed. "You and I are about to stitch up a church out of whole cloth!"

Chapter 17: Over the Hills and Everywhere

Upstairs, Stan was tugging up the pants of his Spider-man suit. If, he thought, Felicia wanted him to be someone else--to join, that is, Double-I/Double-You--why not do it with a secret, superhero identity? He didn't need to be a crime fighter with genuine superpowers, but at least he should be someone out of the ordinary. Secret Security Man, perhaps.

Studying himself in the bedroom mirror, however, he was too aware of the extra weight he'd put on in the last six months. Retirement sloth, he knew.

When he'd last worn this skintight outfit, he'd been able to fool himself that it wasn't so bad. But then he'd been imagining himself the way Felicia was supposed to see him, deliberately failing to acknowledge the drooping belly, the rolls around his waist, an overall absence of muscle tone. It seemed as if his body had sprouted new parts that had never been integrated into the whole. These extra lumps and bulges performed no function.

The Specialized Hardrock GX mountain bike in the garage--perhaps he should start riding it to lose weight? He could wear this costume--under some sweat clothes, of course.

Where had he heard about that rails-to-trails project recently? Ooh, was it at the doctor's office, from that young woman, Dr. Montgomery, who told him he needed to exercise? Would there be information about it on the Internet? Would there be information about her on the Internet?

He bent down to look at the crotch of his Spider-man pants. Shouldn't there be padding there if he goes biking? Might that narrow saddle do damage to a sensitive area? If he were perched on that thin ridge and pedaling for miles, would pressure on his . . . um . . . equipment add to his problems of marital performance? He couldn't ask Dr. Montgomery.

He vaguely remembered that the hiking, biking, and horse riding trail was being built on the bed of an abandoned railway spur west of Fairfield. It wasn't that far from the neighborhood he'd grown up in, west of which were woods and farms. He visualized The Circle, where he'd been young and active. Where this body, much younger, worked so easily he had to struggle to keep it from going off on its own.

The Missouri-Pacific's main trunk line, parallel to Route 66 coming from St. Louis on its way toward Oklahoma, passed through the middle of Fairfield and then ran just to the north of Limestone Street in a deep cut through Piney Ridge. Trains thundered past The Circle's several dozen homes night and day, but they were invisible from street level. (Early in his childhood, he could see steam from the hidden engines rising behind the Limestone Street houses.) On the next street over, Oak, where Stan had lived with his mother, that sound of train traffic was even more muffled.

Circle kids played along the tracks in the woods to the west, where the railway bed had been built up from the valley floor. They stayed south of the railroad, almost never crossing. Still, the children "*kept their watching*" for regular passenger and irregular freight traffic.

The spur, parallel to the main line but a few hundred yards to the south, had been used to park old passenger cars needing repair. Most of that work was

107

done in the little town of Newville, ten miles away, but there was often overflow at that facility. The spur had been abandoned sometime in the late 1970s as Amtrak cut back on service, but the right of way had remained with the railroad until a few years ago. Now it was officially a county park, ten miles long and fifty feet wide.

In his early teenage years, Stan had sometimes snuck into empty passenger cars, intrigued by their mechanics and the romance of travel. In many imagined scenarios, he was not just going to exotic places but experiencing erotic encounters. Love on a Pullman!

He'd seen Marilyn Monroe in *Some Like it Hot* three times at the Uptowne. And in one imagined scenario he added to that already steamy plot his own quirky idea of flirtation. What was the name of that woman in the movie? Not Montgomery, surely! No, Sugar; it was Sugar Kane. What did his son say--"sweet"?

In Billy Wilder's 1959 classic, Sugar/Marilyn Monroe was traveling by train with an all-girl band, trying to escape from men . . . and from her own attraction to men. In a key sleeper car scene, she doesn't realize that two of her fellow passengers, played by Tony Curtis and Jack Lemmon, are really men in disguise.

In Stan's version of that crucial scene--recalled as he gazes at himself in the mirror decades later--he and Marilyn/Sugar are alone in the sleeper car rather than surrounded by a dozen female musicians. He's been hired by the company to see how teenage boys are jumping aboard when the train moves slowly through a residential neighborhood. Instead of boys, though, he finds a beautiful blonde hiding in the lavatory.

"What have we here?" Stan/Joe says, leaning on one side of the doorjamb with an arm blocking her escape. Among the things they have there are her bare shoulders and knowing, provocative eyes. It's just the situation he's longed for.

In the movie, Sugar, finding Joe/Curtis awake, agrees to share a few drinks, passing the time of the journey. Marilyn climbs into the upper berth with "Jennifer." Believing this fellow traveler is another girl, she doesn't realize that Joe's heavy breathing and sweaty brow come from their snuggling into the covers. It's the one-on-one Joe had hoped for from the beginning of the journey. He decides to reveal his true identity only after they've both gone mellow with a bit of whiskey.

"I'm . . . I'm the porter," Sugar tells Stan in his fantasy. Inspecting the tiny space, she announces confidently, "Everything okay here." She turns sideways, as if to slip past him. "Excuse me. I need to turn down the berths."

He continues to stand in her way. "The porter? I thought they were all men. And you're definitely *not* a man." His evidence for this is visible in her blouse with its top button unattached.

Middle-aged Stan sat down on the edge of the bed, reminiscing and daydreaming at the same time. The Sugar in his fantasy is played by Felicia when she worked at the drug store and he was a fire tower guard. Her blouse, too, gaps at the top.

In the movie Sugar's excitement awakens another girl in the band, who is then eager to join the party. Joe, of course, wants to be alone with Sugar. But the second girl offers to bring some vermouth, and her rummaging through her luggage initiates a chain reaction among the musicians.

Another girl has peanut butter, someone else holds up a salami, a third promises cheese and crackers. Glasses (paper cups), cocktail shaker (hot water bottle), and a corkscrew are found. Pretty soon the berth is packed with a menagerie of increasingly tipsy and excited women in night clothes exchanging food and drink--plus a ticklish Joe.

Stan begins to dislike the movie scene when the gaggle of girls crowd into the upper berth with Joe and Sugar. It's the kind of complication that always seems to occur in his own life, confusing roles and eroding boundaries. He longs for the simplicity he always had as the only child of a single parent.

"I'm going to have to see some kind of identification," Stan tells the beautiful stowaway. He's already thinking it will be necessary to frisk her for train property she may have concealed on her spectacular person: little bars of scented soap, courtesy blankets, magazines featuring love making tips. Her clothes hang so loosely on her, he feels such a search would be easy.

As the party continues in the movie, one of the girls wakes Jerry/Jack in the lower berth by asking if he has any maraschino cherries for the manhattans they're now mixing. Soon s/he's in the lavatory with Sugar, who is chipping pieces off a big block of ice they'd pulled from a train cooler. As Marilyn works, she explains her addiction to men, and soon there's a second man in the Pullman who needs to be cooled down.

Teenage Stan had to cool himself down in the abandoned passenger car.

110

After he asked the woman with bare shoulders what happened to the complimentary mints that were to be left on pillows in made-up berths, she leaned close, her lips grazing his ear. A wisp of blonde hair tickled his check and a hand found his hip. She whispered in that sweet Marilyn Monroe voice, "Search me."

Another voice asked, "What have we here?"

Leaning on the doorjamb of his bedroom, an arm blocking any escape, stood Felicia. She saw her husband in a Spider-man suit at least one size too small. "If this is a web crawler trying to behave badly, Spidey, then I'm your worst nightmare."

From a recent choir practice, Stan heard yet another voice: "*behold throughout the heavens / there shone a holy light.*"

Chapter 18: Like Stars His Children

Stan, getting up, tried to laugh this off. "No, no. Just me, checking on . . . on the toilet. I wanted to be sure the leak is completely fixed."

Felicia was embarrassed. She'd actually come upstairs with the idea of romance. Talking with Donna and Meg had made her think she might have been too hard on her husband recently. His physical problem might be psychological, and the last thing she should do is be negative. And, to tell the truth, coming into the bedroom she had imagined her hands on him in spandex and was not put off at the prospect.

"You're being a plumber in your Spider-man suit?"

Stan decided to confess to part of his reflections. "Actually, I was thinking about taking up your suggestion, biking, for exercise."

"Oh. Well, that would be good." She was relieved on one score. "But in that, in public?"

"As insulation, really, under some other things. Say, where is that new trail . . . ?"

As Felicia reminded him of things he was supposed to know already, she thought of Stan as a teenage boy, son of a woman whose husband had died in war. She knew one of the reasons she'd first been attracted to him was the air of loneliness that had surrounded him, especially compared to the crowded family and social life she'd always enjoyed. With two sisters and two brothers, she was almost never alone. And her family's active role at Holy Trinity filled her week with regular services and her vacations with special events.

Stan, on the other hand, spent much time in his attic bedroom on the other side of The Circle. Felicia knew that his mother had been almost pathologically reclusive, but why didn't her son at least try to join in neighborhood games?

"I was reading," she told him, "about exercise and . . . um . . . sexual activity. Especially for older men.

"Older men?" He began peeling off the top of his costume.

"Well, sure, not that you're 'elderly,' by any means. Still, we should both do more to stay in shape, perhaps start going to the Y." The minute she said it, of course, she knew he would balk at joining any organization.

"All those people," he reminded her. "All those people wanting to compare their statistics--their weight, body mass, cholesterol. Everyone an oddball one way or other but thinking you're just like them, one happy family. Count me out."

"Biking would be good for you, though. The bike's in the garage. I could borrow Meg's and go with you." Couldn't the two of them form a group with shared interests?

He had paused in undressing, though he wasn't quite sure why. If Larry had gone, supper would be soon, and he should have clothes on for that. Still, the memory of Sugar left him interested in . . . well, frisking, or being frisked, or being frisky?

"Do you know who invented the bicycle?" he asked, thinking perhaps she'd sit to listen. "There's a debate about that, you know."

Felicia did sit, her smile suggesting she was ready to hear him out. He didn't see yet how he could turn discussion of the celerifere and velocopede into their playing Pullman Car.

"I would have thought it existed before the days of patents. It's just two wheels on a frame."

"Not quite. There had been scooters of sorts in Europe for some centuries before the key element of a bicycle, as a system, was discovered. And descendants of two different men claim a family right to ownership of that idea."

Again, Felicia's heart softened as she listened, believing such knowledge came from nights of solitary reading as other children played. When the weather was bad, marathon games of Monopoly, Careers, Clue went on with her brothers and sisters. Their parents would demand the lively sessions end at midnight so everyone could get some sleep. But sometimes muffled play went on in a closet by flashlight.

"The idea of a bicycle?" she asked. "It's the same as a scooter with pedals."

"Yes and no. That's the difference, but propulsion isn't the whole secret to the bicycle's success, or why the patent was registered originally."

Actually, he wasn't sure about the specific claims of the patent. He had read about this long ago and couldn't remember all the details.

"Two French brothers--Michaux, I think it was-- claimed the central principle in the 1860s or 1870s. But a Pierre Lallement--it's now asserted by his great-great-(whatever) grandsons--had submitted an application earlier, identifying the same principle."

"Did you have a bicycle growing up? I don't remember . . . "

114

She was going to say she didn't recall him with her brothers, racing down driveways, sidewalks, wooded paths. Her mind's eye pictured one group (cops) on red Western Auto bikes, blue Schwinns, a lone silver Batavus Flying Arrow pulling up Hill Street in pursuit of a second group (robbers). Where was her future husband? She thought how even Christ suffered childhood; he *"was little, weak and helpless, /tears and smiles like us he knew."* Why was this tugging at her heartstrings now?

"Sure, sure. I had a bike, though it had 24-inch wheels, and it . . . always needed repair." He stood up and walked to the window. "I spent more time indoors, working on electronics."

Felicia went to stand beside him, a hand on his shoulder. "Maybe you needed a better costume, like this Spider-man suit." She slid a hand below his waist and gave him a slight slap.

Stan chuckled and didn't move away. "Would you have been impressed if I had invented something like the bicycle? A new electronic device, maybe?" He slipped his arm around her waist. How comfortable it felt!

"You did invent devices, security systems that beat out your competitors back in the day."

"'Back in the day,'" he sighed.

Now he too recalled pictures of boys and girls racing through The Circle. He could see them from his room over the garage, hear them in summer months crying out the "1-2-3's on this one" in Hide-'n'-Seek, their "Olley-Olley send that one on over," the "Take three giant steps."

Listening, he knew they had to ask, "Mother may I." He never did at home.

His mother made few rules for her only son because he seemed to know from an early age how precarious her state was. She cried more than he did, slept poorly, and had few joys other than Stan's company. In order to keep her as happy as she could be, he never asked for much. And he joined in her few pleasures: listening to the radio, sewing, reading the Bible.

Felicia believed that all children would one day be "*at God's right hand on high; / when like stars His children crowned, / all in white shall wait around.*" She broke his reverie. "You know what I remember about bikes?"

"Hmm?"

"The seat. It hurt."

"Didn't you have one of those sheepskin covers? They were a good cushion."

"How did you know? It's true; I did."

"Oh, I just seem to remember . . . seeing you, probably on the way to Macy's to get something for your mom." Macy's was the neighborhood independent grocery store two blocks from The Circle. Kids used to be sent there for a forgotten loaf of bread, the laundry soap that had run out, one more box of Kleenex.

She turned toward him thoughtfully. "Well, that helped, but . . . women, you know . . . they're different from men. Down there."

"Hey, Spidey has to be careful about 'down there.' His web powers are, um, connected to 'down there.'"

"Down here?"

Afterwards, surprised at the unexpectedly restored capacity of his aging system, Stan explained the principle of the bicycle cited by the rival inventors: centrifugal force.

The bike's power wheel is really a gyroscope, keeping the machine and its rider upright, even at slow speeds. That was the problem with velocopedes and celeriferes; they fell over. Or the rider's feet had to be splayed to keep them vertical, tipping back this way, then that. But the pedal crank driving a wheel with a chain stabilized two-wheeled travel. And made one man famous.

Stan suspected he wouldn't ever be famous like Nat King Cole, but he wondered if he couldn't at least be stable once again.

Chapter 19: Matchless Gifts and Free

At the Middleman Bakery, Meg gave her report on Mr. Mayle's past. Donna was happy to postpone presentation of her trial jingles for roller rink patrons. And Felicia tried not to think her life was spinning out of control: Stan biking into the woods in a Spider-man suit; she and Larry shaping the church's future in secret; and her suspicion growing that Over-Due's resources were about to be Over-Drawn.

"Fairfield's one time resident," began Meg, a latté in one hand, the other holding a clipboard, "has, at least according to what I could learn, been engaged in a startling number of enterprises, the last being the sale of kaleidoscopes."

"Kaleidoscopes?" asked Felicia. She wondered if eating a cruller or two would be fair since Stan might actually try to get in shape and lose weight. But, ah, everything in this little shop was so good. And the Grays, who'd spent a lot of time cleaning and painting the old building, had created a comfortable atmosphere.

"Right. It was a mail order business, apparently quite successful. Sales were mostly overseas."

Donna said, "That's the tube you look in, right? Turn the end, and get changing patterns of shapes-- triangles, diamonds, trapezoids, whatever. All different colors, never the same thing twice."

"Yes. We all had them, didn't we, as children?"

"Of course. So maybe it ties in with his wanting to bring back the roller rink. He's a nostalgia buff and turns fads of the past into profit . . . I guess. But I don't know why he's been in so many different businesses."

"You mean, if one was successful, why didn't that just expand, go into franchises or something?" asked Donna.

"He may have saturated the market, especially with kaleidoscopes."

"Plus you can do so much more on the computer," Felicia pointed out. "Who needs a mere mechanical toy?"

Meg nodded. "Anyway, listen to what else he's done, which, I guess, has given him enough money to launch a renovated Oval. Mostly, he's had to do with toys. Back in the 1960s, it was the Slide Show-Er (not "shower," as in a bathroom). It was something like the View-Master. You insert a round cardboard disc with 1/2-inch square slides all around the circumference. It rotates to create a sequence of pictures."

"I remember. You look into a binocular type thing and take a tour of the Grand Canyon, or see the history of air flight, heroes of the Old West. My little brother had one."

Meg went on. "I guess I should have mentioned that Mayle enlisted right out of high school, for the signal corps. No one from his class seems to have kept in touch, so all I could find out was from public records. Anyway, he served in Texas and California, then several tours in Germany."

"He didn't ever return here?"

"Not that I could find out. Went to California and started a firm manufacturing playing cards. His came with a special shuffling machine. You put the whole stack in this plastic contraption about the size of a toaster, pull on this lever; they flutter in and come out the other side shuffled. I really don't understand how it worked."

"I've seen one that shuffled together two half-stacks."

"I couldn't find a picture of Mayle's. But I found he was also involved with board games, model train landscaping, croquet sets, an early electronic dart board, some sort of male cosmetics. And somewhere in there came the Paddle Ball for Adults."

"The thing with the ball on a rubber band? You see how many times you can bounce it off the paddle? It's a kid's toy, maybe an office amusement or party gimmick."

"Exactly, though again he had a special twist he used to market his version. It's a bit strange, if you ask me."

"Oh?" Felicia was worried she was seeing a pattern in these varied products.

"The paddle looked like someone's behind," explained Meg. "I don't understand how this was supposed to appeal to kids or adults, at least . . . well, you know."

"A man's or a woman's behind?" asked Donna.

"I'm not sure." she giggled. "You know, they all kind of look alike."

Felicia had been studying the trays of pastry in the glass cabinet, a delicious collection of standard donuts, Danish, fritters, eclairs; but also more distinctive items: almond bear claws, berry mousse pastries, custard filled star puffs, chocolate cream cheese gugulah, Czech walnut pastries, elephant ears, maple long johns, ruggelach, tropical Napoleons, Yugoslav kifle. "*Matchless gifts*" but not "*free*"!

"My son did a project," she mused, "on the kaleidoscope, junior high school science fair."

The others paused to listen. "The basic tube has mirrors and loose colored beads, pebbles, or metallic flakes. Light reflects off the mirrors, which are fixed lengthwise and at certain angles, say 45 degrees. That creates eight duplicate images of the objects at the other end for the viewer. When you spin the tube, the tumbling of the colored objects makes apparently symmetrical patterns, but it's an optical illusion in part--things being reflected and multiplied in the mirrors. A three-mirror model fills the observer's entire field with intricate combinations of colors and shapes."

"Wow! You were paying attention," exclaimed Meg. "Strange, I don't remember that you got an A in 7th grade science."

Donna laughed. "This reminds me of one of my proposed jingles: are you ready?"

"Let's hear it."

"As planets in orbit / spin 'round our suns, / keep yourself fit / while having fun; / make your lover git / after your buns / at The Oval."

"Oooh," said Felicia. "Well, at least we have a theme: buns and paddles shaped like your rear end."

"Believe it or not, I have another: "Round we go / fast and slow, / counter and clock-wise, / at The Oval. / Who's hip gets a prize / whose hips rock you'll know / at The Oval'"

"Nice!" admitted Donna.

"And just maybe risque," agreed Felicia. "You've got more?"

"I've got a dozen so far." She handed out a sheet. "Once you get started, it's not that hard. But not all are exactly the same pattern. They all have seven lines, but the length varies. And the rhyme scheme . . . and the meter . . ."

"No offense, Donna," said Meg, "but we don't really need Shakespeare for this job."

Felicia agreed. "Right. The jingles should be sort of amateurish, camp, tongue-in-cheek."

"Well, at least you're contributing to my body part allusions," laughed Donna. "Look these over and see if you like them enough. I've integrated them with decor sketches embodying the traditions of skating. I've also suggested seasonal variations, for Valentine's, 4th of July, Thanksgiving, things like that. Having a theme, that helps."

"A theme besides rear ends?" laughed Meg.

"Well, there are more body parts . . . " Donna grinned.

Felicia added, "We can have others for occasions like birthdays, graduations, bar mitzvahs. There's always 'National Home Room Parent Appreciation Week' or whatever. We just need to relate everything to roller skating. That *is* the central concept."

"And I've developed a design for the building space--skate rental station, grill, video center, manager's office, etc."

"Okay, then," concluded Donna. "We do have something to offer Mr. Mayle at our next meeting. When is that? Another week? And do we conclude he's someone we really want to work for, this man who capitalizes on children's games directed toward grownups?"

They exchanged uncertain looks, but then shrugged. It was worth going forward, at least for now. Of the poetry they would produce, however, Felicia concluded: *"Better witness to thy worth, / purer praise than ours on earth, / angels' songs afford."*

Felicia was also wondering, after Meg's review of Mr. Mayle's many-faceted past, why her husband had had just one career, one product, one dimension--until now. Now, she worried, he thinks he's going to get his kicks on Route 66.

If she'd seen him at that moment, she might have been even more concerned.

Stan was online registering with ii/w as "Buzz Murdock, high school dropout, fast on his feet and easy with the women." Would, he wondered, any of the site's female members care to ride on the back of his motorcycle?

Chapter 20: Plea and Gift and Sign

Stan/Bud was not mounting a Harley the next day, however, let alone inviting a fantasy guest to climb aboard. Instead he was trying to fit the mountain bike that had gathered dust at the back of the garage for nearly a decade behind the third seat of the minivan. His modest goal was to get in at least one rigorous, weight-loss-inspiring session before he saw Dr. Heady the next day. Much later, perhaps, he would have the body that would attract attractive fellow passengers..

In the meantime, Felicia's recent enthusiasm for Spider-man made him hope he could explain to his physician that a cure had been found for poor bedroom performance. Before choir practice the previous night he had even speculated that he might have one additional positive entry in his medical record. But two surprises had thrown sticks between his spokes, so to speak.

He'd originally planned to bike across town and then head down the trail. But, after a bit more deliberation, he decided it would be best to limit witnesses to this first excursion. So he drove to West Look Park. From there it was only a short walk up to the raised rail bed and the beginning of the biking/hiking/horse-riding path. It wasn't a good sign that he was huffing and puffing after that little bit of exercise.

Wondering where exactly the old Pullman car had been when he'd fantasized romantic adventures as a teenager, Stan conjured up with pleasure the image of Jean Triplet from the night before. Low slung jeans were the fashion for college students, and those of The Perfect Third hung symmetrically on her shapely hips.

When she stood upright, the bottom of the light knit top she wore lay neatly on the waistband of those jeans. But, as she lowered herself onto a folding metal chair, a two-inch gap magically opened to reveal a strip of flawless skin. Stan's eyes opened an analogous amount. Seeming to study the music in his folder closely, Stan was in fact fixated on that ribbon of youth.

No one was in sight on the ribbon of the former Missouri-Pacific train route. Stan adjusted his grip on the handlebars, his left foot on the pedal, the right planted on a fine gravel bed. He remembered how, as a boy, he would swing that right leg easily over the rear wheel, the weight on his left foot powering the bicycle's forward motion as he settled onto the seat: he was off!

The trail was straight for a quarter of a mile ahead of him before the first gradual turn around a small hill. And the grade, though gradual, was downhill, following the land's fall from the Fairfield plateau toward the distant Gasconade River. He was ready to ride into the future!

Stan's contemplation of a woman's waist (perhaps "a girl's" waist, as she had to be less than half his age) had been interrupted by Father Tack. "I'd like to introduce," he began, "someone who will serve as our interim--perhaps Holy Trinity's permanent--choir director."

A stern little man with a neat mustache appeared in the doorway, seemingly the result of some incantation, as no one had realized he had been out in the hall. Poof! The look on the choir's face showed that no one even knew who this was. He did not smile.

"Professor Sidney Hatter," stated Father Tack, pronouncing it "Haeter." "He's a newly retired, highly decorated scholar of choral music, who's recently bought a home in the Park."

The Park was a gated community north of town peopled primarily by couples whose urban homes had sold for far more than similar properties in Phipps County. They were a heterogeneous mix in terms of profession, ancestry, and church affiliation; but they were close in matters of style and politics.

"He's conducted groups in Germany, Austria, and Switzerland and been on the faculty of a dozen prestigious universities in his career. Professor, would you like to say a few words?"

"I'd prefer to start with vocal exercises. Please give me a B-flat," he instructed Karen. For ten minutes they sang scales, arpeggios, chords, and dissonances in different keys, time signatures, and tempos. Stan's throat hurt from the effort.

His rear end hurt from the fall. When he'd swung his right leg over the bicycle seat, lost his balance, turned the handlebars 90 degrees, he toppled onto his side. It was good he was alone!

On his second try he straddled the bike before attempting to put it into motion. With his left foot still on the bed, he rested his right foot on the right pedal. Then he lifted the left foot up and stepped down with the right. That successfully launched the bike forward. Soon he was proceeding--slowly and not necessarily in a straight line--down the trail. He didn't try to look left or right.

In subsequent trips he would encounter many sights along the trail's close bordering cliffs, sweeping valleys, and open plains. He even learned the names

126

of some birds he would observe on his rides: the frequently seen hairy, downy, pileated and red-bellied woodpeckers, less common northern flickers and red-headed woodpeckers, seasonal yellow-bellied sapsuckers. He identified none of the grasses known almost exclusively by the Latin names. The white-tailed jackrabbit, Ozark big-eared bat, masked shrew, and even one black bear were at various moments over the next few months in his vicinity, though they were recognized only as the movement of leaves or passing shadows.

He understood the term "ecosystem" in a general way, a community of interacting organisms and their physical environment; but he had no clear idea of how all these elements were coordinated and interdependent. The only organizing principle he felt was his own passage from just past West Look Park to the trail's end and the return trip, twice weekly. He was the center of this universe.

The Holy Trinity choir learned that Professor Hatter was the new center of their world, if not the Anglican communion stretching around the globe. He presented them with an order of hymns through Epiphany, changed most of the dynamic marks Melody had indicated for the Christmas oratorio, doubled the Wednesday rehearsal time, and told everyone to come another half hour early to church on Sundays.

"The Nazi Choir Director!" whispered Chester. "Or Saddam Hussein." He, like everyone else, had been affected by press reports about the danger he posed to his neighbors and to us.

In front of Chester, Linda Cooper started to giggle but saw Hatter swinging his stern gaze in her direction and swallowed the impulse. The altos were frozen. The Lynne twins, who had hoped for a more rigorous adherence to musical decorum and Episcopal tradition, smiled. Stan tried to take in what this meant for his career as "Get Your Kicks on Route 66" soloist.

Jean Triplet raised a hand in the manner of a shy student, not the outstanding mechanical engineering senior she was. "I'm in school, Professor, and it's not easy to take more hours away from my classes. To keep my scholarship I have to maintain a certain grade average."

"I'm not expecting this choir to be at the same number in the future. All serious music requires a single-mindedness that is uncommon today among young people." He scanned the rest of the group, as if in search of immediate resignations. Stan's mouth opened but no words came out--this time not because he was staring at Miss Triplet's exposed middle.

He did see her back stiffen, though, as she rose. With a different voice, one that might unsettle a teacher not completely sure of his or her material, she said, "I can count the hours in a day, Mr. Hatter, and I've given you every minute I feel is appropriate."

Without haste, the Perfect Third put away her folder, took her coat from the closet, and walked out.

Professor Hatter did not move his gaze from the center of the group. Stan found himself studying these words in the hymnal: "*Love shall be our token; / love be yours and love be mine,/ Love to God and to all men, / love for plea and gift and sign.*"

The words he should have said out loud did not come to him, as is so often the case, until practice was over. An unhappy group of half a dozen choristers lingered on the sidewalk outside the parish house, reluctant to leave without some discussion of what had just happened.

"I'm not sure I want to sing for this man," said Marvin Barnes.

"We're certainly not going to recruit new singers, or former ones like Sharon Rich, with him at the helm!"

"I propose," Stan said impulsively, "the Route 66 Choir!"

Half a dozen puzzled faces turned to him. "What do you mean?"

When he'd explained what he was proposing, most were skeptical that it would work, or even that it could be carried out. But, eying Stan in a new light, they agreed to consider the idea of sedition as a possible response to the new nation of Hatterland.

At home after practice, Stan listened to a phone message: it would be Dr. Montgomery, the female physician, he saw in the morning, not the familiar Dr. Heady.

Interlude:Creation's Secret Force

The search committee's visit to another church gave Felicia an unexpected lift. She went to out-of-the-way Valley Springs in the southwestern part of the state and heard a sermon about the often unacknowledged power of art. It was more in the form of a story, skillfully told by the Rev. Wright.

Two older men stood on a street corner. Neither of them understood what they were viewing.

"Who are those . . . those . . ." The first man, Mike, didn't want to say "people," as he knew at least that what he was seeing in the store window were cutouts or mannequins, life-size representations of, but not real people."

"They're sculptures, I guess," said Michael. The two friends, who shared the same name, distinguished themselves by assigning the longer version to the older man--older by six months, that is, at 88 years of age.

"Eve said it was a garden," Michael went on. "I'm supposed to look at their 'garden.'" Eve was his neighbor's child, a first grader. She and her sister Claire were beautiful and outgoing.

Felicia learned later that there were no friends, Michael and Mike, no family with daughters Eve and Claire in the town of Valley Springs. Rev. Wright had drawn the characters from his imagination, though he may well have had inspiration from local seniors, perhaps even from members of his congregation.

"Well, it says on the sign, 'Mo-nets Garden.'" Mike read slowly, pronouncing the

painter's name as two English words: *mo nets*. The exhibit's title appeared on a banner floating above the store window display. He clucked his tongue. "And that little girl did this in her school?"

"That's what she told me," confirmed Michael. "Well, not all of it, of course. She worked on the wisteria, by the bridge. I think all the classes in the lower grades were involved."

Many of you saw the Monet's Garden set up in the developing Center for the Visual Arts last year, a reproduction of the French painter's famous creation in Giverny. I hope you toured the exhibit yourselves.

Our two elderly gentlemen had met around the corner at Southern States, buying seed for spring planting. And Michael asked Mike to walk with him to the elementary school project. He loved his conversations with Eve, especially after church on Sundays. He was careful all week to store up topics and questions, though she always opened up more to his wife, Anne.

Mike scanned the exhibit, whose many elements didn't, to him, seem to go together: the Japanese style bridge over the Ru, flower clumps beside the winding path, water lilies in many sizes and colors. More startling to the two men were the papier-mâché people observing the scene. Monet was bending over on the bridge, studying reflections in the still water, a world turned upside-down and reshaped by perspective.

Mike's attention shifted from complicated present to a simpler past. "This was a good store, wasn't it, Ben Franklin's?"

"Surely was. They carried good products," *Michael agreed. "If you couldn't find it at Anderson's, it would be here. Of course, there wasn't anywhere else in Valley Springs!"*

Felicia and the others were told the little town's history in bits and pieces during their short visit. Even though it lay along famous Route 66, it had never had more than a thousand residents. From the Depression on, a steady migration went from the county, with its rocky soil and over cultivated fields, to Joplin, Springfield, Kansas City.

Then the Interstate bypassed the town by five miles, and some believed Valley Springs would have disappeared altogether except for Arbor College. Surviving hard times in part because of substantial support from the Episcopal diocese, the campus lay on the southern edge of Valley Springs. The townspeople knew they had suffered from the loss of Route 66 traffic, once directed right to the heart of town, and appreciated Arbor students' business. The Reverend Wright continued his story.

The two old timers, like so many of us, have a tendency to reminisce.

Michael noted, "I also liked Ben Franklin's basement, where the bargains were." They could see the wide stairs beyond the exhibit and paused a moment to remember bringing pennies to the candy counter as boys, spending their paper route money for jackknives as teenagers, taking their own children there to show them what Santa Claus might bring that year.

The store had been abandoned some years earlier, producing another forlorn downtown building until the college leased it for storage of

133

surplus office furniture and outdated equipment. Arbor's current president hoped one day to make it a genuine art center. Right now the old store window areas were used for displays, often advertising their liberal arts curriculum. The preacher continued, winking at the congregation.

We all let our conversations drift a bit, you know; so let's not be too critical of our old seniors if their thoughts wandered back to an earlier time.

"You plowed?" Michael asked his friend, knowing it was still too wet, the clay would clump. To get fine dirt, of course, you have to wait for the right weather. Sometimes too much rain cost gardeners their first spring crops.

"Not yet. Maybe next week. Might need some help this year."

Both men used ancient push plows, passed down by previous generations. But at their age, even with plots made rich by years of adding compost, it was slow work breaking up the rows. Stubborn, they turned down offers of help from neighbors and church friends--church friends like us, who, I hope, know always to offer.

"Any vegetables here?" Michael wondered. "It is a garden, after all." He always let Anne do the flowers in the front of the house, never distinguishing any more specifically than "roses." He was busy from late March into October with peas, squash, tomatoes, corn.

"Mike said, "Can't tell. There's so much!"

The exhibit, perhaps twenty feet by ten, was crowded with artificial bushes, flowering

134

plants, birds and butterflies; and the men's vision had weakened with age. The arrangement seemed random to them, and specimens grown a bit wild. "How did they make all this anyway?" Mike finally asked.

Michael chuckled. "Cardboard and plastic! Anne's been saving egg cartons, toilet paper and paper towel cylinders, cereal boxes all year to contribute. Eve's teacher uses them--see those branches? I don't know how they make everything, like the leaves and petals."

"A lot of work for . . . well, just to make something pretty."

Michael tried to explain. "I guess the little children learn how to use scissors, crayons. But the teachers must do the real work."

Mike clucked his tongue a second time. "Well, it costs money to do extra stuff like this. Students need to learn arithmetic and grammar more." Their own children had been out of school for decades, and their grandchildren had grown up in faraway towns and suburbs, part of the Valley Springs exodus. He asked, "Who did you say the school teacher was?"

Michael rubbed his chin. "Joy . . . Joy something. I can never remember. Funny name for around here. Her husband's at the college."

Mike responded, "Well, whoever she is, she sure uses bright colors."

The morning sun had crested the buildings across the street and now lit up Mo-net's Garden. The variety of shapes and shades was dazzling. "O God, creation's secret force, thyself unmoved, all motion's source had brought the light."

After a moment said Michael. "Eve's mother says you can go in there, walk down the path, even go across the bridge."

"Why would you do that? You can't get anywhere; it's not like a real path."

Having lived in Valley Springs all their lives--except during the war when, miraculously, both survived Normandy--they knew just about every road, street, and lane in the county.

Michael tried to explain. "I don't know exactly. I guess to see it better, from the inside?"

Mike shook his head. "Um. I think some college students went inside a bit ago." Michael looked toward the entrance.

Felicia had seen the building when she drove in and remembered that the double doors opened out to the center of Valley Springs, the crossing of Main (a local branch of what was now "historic Route 66") and Church Streets.

One of the students, a young pregnant woman, who'd gone through the doors earlier, stepped onto the exhibit platform,. She smiled at the men through the glass. They were embarrassed, as if they'd been caught spying. She was going into one of God's worlds made by His tiny hands. "Creation's secret force" was in and around her. May it always find us.

Amen.

Volume Three. Epiphany and Lent.

Chapter 21: All Mortal Flesh

"I've read," Felicia offered tenderly the next morning, "that men, after vigorous exercise, need time to recover before . . . before . . . you know."

They were lying in bed. Every muscle in Stan's body ached from his biking, or from the morning's effort. Felicia thought about skating at The Oval with Tom Baettner once when he'd come from an especially rigorous football practice. Would he have been able?

"I have an appointment . . . with the doctor today. I can ask . . . "

Then he remembered the person he'd have to ask was not a fellow man. How could he convey to Dr. Montgomery what he'd felt pedaling back to the trailhead, with that seat jamming itself into him at every stroke and his jeans removing leg hair with the efficiency of sandpaper. Who could perform after that! What would be worse, of course, is that this might not be the cause.

"By the way," said Felicia, rising, "I'll be gone again next weekend." Then she regretted choosing this moment for making her announcement, both because of Stan's vulnerability and because of the recollection of her first beau.

"Oh?" He rose on one elbow.

"I'm making another visit with Thelma, for the search committee. There's a church in central Illinois, and the diocesan consultant, Fred List, says they might be good for us. We need to leave Saturday, middle of the afternoon. I should be back Sunday in time for dinner."

"I might see if Ben would like to go out for dinner on Saturday. It's been awhile." The rest of the weekend would be pretty empty. As far as he knew, at least, there were no major chores listed on the refrigerator. He was glad that the repaired toilet didn't need attention any more.

"Do call him. I am leaving enough lasagna for two dinners, though, just in case. And there's plenty of bread." She knew better than to give him many options. She paused. "Do see what Dr. Heady has to say. I'm sure stress can be a factor, too. And if you're going to keep up with the biking, we probably need to be more careful about timing."

She had been relieved he wasn't wearing the Spider-man suit, which he'd thrown into the laundry basket. That receptacle was full, in fact, from the last two weeks. Even in retirement, and with her busy schedule, Stan refused to help with the laundry, claiming he never understood exactly what qualified as "white," "permanent press," "gentle," "extra rinse." Everything to him was just "clothes" that went into the "wash."

Still, she could understand how recalling his physical problems, having to amuse himself for the weekend, and facing an extended session with Professor Hatter on Sunday morning didn't put him in a good mood to be by himself, or to see the doctor. What she wouldn't know until much later was how the crowd in the waiting room depressed him even more.

Scattered around on chairs, sitting across the one sofa, and standing at the magazine rack were: a mother with noisy triplets (one male); an elderly couple (he with a cane) whose deafness led to their and others' shouting; a teenage male whose exposed arms were covered with tattoos (was that really a fish coupling with a swan?); a young man in a grey suit talking into his cell phone (Stan at first thought the black thing in his ear was some new form of jewelry for men); and an immaculately dressed girl, perhaps ten, apparently with no accompanying adult. (He didn't add "one aimless retiring retiree whose wife might be tiring of him.") How did all these people belong in one room?

In order to keep his distance from the other patients, Stan ended up standing by the coat rack reading a *Readers' Digest*. Perhaps he would find some helpful lifestyle suggestions in the most widely read periodical in America. The Table of Contents on the cover offered two possibilities: "Twelve Ways to Reduce Stress" and "Men Women Love." He reviewed the first six methods to lower anxiety (all related to workplace stress) and learned that women really loved other women. Finally, he was called by the receptionist.

"So, Mr. Measure, how are we?" smiled Dr. Montgomery, taking up the cuff from the cabinet when she entered the examining room. Stan, having carried his magazine with him, was by this time trying to laugh at "50 Jokes from 50 States."

"We?" he wondered. Shouldn't "he" be the subject of their concern? "I guess that's what I"m here to find out."

"Shortness of breath? Dizziness when rising? Unusual fatigue? Racing pulse? Sense of impending doom?" She squeezed the bulb; the sleeve squeezed his arm; he imagined squeezing her.

"*Sense of impending doom,*" he repeated to himself. Is that a medical condition? Well, if so, he probably had it.

She released the air, took his wrist to count his pulse.

"I take it my blood pressure is up?"

She only smiled, almost as if she didn't at that moment see him. Then she looked at the chart. "Well, I must say, over the past six months, it's been all over the map--one day within acceptable limits, another day something that needs to be treated, but one time-- back in August--perfectly normal. With patients who occasionally experience white coat syndrome, it's sometimes as if we're seeing five different people rather that a single person."

He was pretty sure he didn't want to be the single person defined by his recent actions: grumpy old man, dirty old man, impotent old man.

"We're going to increase your medication," Dr. Montgomery concluded. Stan wondered how "he" was now included in this "we," a reversal of her inserting herself into the "we" whose state they had considered earlier. "You're not experiencing any side effects, are you?"

Side effects? Whatever effects he was experiencing were not in his side.

"You're on a fairly small dose of Lisinipol, and you have no other physical problems that need to be addressed. I think this will get you on the right track pretty quickly."

Stan's breathing was short. "I was reading, in one of the magazines--not this one." He held up the *Readers' Digest*. "But in one of the medical ones, that . . . um . . .

141

marital relations might be improved by taking . . . what is it called . . . ?"

"'Marital relations?'" She paused. "Oh, yes, well, Viagra is the best known. There's a problem?" Her eyebrows lifted with the question.

"Oh, probably not. But I also saw on television, a man my age. It made a difference on special occasions, and I was just wondering . . . "

She folded his chart and set it on the examining table.

"We don't like to go immediately to that option." There's that damn "we" again! "If there's consistent dysfunction, there might be physiological or psychological difficulties we need to consider."

Stan was ready to leave.

"How often have you experienced erectile failure, say, in the last few months?"

Why was he always "experiencing" things? It was as if he routinely selected from a list of "experiences," like choosing a few magazines from the a long list of possible subscriptions.

"Well, not that many times, really. Generally, we're okay." This time he caught himself using the "we."

"Mr. Measure, healthy men much older than you father children all the time. It's true that it may take one . . . It takes any man past a certain age. . . a bit longer to get . . . um . . . ready than it did when you were a teenager."

Was she rubbing it in? Should he think of rubbing?

"And completion of . . . the act can involve more time. And more . . . um . . . effort . . . or patience . . .

from your partner. However, at this age, a woman is . . . usually more than ready."

Stan remembered what Felicia had said this morning before they'd tried to make love: "You *do* know that I have needs?" He assumed she only said that because she believed that it would make him feel his advances were welcome.

He had long entertained a conventional view of women, that only rarely did desire claim them. Felicia, to his mind, would generally *"ponder nothing earthly minded,"* urging that *"all mortal flesh keep silence, / and with fear and trembling stand"* in contemplation of higher things. Perhaps he'd been wrong all these years. Or maybe she was changing, just as he was.

In any case, in addition to the consciousness of failing himself, he now could add a sense of guilt for failing her. He was going to need a Route 66 Husband's Advisory Committee as well as a Route 66 Rebel Choir!

Dr. Montgomery did not give him a prescription for Viagra.

Chapter 22: What Glory Shall be Theirs

Stan had begun the new year in the way he had hoped--as a new man. But he was neither the better husband he wanted to be, nor the talented vocalist he'd hoped his singing in church would produce. Instead, he was more and more often Buzz Murdock, "intimate" Internet friend of Samantha Haute, or whoever was signing herself in under that name on ii/w. Buzz was communicating with Sam daily, and Stan felt transformed.

Ms. Haute was not the only person he exchanged comments with in his new virtual community, but he tended to take in information more than offer himself as a friend to individuals. It was all he could do to create--or borrow--one new identity. And he felt the eccentric personalities he encountered online--the Vietnam veteran who lived in a treehouse, a housewife who claimed to "chat" only while in a bathtub, a teenager insisting he had been raised by wolves--needed respondents who would fit in their worldview.

One online discovery helped Stan strengthen his sense of Buzz and himself. The star of the television series (now his namesake) had apparently released two albums in 1962, one of which included his rendition or "Get Your Kicks on Route 66." Stan had trouble seeing how a collection that included "Witchcraft," "Lollipops and Roses," and "Moon River" belonged with praise of "that California trip," but he decided to order a copy of the CD anyway. It might come in handy in the development of the Route 66 Choir.

Felicia, unaware that this Buzz existed, assumed Stan's happier self was inspired, at least in part, by her own attentions, which were more regular and more often successful.

"What did Dr. Heady say?" she asked him after the latest visit. "And did you thank him!" Coming home from a search committee meeting, Felicia had found him in the den, a stack of oddly sized books on the table by his favorite easy chair.

"He thinks my blood pressure medication can, um, 'affect one's libido.'" This was something else he'd learned on the Web, not from Dr. Montgomery or Dr. Heady. He wasn't sure why he didn't admit to having seen the female physician.

"So, did he, ah, recommend anything? A change in what you take?"

Stan seldom lied to Felicia. Having few secrets and dependent on her to manage everything except his work, he generally confessed his frustrations and desires without disguise. He realized now, however, that, if he was going to pretend he'd not seen Dr. Montgomery, he would have to keep a consistent account. He'd read--again, on the Internet--about the danger of half-truths or untruths multiplying into a web of contradictions, especially in a marriage.

"We'll keep things the way they are for a few weeks, then see."

"Well, I do think your biking will be good, get you in shape. Did he say anything about exercise and . . . and people our age?"

She looked at the books beside him, most larger than a standard hardback. He had folded one closed, with a finger marking the place. What was he studying?

"He said that biking was good." Stan was recalling his latest trip on the trail, another fantasy had risen from his youth. A beautiful woman on the train turned out to be a Russian spy. "And he says that variety is good, tends to spice things up."

Felicia decided to take the conversation elsewhere. "Well, good, yes, different times and so forth. What are you reading?" She came to sit on the chair's arm and look over his shoulder.

"Oh, these. They're hymnals, music books."

Felicia's hip bumped against his shoulder in just the way that blonde spy had knocked into the mild mannered home security expert traveling from a little town in the Midwest to testify in a post-9/11 investigation. (He'd updated his adolescent scenario.) No one but Stan/Buzz knew that former Soviet Union agents were involved in international terrorist plots.

"Music?"

The man on the train, who would save the Western world, had been reading, too. He had to snap shut *Spies Without Borders* quickly to avoid exposure. In the end, of course, he had to give himself to the double agent in order to discover the whereabouts of the transmitting device he knew she carried. It had been hidden in her underwear.

"Yes, rock and roll collections. And hymnals from different churches--Baptist, Lutheran, Methodist, even some nondenominational ones." He opened the book he'd been holding. On the page was a version of "O wondrous type, O vision fair."

"I thought Father Tack brought in Professor Hatter to direct the choir?"

"Technically, yes. But we may have some ideas of our own about the program."

Felicia decided she didn't need to know what this meant. She realized his battle with Professor Hatter had invigorated him. She couldn't say about her husband, *"brighter than the sun he glows!"* But some of their most satisfactory love-making had followed his excited reports of what Hatter had done that day.

On the other hand, she had to admit Stan was contributing to the growing schisms in the church--the choir bickering, a congregation divided on social/political issues, everyone confused by Father Tack's malapropisms. She had been encouraged, however, by other recent events to believe that the selection of a new priest would start a process of healing.

After their trip to Valley Springs, she and Thelma were optimistic about the search. If the Reverent Wright was an indication of the quality of the candidate pool, Holy Trinity could expect to find someone with the necessary ability to pull the church together. Felicia also noticed, with mixed feelings, that, so far at least, no one had challenged the more focused church profile she and Larry had produced and that now guided the search.

Felicia's more immediate concern was Over-Due's involvement in The Oval. A casual comment by retired policeman Marvin Barnes, and overheard by Meg, had increased Felicia's concerns about Mr. Mayle's intentions.

"He's bought the old Stony Court motel," Meg explained early in the new year.

"On Kingshighway?" asked Donna. "It's been abandoned for a decade. Can it be restored?"

Stony Court was a Route 66 landmark, built during World War II in response to increased traffic to and from nearby Fort Leonard Wood. In the 1950s, when Americans started to buy cars again and to travel, it was a convenient stop for families and salesmen moving east and west on America's highway. Built in a style called "Ozark Giraffe," it featured irregularly patterned facing made from stone indigenous to the area, mostly limestone and sandstone.

"Not without sinking some money into it," Donna asserted. "But I heard he wants to link Stony Court and The Oval, let groups come from out of town--you know, high school reunion classes, social clubs, gatherings of former military units--stay in the motel for a skating weekend. He's going to run a shuttle every half hour between the two."

"They haven't even approved our design yet," noted Felicia. "I wonder if he has building permits, licenses--those things you need for such enterprises."

Meg said, "He also wants a 'family restaurant' where that old diner was, across the street. What was it called?"

"The Dining Car," said Felicia. "Of course, we always called it "The DC." She pronounced it Thee Dee Sea. "Our old high school hang out. He does want to take us back in time."

"Well, all that's not our concern, at least so far," concluded Donna. "I mean, whether this follows a conventional business model or not, we've simply been asked to design The Oval as an old time skating rink that will be attractive to contemporary consumers."

"Yes," added Felicia. "And if a '50's theme--a Route 66 theme--ties these enterprises together, that could be great for the Road House. We could even do more to recall Fanny's Dairy Delite's history as a roadside attraction for Mother Road travelers."

Later, folding laundry, Felicia tried to remember the name of that movie where a contemporary young couple falls back into a 1950s television soap opera. Families and communities are harmonious in this black and white world, but the inhabitants experience little joy. When a bit of color--a red rose--appears, everything becomes more vibrant, but new tensions also emerge. Why did our alternatives all have to include a down side?

Mayle's plan for The Oval, The DC, and Stony Court called up nostalgic memories of her growing up with Donna and Meg, Tom Baettner and others-- *"faithful hearts are raised on high / by this great vision's mystery."* But were, she asked herself, the partners in Over-Due closing their eyes to insidious elements of some scheme that lay behind roller skating, ice cream sodas, and family vacation travel on The Mother Road? She smelled danger.

Chapter 23: Manifest in Making Whole

Stan's surprise ally in the creation of The Route 66 Rebel Choir was Chester, the sawmill operator. He seldom took sides in church debates, often finding ways to poke fun at both parties. But he called the day after Stan had impulsively proposed sabotaging the interim director's plans and wanted to see what he could do.

Still ready to have fun even on a matter that he cared about, Chester suggested they have a private meeting. "Let's get together somewhere . . . safe," he said, lowering his voice. "Safe from . . . from . . . well, little pitchers have big ears, if you know what I mean."

Stan didn't know, but an idea occurred to him. "Have you been biking on the rails-to-trails route? It's new, so, when I go, I'm generally alone out there."

"Biking? Like on bicycles?"

"Yes. It's good exercise and you're outdoors."

"Let's see: in the sawmill business, I buy logs and produce lumber. Now, where is it I'm always getting those logs? Oh, yeah, outdoors!"

As a child Stan had hated being out of the know. In The Circle, at school, in stores he was too literal minded to understand irony. Perhaps walling in those cliques that left him out of the loop inspired him in his security business. But he was thicker skinned as an adult.

"If you'd prefer another place, just name it."

But Chester, apologizing for being flip, admitted he would enjoy exploring the new park. He did have an in-between bike (part road, part mountain) and sometimes rode for exercise. So, one afternoon not long after their phone conversation the two choir members were pedaling slowly west on a crisp mid-winter day. And Stan's scheme took on new application at the same time he learned something about trees and wood.

"There are different ways to consider timber," Chester observed. Stan had asked him what species lined their route. "Most folks think each tree is a unit-- an elm, an oak, hickory."

"It's not?"

"Well, it is, but, you see, I'm in the lumber business, so I see each tree as a source of different pieces of lumber."

"But they're all one wood, aren't they--walnut, sycamore."

"Of course, but when I look at any tree, I see how many boards there might be for the construction engineer--seventeen 1x8's, six 2x10's, four good 6x18's. Whether it's cherry or pecan or birch, it yields a certain collection of lumber pieces."

"You make me think of doctors, who see you as a collection of body parts," Stan mused sadly. To himself, he added, "some of which don't always belong to the functioning whole."

"That's taking the negative view. But I think of it as freeing these beautiful boards, which have been trapped inside a trunk and limbs. I envision them coming out of my sawmill operation, where they're beautiful, trim, clean pieces ready to be part of something new as yet unformed--a house, a boat, a fine piece of furniture."

Stan thought about this a bit. "We can't see the boards for the trees, you mean?"

Chester laughed in agreement, and Stan went on. "So, for you, the tree that nature made is an artificial or irrelevant organization of wood; it's temporary. Each part has a separate destiny not foreseen in the grand scheme of Mother Earth."

"Something like that. Now, I do understand there are other ways to look at trees, as living organisms and as parts of a functioning ecosystem."

They were both breathing heavily in the cool air, and their pace was slowing.

"I wonder," Stan continued, "about the choir. We might say we're all of us bonded into Hatter's shape, none of us free. We could want separate destinies." He imagined Nat King Cole singing, or was it Buzz Murdock?

"We certainly don't belong in the roles he's given us," agreed Chester. "That's why I want to join with you to liberate each voice."

"Well, you know I haven't been singing that long, and I don't really know the etiquette of a situation like this. It does seem he's hammering us together into something that belongs in another place, and maybe another time."

"A concert choir in the European church of the Middle Ages, if you ask me! He badgers us like we're professionals, trained singers from childhood, folks who have no other life. Shoot! We're amateurs. We're a church choir, for heaven's sake (pun intended!)."

"I guess that's why I think a rock and roll rebel choir is going to drive him crazy."

"So, let me get this straight. You say we all come half an hour early. You'll have some sheet music-- country, the sort of thing you'd hear on KTTF early Sunday morning."

"That or worse," agreed Stan. "And we sing it with amateurish gusto."

Some newcomers to the area, having trouble adjusting to local color, claimed the radio station's call letters mean "Keep Traveling Through Fairfield." But KTTF had a loyal following among county farmers (who listened daily for farm prices) and businesses (which relied on radio for advertising). Their music was relentlessly Branson.

Chester chuckled. "So we'll be singing 'Goin' to the Chapel,' or something like that, with all the twang we can muster when the Nazi Conductor comes in."

Hatter had seemed so far unaware of music composed in the twentieth century, or at least anything written before the 1916 Episcopal hymnal. His favorite composers were from the fifteenth and sixteenth centuries. He remained a distant figure himself, appearing for rehearsal at precisely 7:30 (as magically as the night he had been introduced), expecting the choir to be seated, hymnal already open to the first Sunday hymn (a list was posted by the door), and prepared to work without pause until 9:00. Of course, they didn't begin by singing that hymn; twenty minutes of vocal exercise preceded anything that might give pleasure to a listener.

"I think," Stan added, "that the small group coming early can actually benefit from the practice. We can concentrate on hearing the different parts, the blend. With the full choir and the complex pieces Hatter has us working on, I can't tell what's happening overall."

"Close harmony is hard, so you may be right."

Stan admitted to himself that he thought he could improve if he could get away from the Lynne twins, such dominant voices. He had learned to sing what they were singing, but a Nat King Cole soloist needs to carry the part on his own.

"I'd like to do more *a cappella* work," Stan added. It would have surprised Felicia to know that he had learned to appreciate the way strong individual voices disappeared into one communal sound, the chord.

The rebel choir, of course, was as likely to cause disturbance as to unify resentment of a director imposed on them by the interim priest. Would it produce *"anthems be to thee addressed, / God in man made manifest"*? Stan decided not to dwell on possible side effects.

Chester continued, "I'm not sure which will be more irritating to Professor Hatter, my guitar or my harmonica. In fact, I can play the two at once. I have the neck holder and can wail with the best of them. I don't suppose anyone else knows how to clog?"

Stan certainly didn't. His taste for country music had come from waking up early and hearing gospel groups on his mother's kitchen radio.

Karen, who depended on the small salary she was paid as accompanist, was not willing to come early and anger the director; so another instrument would allow the singers a way to hear the proper pitches. But Robin Shure had seemed interested; and Linda Cooper was enthusiastic. That, at least, would mean four voices, soprano, alto, tenor, bass.

It wouldn't be fair to say Stan actually appreciated the style he had proposed, but he associated it with his mother's memory. While his own children were growing up, his clock radio also began the family's day with "His Hand in Mine," "I'm Gonna Walk Dem Golden Stairs," or "Where Could I Go but to the Lord."

When Stan started Wall-All, he would carry a portable radio on jobs. The local station's gospel hour led into a day full of Nashville hits old and new, interrupted by short newscasts read from the wire, locally produced commercials, public service announcements. KTTF's music soothed many of Stan's residential customers, and businesses associated it with local craftsman who would still be in the community if their services were needed at a later date. So, without his intending it, the sounds of country music had connected his childhood to his adulthood. Now he might be carrying it into his Golden Years.

And if the Route 66 Choir didn't drive Hatter away, maybe he could sing with Samantha Haute at the Internet Cafe. As he said about security systems, there should always be a backup.

Chapter 24: A Thousand Tongues To Sing

The next day Stan steered his morning virtual dialogue with Sam to the question of music.

"Who's your favorite singer? I like Nat King Cole." Buzz wrote, then regretted that he might too clearly show his age. He had been evasive about his true identity, assuming she was also.

"Don't you love the duet with Natalie, 'Unforgettable'?"

A good sign. She at least knew who he was talking about, but was she of the father's or the daughter's generation?

He had to believe she was some years younger, as she understood what he wrote in unexpected ways. And her side of the conversation was often ambiguous to him, capable of a variety of interpretations. Habitually straightforward, he worried about her elusiveness. But he had to admit that it sometimes excited him.

Whenever he tried to picture Samantha, she generally came up in his mind's eye as Jean Triplet. The Perfect Third was lost to Holy Trinity's choir, presumably forever. She did, however, come to church regularly and helped a congregation that might be termed "musically challenged" by singing the melody confidently.

"I like other kinds of music, too," Buzz wrote. "What do you think of Chuck Berry or the Rolling Stones. I know we're talking 'golden oldies,' but they have a distinctive sound."

He was trying to nudge the conversation toward country singers, rejecting from his list of those who had recorded the Route 66 theme song Mel Torme and Bob Dylan.

"Well, I like different styles. And not just in music, if you know what I mean."

He didn't. This was what happened in many of their online conversations. She treated his literal statements as metaphors and slipped in double entendres he wasn't quite sure he understood: what, for instance, were "missionary hugs"?

"Some say my vocal style is a throwback to the 40's," he offered. "Of course, I'm not the lead in my little ensemble."

"You're in a group?"

"Well, right now we just perform for small functions, mostly weekend gigs. I'd like to do more, maybe go on the road when the time is ripe."

Good grief! He was becoming a practiced liar. It was a stretch to call the church choir an "ensemble." And "weekend gigs"! He was going to be struck down, if not by Felicia or some Internet police, by one of God's angels. He signed off ii/w and returned to the question Chester had unintentionally put before him on their latest bike ride: the fog-free mirror.

Apparently, this was a special kind that didn't cloud up in the bathroom when you used plenty of hot water. Chester had touted it in talking about his recent house renovation. Stan, who had not changed his bathroom configuration or routine in over thirty years, was intrigued.

Since whiskers are softest when warm and wet, Stan always shaved right after his morning shower.

The mirror on the medicine cabinet had to be wiped clear with a towel before he started and could still film over again while he worked; so there were disadvantages to his regimen. This fog-free mirror must be the latest in technology, he concluded, a mirror that stays clear even in a hot, moist atmosphere. Where could he find one?

The obvious answer was to go online, and it didn't take Google long to show him the basic options: those that attached to the shower nozzle, circulating warm water through the frame and back of the mirror; and those with some space-age surface to which fog could not adhere. Instinctively, he went for the second, less expensive option. (He also didn't want more places where water might escape pipes and threaten the security of his house.)

While he could order one instantly, Stan remained reluctant to send credit card information over the Internet. He decided to see if such a thing as a fog-free mirror could be purchased in Fairfield. His search confirmed a favorite newcomer's thesis--that this was indeed a town that did not hear the voices of progress.

"Free? No, all ours costs something," insisted the large clerk at Walgreens, "Betty," according to her bright blue name tag.

"No, *fog*-free."

"Well now, ours all come without fog, if that's what you mean."

"No, no. They don't fog up; um, they stay clear."

"You mean one of those mirrors you use on a camping trip?" she leaned an absolutely huge bosom over the counter. "If you were huntin' or fishin', and the morning' was damp and some fog come up on the mountain, you'd want a special mirror?"

Before he could get away, Stan looked at a metal camping mirror, a handheld mirror to be carried in a purse, and a small mirror for car use.

He did no better in the town's finest jewelry store, where a clerk (no name tag here, only an incessant smile) showed him a magnifying mirror, several gold- and ivory-handled mirrors, and a rectangular mirror with another smaller, round mirror in one corner. Images of images were multiplying, thought Stan, but each would be clouded in the shower.

The young hardware store clerk, in matching denim pants and jacket with stylish hiking boots, who introduced himself as Chip, thought they might be able to get him a two-way mirror, or even one of those three-panel mirrors found in clothing stores for customers to inspect themselves from all angles. "Perhaps," he added, with a wink, a look to the back of the store, "a mirror for the ceiling of a master bedroom?"

At first Stan thought this kid knew he was seeking extra excitement in bed and started to get angry. Then, he realized, to believe that would be pretty close to paranoia. He shook his head sadly and went home.

Later he wondered idly if Felicia knew what a fog-free mirror was.

"You want one?" She was ready to be distracted from the latest church gossip: long-legged soprano Linda Cooper had quit her job at the bank to start her own financial consulting firm.

"It's just an idea. Chester was telling me about his, saves time and mess. Just shower away lather and whiskers."

"Shower away?" Linda had told Felicia she was not leaving Holy Trinity or the choir, but the chair of the search committee worried that changes in professional life often lead to changes in personal affairs. Another worry for the new priest, whoever he (or she) would be.

"Yeah, it goes in the shower . . . in, um, our shower." Stan realized there could be different views of this project.

"How do you hold it while you're in there?"

"Hold . . . ? No, it's attached. It's permanent."

They had a second bathroom on the main floor, and Stan realized she might prefer it go there. But no one would want to go downstairs every morning, then troop back up where his clothes were, would he?

"You would have Tony install it?" She saw this project ballooning into another of Stan's obsessions. A little thing expanding to fill the vast spaces of his boredom and frustration.

"Ah, simple procedure--epoxy, a few screws. It's not that big." Was he hearing the toilet running? "And, as I said, I haven't found one. I was thinking about all those catalogs you get in the Christmas season. Weren't you stacking them up for a trip to the recycling center?"

Marvin Barnes had started a campaign at the church to get receptacles in the parish hall, where they had their potluck suppers and congregational meetings. He'd survived the typical initial resistance and was now combating a campaign of benign neglect. Felicia was 'priming the pump' by bringing in some things she could have put out for the town's collection.

"They're in two of Ben's moving crates at the back of the garage. Before you order anything, though, maybe we'd better discuss where it goes."

Stan decided to settle for this as less than a veto. He knew there would have to be negotiation if he was ever going to shave in the shower. Rummaging through Felicia's store of catalogs, he reviewed the post script to his recent Internet chat with Sam. She'd asked him if he sang in the shower.

"Not really," he admitted. "You?"

"Only when someone's there to make music with."

"Oh, '*tis music in the sinner's ears,*'" he thought, "'*tis life and health and peace.*'" Could he make it happen in reality?

Chapter 25: Song of Sweetness

Linda Cooper's starting her own business could affect not only the church and its choir but also Over-Due. As long as Ms. Cooper represented the bank, concluded Felicia, she had to follow established industry guidelines. Would her breaking away free Mr. Mayle and his backers to run higher risks in developing The Oval? Well, The Oval and its possible related units, the DC and Stony Court.

"You see," she explained to Donna and Meg at the Middleman Bakery. "A bank has clients, all of whom must be treated similarly, with the rules established by the bank's officers and in conformity with other banks nationally. And a lot of times, a larger company owns a number of financial institutions, and they come under a common set of policies."

"Aren't all lending companies subject to the same regulations?" asked Meg. "I would think Linda wouldn't be able to bend the rules just because she's on her own."

"She wouldn't be bending them herself, but perhaps recommending ways to get around certain obstacles that First Fairfield wouldn't allow her to. Then Mayle does whatever he wants to. She's technically only an advisor."

"I think you're worried about things we don't really have to deal with," Donna insisted. "Over-Due does design. Wherever Mayle gets the money is up to him."

"I hope you're right. Still, I'm always afraid of the outlier. Freelancers can spin out of control. And I'd hate to put in a lot of time and effort and then have the project blow up on us before we get paid."

"I think you're writing a song," Donna laughed. "'Freelancers are dancers that spin on their own.'"

Meg joined in. "Yes, it's part country, part rock and roll. 'I'm bettin' they're steppin' out on the town.'"

"Hrumph. I wonder if we couldn't return to the business at hand."

"And that was . . . " Donna paused dramatically. " . . . ah, yes, choosing another pastry to help me think. Sugar high, you know."

"What would a freelancer order?" Meg asked. "Ah, I know: bear claw!"

Felicia sighed. She thought of Stan messing up her bathroom with a fog-free mirror; the Holy Trinity congregation challenging the profile Larry had put together; the country realizing they might be approaching another war far from home. "*Alleluia cannot always / be our song while here below.*"

Even Over-Due was starting to show the strain from The Oval project. Perhaps her partners were realizing they had fundamentally different opinions about the project. Donna was for just getting the job done, pocketing the money, moving on. Meg wanted to put enough into the design that it would establish a template and earn them more contracts. Felicia was worried that they were falling into something they didn't understand.

Maybe their different core personalities were emerging. Despite the fact that they'd grown up together as fast friends and took pleasure in rediscovering each other when Meg and Donna came back to Fairfield, they couldn't expect to agree on everything. Felicia felt, for instance, that she was the only one worried that President Bush, after his "Axis of Evil" talk, was already contemplating another Middle East war to finish the job begun by his father.

Years ago, their disagreements were trivial: what's your favorite song? "Soldier Boy" always made Felicia weepy. Donna, the most rebellious, played wild air guitar for Chuck Berry's "Johnny B. Goode." And the group's best singer, Meg, could do a fine rendition of Patsy Cline's "Walking After Midnight." Now personal preferences could have global consequences. Rock and roll had been a joyous celebration when they were young, but now fundamentalist societies, even Saudia Arabia, an ally, could say it was undermining their basic values.

Over-Due was not, of course, a musical group, so the three partners could differ in their tastes for song. Holy Trinity's choir, however, needed to work with a shared sensibility, as Felicia was reminded that evening. The temporary, but perhaps soon to be permanent, conductor had made it clear this group had to march to a single drummer.

"You know what our Nazi choir director had us do tonight?" Stan asked. "He told us to put our hands on someone else's belly to make sure they were breathing properly."

"That make's sense, though, doesn't it? Supporting the sound rather than squeezing it out." Felicia was immediately curious about whose tummy her husband had been fondling. If it was one of the Lynne twins, who, she knew, he'd didn't get along with, the picture was humorous. "I remember my high school chorus director saying singing comes from the gut, not the head."

"Well, I think we could each check our own diaphragm. And might I point out that the human belly no longer stays in one place."

164

"It doesn't?" Involuntarily, she touched hers.

"Oh, no. Styles have changed, as you might have noticed. So not everyone wears his or her belt at the same place. But always--well, almost always--belly's go below belts, which means some are mighty, *mighty* low these days."

Felicia considered two examples: the aging male with drooping beer belly that strains the buttons of a shirt, and the young female with pants riding so low on her hips that heads turn to follow. Both belts were well beneath the traditional mark of the bellybutton. Stan's mind's eye saw a female lion tamer, whose belt cinched a perfect waist. Then he went back to what had happened at choir practice.

"But that's not all. Then we had get in a tight circle, each person behind the one he's putting a hand on, so we're all linked up, belly to back, feeling muscles tighten . . . or not. I won't tell you what set of adolescent male jokes this calls up."

"Please don't!" She paused. "I'm not sure I want to imagine this as boy-girl, boy-girl or the other way." Oh my gosh! Was her husband feeling up leggy Linda Cooper?

"By the way," she said, in part to distract him . . . and herself, "I found your mirror for the shower in one of these catalogs." Felicia pointed back to the dining room side table. "I skimmed some before I dropped off most of them at church. Let me get it."

In her cursory review she had been amazed once more at the variety and quantity of stores inundating America with sophisticated sales pitches for the holiday season. She decided that sending the catalogs through Holy Trinity and on to the recycling center might be viewed as following the dictate of rendering unto Caesar.

Opening "Bins and Boxes" to the earmarked page, Stan found a fog-free mirror with built-in radio and soap dish, only $39.95 (plus shipping). Eighteen inches tall, ten inches wide, it could be fastened to the shower wall with adhesive patches (included). It was a little more expensive than he had been expecting (shipping added $3.95). It was also going to take up a lot of space in the shower (where no one else would be using it). And the notion of playing a radio in water while shaving troubled Stan, who always thought of security.

For a moment, he envisioned himself standing in the shower one morning. Although he customarily used a safety razor, the image he created featured him with a straight razor poised ominously at his ear. As he listened to Fairfield native Willy Hunter itemizing the grocery specials at Big Star, Stan's whole life flashed before him. A moment of depression, an announcement that it was national Clean Your Gutters Week, the razor--not good!

Felicia checked her phone messages: the committee had approved bringing in two candidates for interviews over the coming weeks. One was Reverent Wright, from Valley Springs, and another was a couple, both priests, who would, if called, share the position. She and Larry had raised questions about that. Some would not want a woman priest; others would object to a having two people in one position. Oh, may I hear a *"song of sweetness"* she prayed: *"ever raised by choirs on high; / in the house of God abiding / thus they sing eternally."*

Now that Stan had seen a fog-free mirror, or at least the picture of one, he wanted it even more than ever. Having absorbed a favorite advertising motif, he felt a "new and improved" self might be reflected back at him.

Although the write-up did not explain how the device worked--that is, how it stayed clear in the shower--Stan was pretty sure he understood it sufficiently to continue the search. He would save this order form, keep looking at any more catalogs that came in over the next few weeks, and perhaps succumb later if he found no suitable alternative. Perhaps Nat King Cole would look out as he shaved, and they'd sing together "Get Your Kicks on Route 66."

He recalled his hand on Robin's stomach, while the palm of Melody (on one of those rare occasions when the former temporary director did return to sing with them) pressed his own. What music he could make with the appropriate encouragement! Samantha Haute?

Chapter 26: Just As I Am

That night Stan dreamed of his mother.

In his retirement, dreams came more frequently and went on longer than at any time in his life. Unlike the dreams he heard others narrate, his were less fantastic and more often peopled by those he knew. In this case, though, he himself was the chief element who didn't conform to the laws of reality--he flew in on the scene.

Stan was back in--well, he was above--his old neighborhood. Unlike Superman rocketing through the sky, he floated gently down toward the house on Oak Street in The Circle. It was night, bright and clear with moon and stars. He saw the shingled roof of the two-bedroom house, its fenced back yard neatly tended--by Mr. Jackson, he assumed, who'd been a friend of his father and did a lot of chores for Stan's mother.

When the houses that became The Circle were first built, during World War II and the boom years that followed, there was little variety in design. All buildings followed one of two basic blueprints: bedrooms at the back separated by the bathroom; or two at one end of the house with the bathroom at the back. Living room, dining room, and kitchen faced the street in the former case; and the kitchen and dining room were situated behind a living room in the latter. With continuing prosperity, of course, additions to these fundamental shapes led to a striking collection of structures by the time Stan married and moved across town with Felicia.

Families added wings out the back, turned garages into recreational rooms, raised the attic for more bedrooms. Basements were finished (some with bomb shelters--it *was* the Cold War), porches were added, exteriors were converted to brick, asbestos shingles, faux logs. From the conformity of the 1950s The Circle moved through the revolutionary '60s, complicating the simple framework that had given Stan comfort in childhood, even while he struggled to find his place outside the home.

As he floated closer to his house, he was--by the magic of dreams--able to see through the roof into his own attic bedroom. It was empty, the bed made and only some of his childhood toys artfully displayed. Yes, this would be after he'd left for college, or later when he was married, perhaps had children. Where was his mother?

He drifted toward the other end where her room had always been. The bed was empty, but the covers were pulled back. At this wee hour, was she roaming about, not sleeping? A pang of sorrow at her probable loneliness touched him. He flew over the living room, where a light burned, but he saw no one sitting in a chair or resting on the sofa. The kitchen?

Like Stan, Mrs. Measure had been a creature of routine, a characteristic intensified after she lost her husband early in the marriage. From all the years Stan had lived with her, he could predict where she'd be at most times of the day: Tuesdays were her grocery shopping days, Saturday major cleaning, Wednesday night and Sunday church. On all days she knitted. She was famous for the little booties she gave to each new baby at Fairfield Baptist, but she also did pullovers, scarves, slippers. She was always finding new patterns.

Even while flying in his dream, Stan recalled Felicia's astonishment when his mother--on her first visit--presented Stan's sudden fiancée with two shawls, a handbag, and three sweaters. When Fel gushed appropriately, Stan had to stop his mother from running back to her room for more fine items to give the woman whom he had said he loved and who would marry him.

Felicia had been tireless in including her mother-in-law at family birthdays, performances, celebrations. Stan took his wife's efforts for granted, busy always with his developing, one-man security business. Deep down somewhere, however, he understood that he should have done more himself for his mother. And there had been times lately when he wondered what his mother had done alone in the house those many years, as he was now whenever Fel was out, his children having flown the nest.

Mrs. Measure was friendly to her neighbors and faithful at all First Baptist events, but, Stan realized, she spent most nights at her home on Oak Street utterly alone. She wasn't, as far as he knew, a great reader, except for the Bible, and she did not like to gossip on the phone.

The kitchen light was on, and Stan could see the door to the landing beside the garage entrance was open. Stairs went from there down to the basement and one semi-finished room. It was used for storage-- old clothes on several racks, boxes of letters and photographs, several shelves holding Stan's school books. For years, a number of large crates held discarded electrical equipment, the material of his childhood and the basis of his later security business. Was she down there, rummaging through the past?

"I think she ran away to the circus."

170

Stan jumped (if you can jump while flying). Felicia, apparently, had been flying just behind him in his dream. Now she dropped down to his side, smiling.

"The circus? What are you talking about. She doesn't leave the house any more than she has to. And she certainly wouldn't go on the road with a performing group."

Felicia giggled. "She heard there's this woman lion tamer traveling with the Big Top who's interested in her son--Miss Whipbite."

Stan looked over. The dream Felicia was wearing a lion tamer's costume: black corset with tuxedo tails, red garter skirt, and short jacket.

"Um, so Mom's going to stop you from taking me?"

"Well, she doesn't want to be alone. And I do want you." He saw the whip coiled into loops attached to her belt the way Wonder Woman wore hers.

Mrs. Measure hadn't wanted to lose her son, of course, but when Stan brought Felicia home to say they were getting married, she glowed with pleasure.

Felicia was known throughout the neighborhood for her volunteer work. She visited shut-ins, babysat for mothers who couldn't afford help, tutored children who missed long periods of school with sickness. She was Holy Trinity's local missionary.

Stan, in bed, stirred. The immaterial, lion taming Felicia was inspiring a material reaction.

"Would you like to perch on a stool?" she asked, arching an eyebrow.

"I . . . no. I mean, I have to find Mom." And Felicia floated off.

Stan concluded his mother must be in the basement, and his dream allowed him to pass through ceilings, floors, and walls to hover over the stairs coming down from the kitchen. His mom was down there.

In slippers and a robe, she had pulled a stool in front of an old, metal file cabinet, tall and deep. At first, Stan thought this must be the repository of his father's effects: the records of his school achievements, Army papers, letters he'd written faithfully until the last mission. But it wasn't.

Coming closer, he could read the labels, neatly printed on little cards and slipped into metal frames on each drawer: "Mittens, Gloves, Ear Warmers"; "Sweaters and Vests"; "Scarves and Mufflers"; "Baby Clothes"; "Afghans"; "Table Runners and Tidies"; "Odds and Ends." Ah, this was where she kept her knitting patterns!

But why was she rummaging through this material late at night? Why had he come to witness her search? Stan floated lower as she thumbed through manilla folders in the "Odds and Ends" drawer, again each tab at the top hand lettered, precise in black ink.

He assumed the order of folders would be alphabetical, the A's in front and Z at the back. As she pulled the drawer out, Stan realized it was remarkably deep. His mother even had to scoot her stool back as she tugged on the handle, and Stan felt the drawer not only went back far into its cabinet, but on into the wall, into the very structure of the house.

The order of folders was chronological not alphabetical, from the present toward antiquity. Each folder had a woman's name on it. Because his mother was thumbing through them steadily, obviously looking for one in particular, Stan couldn't read all the names, but he saw, flipping past, "Eleanor Roosevelt," "Annie Sullivan," "Susan B. Anthony," "Harriet Beecher Stowe," "Abigail Smith Adams." These, he knew, were American.

But then came, along with others: "Daw Aung San Suu Kyi," "Marie Curie," "Tz'u Hsi," "Catherine the Great," "Margaret of Anjou," "Joan of Arc," "Sappho." He didn't know half of these names. Who were they? Why was his mother keeping files on them?

His mother pulled out a folder, very close to the back, but, when he looked, Stan couldn't make out the name printed on the label. The harder he stared, the fuzzier the letters became.

His mother's beatific smile eased the pain Stan had been feeling at her solitary state. She was humming one of her favorite hymns: "*Just as I am, though tossed about / with many a conflict, many a doubt; 'fightings and fears within, without, / O Lamb of God, I come, I come.*"

Chapter 27: I Cry to Thee

Robin Shure had wonderful breath control, which wasn't a surprise to Stan, having admired her lean form, her tight stomach. When his hand had been on her (sure!) tummy, he tried for once to do exactly as Professor Hatter instructed--concentrate on the columns of air supported and sustained by posture and attitude. But he knew his hand was shaking.

After practice she startled him by catching his arm as he was going up the stairs in front of her. "I need you to tell Felicia something."

He blushed. "About . . . about . . . uh . . . the search?"

"No, it has to do with The Oval, the skating rink she's working on. I think it would be good if we met somewhere to talk more about it."

Felicia didn't know it, but Donna had contacted Robin about one aspect of the project. And Robin was puzzled.

Stan was relieved that Robin was not accusing his hand of doing something it shouldn't have, even though it would have been against his will. Why did the word "palpitate" drift into his mind? Had Dr. Montomery talked about palpitating something? Lord, he was positively coming unglued!

Still, he knew he should take advantage of this opportunity to determine if Robin was going to help the rebel choir. He gathered himself. "Oh, by the way, Chester and I, and--um--Linda, are coming early next time, the rebel choir I proposed. Can you . . . would you come?"

She brightened. "I think it will be fun! Our guest conductor is downright tiresome. And maybe we could sing some bluegrass as well as country. Shall I bring my ukulele?"

Stan's heart went pitter-pat. He hadn't palpitated anything. And, who knew that others beyond this central group might show up as well. He headed home convinced the campaign was under way!

What Robin wanted to go over with Felicia was part of the design for The Oval. They chatted at the after church social hour.

Mayle had apparently proposed a configuration of life-size figures at the center of the skating rink. Not animals, as Robin had created and placed on her farm, but famous movie stars of the 1940s and 50s. She talked with Felicia at the coffee hour after church.

"If we can use Jane Darwell from *Grapes of Wrath* and, maybe, Martin Milner from the Route 66 TV series, that might fit in with what we've talked about," mused Felicia, sipping coffee from a church mug. "So Donna asked you about this?"

"Don't get angry with her. She admitted she'd hadn't cleared it with you or Meg yet, but we just ran into each other at Krogers. And she's worried that you're starting to balk on the project, so it was just raising the possibility of my becoming involved."

Felicia studied the snacks laid out on a conference table. "But why did you come to me? Is there something making you hesitate? I mean, you'd get a lot of exposure."

"There are two things, I guess. As you know, I don't really advertise my art. It's more for my own pleasure, a private collection. And one of the things I like is the complete freedom to add to it anything I want."

"You do have some creatures that don't belong in the same habitat!" laughed Felicia. "Kuala bears and the American bald eagle, for instance."

She realized Mrs. Green must have been handling refreshments this Sunday: none of the usual ham biscuits, sausage balls, or microwaved chicken nuggets were visible. Mrs. Green, at 89 years of age, had given up meat and was, two years later, an enthusiastic champion of alternative lifestyles. So the snacks were all vegetarian.

"The other reason you might have reservations?" asked Felicia.

Robin, stirring some roasted mushrooms with a cold asparagus stalk, clucked her tongue. "One little thing about the figures. She said the owner wanted flexible joints, so their poses could change."

"Ah, I bet that's for special events, the different seasons, theme parties."

"Right. The thing is . . . the figures would have to be constructed nude, so I'm not sure why they wouldn't want manikins. They would be cheaper than having me sculpt them. And I would want to make each one distinctive, an individual, not a sort of robot human body."

"That is odd." Felicia held a tiny carrot between thumb and forefinger. "I also wonder why I didn't know about this as part of the design. It would be central to the whole building. Everything else radiates out from there, and everyone's gaze is drawn to that spot."

She decided to give Donna a call later. She wasn't opposed to the figures, which, if handled properly, could draw together The Oval's interior. Right now she felt she should be home. Stan was acting

176

increasingly odd, and he had hurried away without her after the service.

She knew about his small vocal ensemble. He'd started calling it "The Route 66 Choir," although he didn't explain why. She assumed this was simply because he was thinking of himself as another Nat King Cole traveling the Mother Road. What really troubled her was the time he now spent surfing the Internet.

She would have viewed it as a good thing if he'd been caught up in the news, especially the increasingly militant threats of American officials who had proclaimed a "War on Terror." Felicia believed this rhetoric was isolating us, not solidifying the deeper alliances necessary for the future. She had been upset, too, at how we were treating some of our own citizens. There were reportedly pictures of that boy, John Walker Lindh, being tortured.

If Stan's search for a fog-free mirror required extensive Yahoo-ing, she wouldn't have been concerned. But there was so much typing, he must have been writing to someone.

"Double I/Double You!" she said to herself, turning into the driveway. "He's created an alternative life for himself. Just what Donna suggested."

At first, she was relieved. He needed more outlets, and she believed his underlying shyness would prevent him from revealing too much or embarrassing his family by following a virtual connection into the real world. Then she remembered his saying Linda Cooper--and her legs--would be joining his rebel musical group. Did she also have a virtual self? Was she prowling the Internet looking for kicks on Route 66?

Stan was certainly more capable of change at this time of his life than he'd ever been. And these days he was easily frustrated when things didn't suit him. He'd been too angry when the right fog-free mirror wasn't in her catalogs. But what more could she do for her husband and his possible identity crisis? Should she spy on him or trust him not to do anything foolish?

The new Buzz Murdock was wondering what to do about himself as well. It had occurred to Stan that, having proposed a rebel choir--which, at the moment, was only a quartet--he had assumed he could carry the tenor part on his own. Linda, Soprano; Chester, bass; Robin, alto; Stan, tenor. But could he really handle that role? The other three had sung for years, and he knew, when each was the only person for that part, he/she was secure. But Stan had only a few months of experience and no formal training.

Thinking vaguely about Samantha Haute's idea of "making music" earlier in the week, he had devised a way to test his ability. In a closet of the guest room, Stan recovered an old cassette recorder. While Felicia was out (OverDue? search committee?), he recorded himself. Then he played the tape back to see how it sounded. The results were not encouraging.

If he sang melody, it was not so bad. He was certainly loud enough. But when he tried the tenor part, he felt he was sliding back to melody. He needed a way to check, but without, of course, asking someone--certainly not Sam--to help him.

He went to his own storage closet and found some of the tapes Melody had prepared for the choir when she was the temporary director, pounding out each line on her home piano. He was supposed to have only tenor tapes, but, bless her, Melody had sometimes mislabeled or distributed hurriedly, so there were also some soprano recordings mixed in. He realized he could play the melody on one cassette, sing tenor, and record both sounds together on a second machine. The two could be played back to see if harmony resulted.

At one point he asked himself if he had turned into a ventriloquist; or if his former choir director and he had become a duet; or if he was morphing into several different shapes all on his own. No matter which way he looked at it--or listened to it--he was no Nat King Cole.

Just as one of the hymns he sang explained, his *"best hope"* lay *"not in [his] own merit."* Somehow he would have to develop a *"contrite spirit,"* which was not a regular process for him. Putting away both recorders, he hummed (the melody, not the tenor part):*"here is my comfort and my trust; / his help I wait with patience."*

Chapter 28: Stand Up, Stand Up

"A package came for you," Stan told Felicia that Saturday afternoon. "It's on the dining room table."

"It says it's for you." She was hanging up her coat and scarf. She'd been meeting with others on the church committee about the visit of the Rev. Wright scheduled for later in the week.

"But I didn't order anything." He walked over to the table and looked at the label: "from This and That, Them and Those."

"Go on. Open it."

In a moment, he asked, "You bought this . . . for me?"

The fog-free mirror was a leaner version than the one he'd found in the Bins and Boxes catalog. A plexiglass frame, perhaps 5 by 7 inches, held a metallic mirror. No radio, no little shelf to hold razor or scissors, but sturdy and attractive in its simplicity.

"Well, *I'm* certainly not going to be using it," said Felicia, "unless my hormones go even crazier!"

He grimaced, always made uncomfortable by any reference to her aging or changes. "And you're going to let me install it . . . in our bathroom?"

"Of course! You're good at that sort of thing."

Odd. A change in Fel's attitude about home repair. After the toilet tank episode, he assumed his domestic maintenance career was over. Perhaps she was so distracted by church and business matters these days that she had no energy left to keep him in line. Whatever her reasons, he was pleased.

It didn't occur to him that the fog-free mirror was the distraction he needed, a way *not* to think about how he was going to sound in the Route 66 Choir Wednesday night.

When Felicia stepped into the kitchen to answer the phone, Stan carried his package to the den. The unit came with all the screws and brackets necessary for mounting, and he found the directions were like most these days--marginally adequate because they had originally been written in another language and then poorly translated.

At first he'd thought he'd put it up right away. But there was, he reasoned, wisdom in studying the situation before putting holes in anything or using a permanent adhesive. Patience had been a key in his success with Wall-All.

It would make sense, for instance, to survey the layout of the entire bathroom, making sure he would be putting the mirror in the best place. It wasn't just a question of where on the tiled wall around the bathtub it would go, but also where in relationship to the bathroom's arrangement of fixtures this new element should be positioned. After all, one hoped for a coherent ensemble in this most private room.

Flicking the switch by the door, then the one at the side of the medicine cabinet (flanked by two florescent bulbs), he gauged where he would benefit most from overhead and wall illumination. How would light reflect from the mirrors over the sink and on the back of the door? After all, almost every day of his life he composed a self in front of the mirror in which he shaved.

He also regularly composed Buzz Murdock these days, his alter ego traveler/crooner. But that was in front of the computer screen. He was less conscious of how he performed the second process, since he didn't use the webcam to show himself in a smaller window while he chatted with his virtual companions.

Felicia meanwhile was being badgered on the phone by Father Tack. Although he was supposed to serve only as an advisor in the search process, it had become clear along the way that he had a favorite he assumed would be the committee's logical choice. He was furious that the Rev. Hamm wasn't even on the official short list.

"The committee can't count their chickens before they're born," he argued.

"We haven't made a final selection, you understand. But we liked these candidates so much, we didn't want to wait too long before having them visit. If we don't move swiftly enough, we could lose the opportunity."

"Well, if you're planning to invite more men in, of course . . . if the review process isn't completed . . . we just don't want to close the barn door before the cows have gone out."

Felicia attempted to digest yet another idiomatic expression gone idiotic. "We've been working closely with the Rev. List, from the diocese."

This wasn't exactly true, as she and Larry felt the consultant was obsessed with procedure rather than results. The career bureaucrat was less interested in the church's finding a good rector than, as Tack might put it, dotting the t's and cross the i's on his own detailed resumé. Larry had seen it in law firms; another reason, he said, to work with worms.

"That's good, that's good," intoned Rev. Tack. "And I realize I'm here just to offer advice, to answer questions, to suggest ways forward. But I do happen to know Paul Hamm, Father Hamm--we went to seminary many years ago--and a personal relationship can mean so much. There are many fish in the sea, but only some are a catch."

"Of course."

"My friendship with Professor Hatter, for instance . . ."

Felicia had had enough. "Rev. Tack? I'm sorry, but I have something on the stove. I must run, but thank you. Thank you *sooo* much. "

She praised herself for not having slammed the phone down.

Meanwhile, Stan was measuring the width of the tub to make sure his mirror would be positioned in the exact middle of the space. He didn't want to make more than one set of screw holes in the tile grout. He also stopped to consider the mirror's height: too high and it'll be a lifetime shaving on tiptoes; too low, stooping forever. Discomfort either way would lead to slips, cuts and scratches--not a pretty face to see.

Should the mirror be right for any one else, he wondered, guests like his son? No, this was his own, personal, private shaving mirror. A man's bathroom was still his castle, or his castle's water closet, or something like that.

By 5:00 that afternoon the fog-free mirror hung in place, level, with no scars on the neighboring tiles, no extra pieces left around the bathroom, even the packing already out in the trash can at the back of the garage. He would take his shower and enter into a world of frictionless shaving, a privilege for decades.

The preliminaries of getting ready added to the anticipation of the event. He took a clean towel and washcloth into the bathroom and started the water in the tub. He let it run to get hot.

Although there was still a visible roll at Spidey's waist, he had lost a few pounds recently. He stood straight, flexed and relaxed, pleased to find no huge places of conspicuous flab or sag. He looked more closely at the face. Yes, there were some tiny wrinkles around the eyes and at the corners of his mouth. But the overall look was still fresh and interested, alive and active, the new Buzz reborn to ride a mean Harley down Route 66.

He leaned into the tub, diverted the water up to the shower, and then stepped into the warm steamy enclosure. First, the hair: rich shampoo, heavy lather (try to fluff up that thinning band); rinse, lather, and repeat. Then the body purified with 99.7% pure Ivory soap. And finally, whiskers wilted, skin soft, it was time to shave.

He wrung out the washcloth, draped it over the shower curtain. He took his shaving brush, rubbed it into a bar of special shaving soap in an old coffee mug, creating a rich, bubbly lather. He began to cover his face and chin liberally even as he turned around to connect with the new representation of the world's and his own progress, the fog-free mirror.

The mirror was, of course, completely fogged over.

He could not believe it! His space-age, fog-free mirror was not just a little bit misty but completed socked in. It was even more throughly clouded than the medicine cabinet mirror, which was outside the swirling steam of the shower. How could this be?

He sagged against the back wall of the shower. Why had technology failed him? What sort of trick was fate playing in his grand dream of rising to the plateau of stately wisdom and competence? *"The trumpet call obey!"* he commanded.

He stood up straight, rubbed the mirror with his washcloth, thinking *"when duty calls, or danger, / be never wanting there."*

It re-fogged immediately. He blew on it, tapped it with his razor. He whistled, clapped his hands, demanded, "Mirror, mirror, on the wall, where's the clearest face of all?"

Nothing changed. He could see nothing.

Chapter 29: Wilt Thou Forgive

Stan was so angry at his clouded reflection that he went back to shaving in front of the medicine cabinet and even contemplated a return to the use of an electric razor. Of course, he couldn't take the fog-free mirror down. So well had he glued and screwed it that it would probably be found in place after a nuclear attack on Fairfield.

He told Felicia (yet another lie!) that it worked perfectly, "Thank you *sooo* much!"

She seemed pleased. Since it was unlikely Felicia would test her husband's gift, he felt he could leave things as they were. Some miracle might occur that would heal the flawed mirror.

Just before choir practice the following Wednesday, Stan checked in at ii/w. There he learned Samantha Haute was, or claimed to be, one of four.

"You have three sisters? You're not quadruplets, are you ?"

"We look alike, but have different tastes . . . if you know what I mean. :)"

"Do any of you sing?"

"Of course, we sing: first and second soprano; first and second alto--an ideal quartet. We're full-throated, big-chested, lush-lipped beauties. By the way, what are your lips like, Buzz?"

"My lips are tight. 'Loose lips sink ships.'"

"What?"

"Oh, it's an old saying . . . from the Navy, I guess. I must have heard it somewhere, probably an old movie."

"Well, I'd like to see another picture of them. Your profile photo looks more like some movie star from the '50s. Is that really you? Or are you pretending?"

Stan was pretending, of course, or at least speaking out of both sides of his mouth. But then again, Samantha was offering possible versions of herself in what were probably fictional (virtual) siblings. Still, the strain of presenting himself was starting to show in Stan's face (which she couldn't see), in his prose (which she could), and in his heart (which he could not see).

"The profile pic--oh, that's my head shot, you know, for the Route 66 Choir, my performing group."

"Ooh, I see. It's put out by your agent, for publicity, a bit touched up for professional reasons. We need to do that, too, just like the Andrews Sisters."

The image of real or imagined singing sisters made Stan cringe. In one hour he would be attempting to perform in an actual quartet, and he knew he wasn't another Drifter waiting to be discovered. He feared exposure, embarrassment, laughter.

Not that he hadn't practiced every day with his multiple tapes, his own voice doubled and redoubled. Because Felicia had been out a lot that week, meeting with Donna and Meg or with the search committee, he had time to record, listen, repeat. And at least one good thing resulted as he tried different arrangements: he found the perfect song to sing for Hatter.

Thumbing through the hymnal in his solo rehearsals, though, he kept landing on mournful hymns that underscored his current unhappiness. The words of John Donne tugged at a guilt he could not acknowledge: *"Wilt thou forgive that sin, where I begun, /*

which is my sin, though it were done before? / Wilt thou forgive those sins through which I run, / and do run still, though still I do deplore?"

Was he using the opportunity of retirement to build or to tear down, he wondered? Did he want to find his voice as a singer or just get attention from others, distraction from the worries of aging? Dressing up as Spider-man, pretending to be Buzz Murdock, and umbrella-fighting an imaginary herd of toilet-tank floats--he was hardly entering his senior years gracefully.

Was this idea of a core musical group meant to hone his skills and inspire him to greater things, or was he just resenting the abilities of a man who knew more about music than he could ever learn? Did he really expect experienced vocalists to coalesce around him and invigorate the whole church?

And, of course, there was Felicia. Here she was laboring to find a new rector for Holy Trinity, worrying about Over-Due and The Oval, hearing a toilet leak and wondering if Stan was about to demolish the bathtub. He recalled how patient she'd always been, waiting for his business to succeed, to grow, to weather new challenges.

For years he'd been allowed to leave the house at any time, for regular work or to take care of an unexpected problem. He let members of her large family babysit his children when she was sick or needed as volunteer. He denied her vacations not because they couldn't afford them (which he claimed) or because there was nothing worth traveling to see (another assertion), but because changes in his routine unsettled him.

"I can't think of all these things at once!" he had shouted when she tried to corner him, worried about

Ben's hitting slump in high school, Marian's flirtation with gothic dress, her own, often severe headaches. "I pay the bills. I deal with recession and competitors. I'm putting aside money for retirement."

Of course, he'd been spoiled, only son of a doting mother, so shy he grew up with no close friends, a workaholic because only in that mode could he control his world.

He began the first meeting of the Route 66 Choir with a confession.

"You know," he told his three co-conspirators, "you know, I'm not that experienced as a singer." Linda nodded in quick agreement, and Chester grinned.

It was just after 7:00, and they had the choir room to themselves. Karen was upstairs in the office xeroxing scores.

Robin thumbed her ukulele. "We might be able to give you some tips, though, help you along. A lot depends on singing with confidence. You need to not hold back so we can see what parts need work."

"Whoever has the melody," Linda noted, "can carry the song. You always need a lead."

Robin added. "And, remember, with this kind of singing, perfect pitch isn't always the goal."

"We need to do some wailing and some honking." Chester demonstrated with the harmonica. "You can't have too much nasal twang."

"I do have a song," Stan offered, handing a sheet to each. He hoped they were legal copies, but, as they weren't going to perform outside of this room, he felt they were safe.

Robin smiled as she read the lyrics. "Where did you find this?"

Linda frowned. "'They have sinners in their crosshairs'?"

"Woo-hoo! '" laughed Charles. "They'd mow down the low down."

"It's a familiar tune, though," Stan explained.

Chester, putting the sheet he'd been given into his folder, suggested. "Let's practice on a few hymns we've sung lately, get loosened up. Then we'll take on our signature piece."

It was a good idea, as Stan needed to relax with songs he'd sung many times before trying the new one. Chester plucked the beginning notes on his guitar, and they sang three verses of "Stand Up, Stand Up for Jesus" to generate energy. Then, more carefully and slowly, all the verses of "Just as I Am."

After ten minutes of enthusiastic effort, Stan had loosened up. Not every note was smack on pitch and his timing was sometimes hesitant, but his throat was relaxing and the air came from deep in his middle. He began to feel as if they were a group, four individuals creating harmony, like Hawkeye and the others in *Last of the Mohicans*: *"we are not divided, / all one body we, / one in hope and doctrine, / one in charity."*

Robin especially knew they were not yet blending as they should. But she was surprised at the potential. They could, given practice, perhaps become a unit. While Stan lacked experience, singing opened up a realm of repressed emotion in him that, every now and then, gave a distinctive quality to his voice. As the rest of the choir filtered in, picked up their folders, and took seats, she could see that he felt an unanticipated joy.

190

Professor Hatter made his dramatic entrance to the choir room at 7:30 as always, so their timing was perfect. Chester had just put up a hand to the quartet-- wait, ready, sing!--and the four sang out the first line: "If the disciples had their rifles, they'd be thinnin' out the herd."

He beamed at the other choir members--Marvin Barnes, the Lynne twins, sweet Melody Robinson. *"Onward, then, ye people, / join our happy throng; / blend with ours your voices / in the triumph song."*

Glancing up at Hatter's stunned expression, he almost giggled. "Right between the eyes!" he thought. "Thinned, Mr. Nazi Choir Director.--thin-néd."

Chapter 30: Why Cast Down, My Soul

"How it'd go tonight?" Felicia called to Stan when she heard him come in. She had had a good session with Donna and Meg earlier that day, reviewing the now substantial number of jingles they had composed, the slide presentation of the revised design they were to deliver next week, and an itemized invoice for services rendered to this point.

"If I do say so myself," he responded from the den, "the choir was outstanding--the Route 66 Choir, I mean."

She came out to meet him. "You've told me about the small ensemble, I know, but why is it called that? Shouldn't it show you're a part of Holy Trinity."

"Oh, that's not an official name exactly. It's what I call it." He dropped down onto the sofa. "Did you take part in homecoming parades back when we were in high school?"

"Yes, sure." What was this about? "The Latin club always had a float, and I know I rode on it at least once. And we girls would always go to the game, even if we weren't dating football players." Felicia realized she had no memory of Stan at any of those kinds of event.

"Did I ever tell you about Tom Baettner getting me to help with the Senior Class float?"

"Would you like a glass of wine while you tell that story? Or a beer?"

He accepted a beer, struck by the story he was about to tell, the meaning of which had never occurred to him until he was coming back from rehearsal that night. Odd that you can carry events around in your head for decades without asking why they've hung on in memory. He could almost touch the hand of Suzie Bell.

Felicia also felt good about her day because the visit of Rev. Wright was fully arranged--meetings with the search committee, the vestry, and Rev. Tack, the witless.

"I don't think I ever went to a homecoming parade until that last year. Of course, Mom had taken me to Christmas parades when I was growing up. But I didn't like it. There were so many groups represented: the Future Farmers, the Cub Scouts, Lions Club. It was all a jumble."

"Not really. They're all elements of the community, local organizations that take pride in Fairfield and the county. They join in the celebration of the holidays."

"Hmm. I suppose. But one group is about raising the biggest pig, another wants to be canoeing down rivers, the civic clubs try to end blindness. It's a hodgepodge, a wagon train of miscellaneous people not really going anywhere except up Main Street and home again."

Felicia sighed. He'd always been this way, dense about organizations, about connections. She'd hoped in retirement he'd come to see the value of banding together with others--to accomplish common goals but also to make use of your individual talents. She recalled his famous Trick or Treat story.

"The church is that way," she insisted. "We come from all walks of life, all age groups, different genders, but we make up one body."

"But how do you--how does one, I don't mean you--how do we find the places where you can latch on?" He took a long sip of his beer. She hoped this was a rhetorical question, as she didn't know how to answer him. And he did answer himself. "I found out tonight."

Felicia's eyebrows rose in interest even as she worried about his frowns. "Tell me about it."

"See, Tom got interested in short wave radio, something I'd played with on my own for years. In those days you had do it all with Morse Code--dots and dashes."

"Sure. My dad was a signals officer in the war, as you know, communicating with other ships at sea. It takes a gift to send and receive."

"Yeah. In fact, I was never too good at it. Anyway, one day Tom came by to talk about how he could put an antenna up at his house; he wanted to listen in on overseas traffic. I had a wire running out my bedroom window to a twenty-feet high pole in the corner of the yard."

"He probably wanted to spy on the Russians."

"The Russians?"

"You know, back in those days . . . " She trailed off, but Stan didn't seem to notice.

"I went with him to his house, over there by Fairfield Gardens, But I found out that Tom was looking for short cuts. So I told him what to do, but he didn't want to put that much time into it. On the way back to town we saw people out by Mike Davis's house."

"On Salem Avenue, that's where your class always built your floats, on the turnout spot by the garage.

194

His sister was in my class, so we'd sometimes try to flirt with the guys there."

"Hmm. I suppose you could have even been there that night . . . "

She laughed. "Another of those times we passed each other by, two ships in the night, without connecting. We should have been sending out radio signals!"

Rather than smile, Stan grimaced. She was puzzled. Why was he troubled when the night apparently had gone so well? Was he still seeking some unknown connection? *"As pants the hart for cooling streams / when heated in the chase, / so longs the soul."*

Well, Tom said we should stop and help. I'd never done anything like that. I didn't know the first thing about how you put together a float--the decorations and all."

"It's not that hard--a flatbed truck, usually, two-by-fours and chicken wire. Of course, it depends on how complicated you want the scene to be, how many figures and their relationship. Sometimes you go can overboard."

She recalled the Looney Tunes design the 4-H club had tried one year. They wanted to get every major character in a space about fifteen feet by fifteen feet. Come to think of it, those cartoon characters were a bizarre menagerie to begin with--bunnies, mice, birds, frogs, coyotes.

"What got me that night were the cartoons of Kleenex, all different colors."

"Of course. We always used them. Not that many shades, though, in those days."

"Well, I did learn how you use them: you stick them in the chicken wire to make letters, background, shapes--a mural down the side."

"Right. What was the theme for the Senior Class float?"

He tipped his beer and found it was empty. "I don't remember. But I worked on it for hours with Suzie Bell. You knew her?

"Well, of course. And know her now. She's Larry Thornton's wife, silly!"

"Ah, yes. Yes, I guess I wasn't thinking. But here's the thing." He set the bottle down on the end table, leaned forward on the edge of the sofa. "Here's the thing. Tom had started talking with some girl--again, I don't remember who--he forgot about me, so I was standing up by the back of the float wondering whether I should just go back home now or what."

Felicia prayed it wasn't her that Tom had been talking to.

"So, Suzie must have seen me, and she said, 'Take this,' giving me a box of blue Kleenex. Then she waved her hand over a section of chicken wire and told me to make an oval, longer than wide. She said just poke a tissue in the wire, and she showed me."

"Well, that was nice of her."

"That wasn't all. She slid a waste basket over, upside down, and told me to sit on it while I worked. She had another basket and sat down beside me. She was doing FHS in red against a white backdrop on the side of my oval."

"Yes, you had to have the school initials on the float."

"So, I poked tissues and more tissues, without thinking for a long time. Then I told her that I didn't think you should push them in too much or they looked too scrunched. She agreed and pointed out that not all the openings in the chicken wire were exactly the same size. Some were bigger, others smaller. And I told her I'd hadn't noticed before she told me. Then I said some of the wire had little loose ends; you had to be careful not to poke yourself. And she said if you perched on a waste basket too long you got stiff. And I said as it got darker it was harder to see what you were doing. She said . . . "

He paused, looking off into space. Felicia prompted him. "You said you learned something. It wasn't just how to poke Kleenex into chicken wire or how to build a float, was it?"

"No, it's . . . it's how you make friends. You don't make that the main object, see, you don't work at saying 'Here I am. Look at me. Like me.' You just do something together: crumple up Kleenex, balance on waste baskets, see letters take shape. It changes the focus so that you can keep talking and getting to know the other person without feeling the stress, without trying to figure out what to say or what not to say. You're just there with the other person, and after a while you find out you like that person or you don't. Anyway, I guess, after a while they're a friend."

She came over and sat beside him. "And church choir is just like that, isn't it? It's a way to make friends." And she thought to herself: *"Hope still, and thou shalt sing / the praise of him who is thy God, / thy health's eternal spring."*

Volume Four: Easter and Pentecost.

Chapter 31: The Company of Angels

Before the next choir practice--for which the Route 66 Choir performed again as the raucous warm-up group--Stan went bike riding with Chester on the Oroginee Watkins Trail.

Stan was pleased at how much more easily he rode now, feeling less winded even though they had increased the pace. Their goal was to cut a certain number of minutes off the round trip each time they went, and since there were no hills, a steady rhythm was the key to better time.

"Did you see Hatter's face," he asked Chester once they had established their cruising speed. "It was like the witnesses to the fire bombing of Dresden in *Slaughter-House Five*!"

'What?"

"You know, Billy Pilgrim and other prisoners and their German guards? Kurt Vonnegut? They had been holed up under ground during the bombing--incendiary bombing that destroyed the city. And when they came up and saw the burned landscape, and the charred bodies, it looked like the surface of the moon. Their mouths opened as if they were a barbershop quartet singing, but no sound came out."

Stan decided this must be a scene in a book or movie. "Well, I don't think we were that bad!" The image also recalled something else, but he couldn't pin it down.

"I know, I know. But we did take his breath away."

"I'll say, though he recovered pretty quickly." Hatter had gone on with the rehearsal once the small group finished their rendition.

"Still, he couldn't really figure out how to deal with us. I mean, he just ignored us and was tentative for the first five minutes or so."

"And we were cooperative, once he started up." Chester nodded. "It may be we have to escalate things a bit."

"How so?"

"I have some ideas . . . " He trailed off with a mischievous chuckle. "By the way, I learned something about this skating rink project. Isn't your wife involved with The Oval?"

"Yeah. She has two friends, and they do design work. I think she's worried about some parts of the project."

"Um-hm. Well, I have a friend, another sawmill operator down in Arkansas. He said he had received inquiries from someone in Fairfield about supplying high grade mahogany for a roller rink."

"Makes sense. They're going to need wood for the refurbishing."

But not mahogany. That's expensive stuff, not what you'd think of. I mean, you wouldn't choose it for a bowling alley or a video game parlor, places that specialize in family entertainment. You might see it in the lobby of some fine hotel, say, in Paris."

"Hm. I don't know what that means, but I'll pass it on. I think Fel and the girls are talking about materials in their design. And speaking of design: I've got a question for you about the fog-free mirror."

"Oh, you got one! They're great."

"Well, it was supposed to be. But mine fogs up in the shower. Is there some trick to it I don't know. How do I make the stupid thing work?"

"Oh, that! Easy. Just splash some water on the mirror; clears immediately."

And it was that simple, as Stan learned when he got back home. If water hit the mirror, it rolled off in sheets. He supposed it might have something to do with the size of drops needed to cause the sheeting action. Tiny ones remained as fog or mist; larger ones had enough mass to be pulled by gravity down the mirror. Whatever the science, Stan found himself in the bathtub of his own happy home at six o'clock that evening staring at his own happy face.

Believing himself to be thinner and more fit, he smiled at the sharp image of himself. Rubbing his shaving brush into his cup of soap, he chuckled, lathered his face, and began to shave.

Then, for no particular reason, he wondered about science and technology and how they did work. If people could do this, he thought--create a fog-free mirror--why couldn't they invent a mirror that was even better, had yet more amazing properties? Why not a mirror that could give you a two-day shave, for instance, so effective it allowed your razor to get way down to the base of each whisker, showed it the way, sort of?

Hey, better than that, let's have a mirror so penetrating, so exacting in its reflection that when you shave before it once, you don't need to shave again--ever! It stops growth by neutralizing some fundamental chemistry at the root of the whisker, letting light in at the core, perhaps. Well, unless, of course, you want to start a beard, in which case--what?--um--you rub a special compound on your face and whiskers began to grow again.

Hmm. He thought some more, shaving neatly below his sideburns, around the mustache. Wait a minute, if they could do that--make a one-time, lifetime shaving mirror--why couldn't they come up with a mirror that cured cancer! Sure, you looked in it, spotted any growths or malignancies, circled them with a special grease pencil attached to the mirror by a thin electric cord, pushed a button on the side of the frame, and they were finished, done away with. Yeah. A heal-all mirror.

Well, shoot! Why stop here?

He rinsed the lather off his face, rubbed with his fingertips to see if he had missed any spots. If they could make a mirror that fantastic, why not invent a mirror that, when you looked into it, you saw the self you ought to be, the person you'd always thought you were (generous, strong, talented). Yes, you met the person who had always been surprised to learn that anyone saw him otherwise (egotistical, conniving, insecure).

Even the physical qualities you wanted would be available, the mirror translating your desire--what you hoped to see--into reality, what was looking back from the mirror. Away with those wrinkles, more hair on the top, please. And a stronger jaw, youth and intelligence gleaming out at you as your heart filled with joy at mankind's potential finally realized. And, and, . . . that's not all.

Stan cut off the shower, pushed back the curtain to reach for a towel. But before he could lay his hand on the towel, he saw in his fog-free mirror--instead of the rest of his bathroom over his shoulder--he saw the world transformed. The universe had been made beautiful by the greatest technological device ever conceived--the heavenly mirror.

He saw before/behind him a serene pastoral landscape, valleys in which lambs lay down with lions and swords were turned into plowshares. Flowers were blooming on bush and tree; everywhere nature was bountiful.

History was made known to him in this vision too, and he realized that what had once been desert was now greening, waste lands come rich with life. Strife had been eliminated as the earth teemed with plenty for all its creatures.

Envy and sloth and all those human failings had also faded away, leaving productive, fulfilled citizens to enjoy their world and each other. A garden stretched out before (beyond) Stan as he hummed softly to himself his version of heavenly hymns, the music of the spheres: *"The company of angels / are praising thee on high; / and mortal men and all things / created make reply."*

So there he was, wearing only a wedding band more than he had been born in, standing in a bathtub, his eyes misty with fantasy, when his wife stepped into the bathroom. Felicia said--and as soon as he heard her say the words, it occurred to him that she had probably been thinking them a lot lately--she said, "What in the world are you doing?"

Stan knew the moment he heard her he had no answer that could possibly be adequate to the situation.

He looked at her, framed in the doorway--my goodness, she looked wonderful! She was wearing a pair of old blue jeans and was about to fasten the top two buttons of one of her favorite flannel shirts. There was no Wonder Woman outfit, no slinky negligee. She hadn't just had her hair done, no bubble bath or sea weed massage. But she was the girl who'd come to the fire tower with him many years ago. "Surely there's a telephone?" she had asked, her eyes sweeping the little room. "You could call someone? If you were lonely."

"Doing?" Stan said now, grinning like a crazy person. He pointed to his fog-free mirror, "I, well . . . I'm just trying to put the best face I can on things." It was a landmark in his life.

Chapter 32: To Canaan's Land

"I want you to read this," Felicia said the next morning. Both what he read and that she gave it to him would confirm Stan's sense of arriving at a new place.

"It's about security equipment?" he asked, actually worried that it was something political. She wanted him to pay more attention to how Bush was linking Iraq to Al Qaeda, suggesting a need for more military action. He really couldn't care less.

"Oh, no. But you don't have to read the whole thing, just this one piece--I really liked it."

She'd folded the pages back to the beginning of "Jesse James," a story in the latest *Journal of the Mother Road*. Over-Due had subscribed to the periodical for the Road House museum project. Stan surprised her by taking it. After the Route 66 Choir's debut, though, Stan was more willing to try new things.

"Jesse James" was about a retired couple's summer vacation in New Mexico.

> *Martin chose the place because it offered a stark change from their life in Plain, Missouri. He felt he and his wife Elizabeth had gone stale in their tiny Bootheel town, their routine so fixed that they couldn't see each other against a too familiar background.* (Stan understood this as Fel's message to him.)

> *Santa Fe was dry where Plain was wet, high if it was low; semi-arid where the Delta was lush, wide open if it was closed-in. And Martin wanted to get away from what seemed to be suffocating in his daily existence. Why Elizabeth accepted his proposal was a mystery.*

That the James's ten-day vacation would be radically unlike an ordinary time for both of them was evident the moment they stepped onto the parking lot of their motel in New Mexico. From Plain they'd crossed the flatland to reach Highway 60 in Popular Bluff and followed it across the state to Springfield. From there it was the path of famous Route 66 all the way to Santa Fe, most of it now, of course, covered over by Interstates 44 and 40.

Against the red-oranges of desert sands and mesa rock their two-story, white framed, Missouri house, surrounded by magnolia and crepe myrtle, faded immediately from memory. In the Boot Heel they had been set back in a green grove of willow surrounded by dark bottom land. Here low adobe buildings sat on sandy lots, and hot winds blew dust and dry vegetation down the canyons. They shaded their eyes in the bright sun as they inspected the motel.

"The sun's bright, but you don't feel the heat," he told Elizabeth, shutting the car door behind her. "No humidity."

"I feel it," she responded from under the motel's canopy.

"You do?" he said, squinting down the street at an adobe bank building baking in the sun.

This was the way things had been going recently, though. He and Elizabeth moved in separate frames of reference, making opposing assumptions and reaching different conclusions. They had lost connection and needed a change of scene to rediscover each other. He recalled their honeymoon thirty-five *years ago in St. Louis. He'd been wild in his love of her. And she, a minister's daughter, was excited by his energy, which at times bordered on excess.*

Stan suspected the Casa Grande would not be the place for Martin's breakthrough. Although the beige stucco walls and red tile roof were meant to represent a Spanish character, the rooms, restaurant, and bar inside resembled those in the hotels of a hundred American cities.

Martin had arranged a series of driving excursions to the surrounding countryside, each designed to jolt him and Elizabeth out of context, to open their eyes to an exciting world around them. On dusty local roads they would see that they both still had foreign territory for the other to explore. They would be following the map's "blue highways."

At the motel before their first trip, on 84 and 68 to an Indian pueblo at Taos, he double-checked the camera equipment he had packed in an elaborate carrying case. Once a talented amateur photographer, he seemed recently to have lost faith in his only hobby. The latest pictures—of their yard covered by a freak, light snow in April; of grown and married children with two grandchildren; of a weekend outing in Memphis—all seemed false, the product of someone else's artistry, not experience. He wanted to try again to capture who they really were, what they did together. For honesty he would use black-and-white film.

"Do you have my asthma medicine," asked Elizabeth. She had developed problems

breathing in late middle age, after the children had left home.

"You won't need it here," he responded. "This is where people go who have allergies."

"I feel tight," she returned. Martin shrugged and held up her bottle of pills.

Why couldn't they at least agree on the basic ground they occupied? She challenged his every premise, evaded his first principles. He recalled all of a sudden a scene from their honeymoon, when he had strapped on a pair of toy six-shooters, purchased secretly while she shopped for lingerie at Famous-Barr. She came out of the bathroom in their hotel suite to see him wearing only the guns and a cowboy hat, a mustache drawn with an eyebrow pencil.

"You're not one of those bad James boys, are you?" she had asked, pretending fright. (Stan thought of himself in his Spidey suit.)

At the pueblo they stood by a stream that came down from mountain springs, its origin magical in Native American lore. "This river has never gone dry," their dark-eyed, black-haired guide told them. "Even when the hills go brown, there is enough for our crops." He gestured at the green mountain rising to the west. The source was sacred, never seen by a white person, though on the other sides of neighboring peaks new roads climbed up to fashionable ski resorts.

"Look how clear the stream is," Martin told Elizabeth. They stood on a bridge that took them from one section of the pueblo to another. The water rippled over smooth rocks.

"Do people really live here?" she asked, looking past the stream. "In these conditions?"

"Most live in more modern houses," Martin admitted. "They come here to run the shops."

"Let's buy something to take home." She entered the dark front room in one of the buildings, where clay pots were on sale. The pottery glittered with mica, characteristic of Taos.

Martin used a whole roll of photographs, most of the landscape, but, later, some of himself and Elizabeth. They paid the guide to take a picture of them at the foot of a log ladder rising to the roof of a mud building, one of the oldest occupied structures in America.

Would they, looking at the picture, be able to see themselves anew? At the end of the day he decided to drop the film off at a 24-hour developer, one block from their motel. Main Street of America Pictures would have the prints tomorrow. Santa Fe featured the Mother Road in tourist advertising though the highway was moved south through Albuquerque early in its history.

Day Two took them back in Taos shops and artists' galleries that catered to tourists, but also northwest on 64 to a great gorge twenty miles from town in which the Rio Grande meandered. The land was perfectly flat for miles in every direction. The river had cut its way a thousand feet down, making a deep crack in the giant table. Kit Carson made his last home in this area long before there were any paved roads.

Stan wondered if Nat King Cole would appear in the story: "*Go down, Moses, / way down in Egypt's land; / tell old Pharaoh / to let my people go.*"

"*Where are we going to eat?*" Elizabeth asked her husband. *They were at a pull-off on the side of the canyon, where the suspension bridge stretched across the gorge.*

"*Not at the hotel,*" he insisted. "*I want to try something authentic.*" *She raised an eyebrow.*

They got out of the car onto a pedestrians' walkway. Tourists went out in pairs and small groups to gaze down, the river at one point nearly a quarter of a mile below. Signs told them not to drop anything, as campers might be rafting on the water far beneath them.

Squinting against the afternoon sun, Martin wondered if, from this height, he could see people on the river below. He thought of taking pictures with his telephoto lens. Then he worried that the pictures he'd taken yesterday would not come out, that there would be some accident in developing, that the studio had already misplaced them.

In his imagination he saw a couple in a rubber raft bouncing over rapids far below the bridge. An older man in the back tried to steer clear of hazards. Up front a woman wearing a life jacket tore photographs to shreds and flung the pieces out over the water.

They got back to Santa Fe well before dark. Surprisingly, the photo shop was closed.

"*At 7:00 o'clock?*" Martin wondered. "*This is a tourist town. They should be open until*

*midnight." But the schedule posted on the door
confirmed this closing as regular.*

*He would have to wait until the following
night for the pictures because they were getting
up early the next day to drive along Route 4 to
Valle Grande and Bandelier National
Monument, home of ancient cave people.*

Stan put the magazine down to answer the door. It
was Professor Hatter wanting to talk.

Chapter 33: Until My Heart is Pure

"I want to tell you a little story," Professor Hatter said. "May I come in?"

Stan could not think of a reason to say no, though he was usually efficient in turning uninvited visitors from his door.

"Uh, sure, I guess. Come in. But," looking at his watch (or at least at his wrist where a watch might have been), he added, "I just have a few minutes before . . . before I go out for my piano lesson."

Good grief, the increasingly outrageous liar! How many years had it been since he and Ben had gone across town to torment Mrs. Barr, having failed to practice scales, arpeggios, chords on their "grand piano"?

"I will need only a few minutes of your time."

Stan ushered him into the den. Felicia was wisely staying out of sight. He didn't want this to be ugly, but he'd never considered what might happen if he were directly confronted by the Nazi Choir Director.

"In the first King Leopold's reign, in the 17th century," Hatter began, not even sitting, but standing with his back to the fireplace. "In the 17th century of my mother country there was a jester, Karl, who kept a high place at court by amusing the nobility."

Stan decided not to sit either. He planted his feet and crossed his arms on the other side of the room. Maybe he should call Felicia in?

"Karl came early to court events--banquets, receptions, audiences--and told stories to the guests, often containing thinly veiled references to actual happenings in Frankfurt. He invented a pretend King and Queen--Leonard and Maria--who were . . . well, bunglers. But he was careful to insist on the differences between his fallen, imagined world and the purer, actual world in which he was privileged to play a special role."

Hatter sighed, apparently anticipating a sad future for Karl.

"Sounds like a dangerous line to walk," Stan observed. "One false step and . . . I wonder, was Karl a musician, by any chance? Perhaps a singer?"

"He thought he was, but the truth is he had no talent whatsoever. He lacked--how shall I say it?--the ability to receive instruction. There was no polish in anything he did, and his musical education was severely limited in the first place."

"Ah, quite so, quite so." Stan felt himself falling into Hatter's own formal mode of discourse. "Still, his talent for comedy insulated him from criticism. I've known people like that." Stan was trying to decide if he could redirect this story. Was Leopold to be Hatter's alter ego, or would some other figure represent the authority who should be respected? He had no doubts about the moral of his visitor's tale.

Hatter went on. "Karl's gift of gentle mockery protected him for a time, but only a time. Like all fools, he pushed his privilege with the King too far. He made fun of Leopold's chief minister of music, Ferdinand, a disciple of the great Johann Sebastian Bach."

"Um-hm. As I understand it, wit was much valued in those aristocratic circles." Stan was, of course, making this up. "A good jest was always appreciated, even if it made a few people squirm. After all, some

213

folks get so high and mighty they need to be brought down a bit."

"A *good* jest can be appreciated, yes. However, Karl did not understand the nature of his monarch, who was benevolent but would not tolerate anything that undermined the natural structure of society. And that includes music."

"I guess by 'the natural structure of society" you are referring to the divine right of kings." Stan surprised himself with this scrap of memory from high school history--or was it civics?--class. But then again, hadn't Felicia been talking to him recently about limits to Presidential power? Had Congress, she worried, let the executive branch take away its role in government, especially in declaring war? Was the country experiencing a return of the Imperial Presidency?

Hatter didn't respond to Stan's assertion. "Karl learned to impersonate Ferdinand, copying the voice and the speech pattern of Leopold's favorite. If he wasn't seen, listeners couldn't tell if they were hearing the minister or the clown."

"Well, there were no telephones or electronic modes of communication in those days, so I wouldn't think he could carry out much of a prank if others were watching. No one is that good a ventriloquist."

"Karl didn't succeed, you're right. But he tried, Mr. Measure, he tried." Hatter's lips formed an unpleasant smile, though the rest of his face and his posture remained unchanged.

"Ferdinand was to conduct a motet for double choir *a capello* . . . "

What Hatter said next was lost on Stan, as his guest probably intended--another part of the lesson to be learned. The director knew the neophyte would not

214

comprehend "contrapuntal treatment of each line in the chorale," "antiphonal repetitions," "strict contrapuntal treatment of the upper voices." Stan, in fact, thought he had said "motel" and was wondering what travelers would be coming together at such places in those far off days--itinerant merchants, troubadours, government officials?

"Not only did Karl interject his instructions to the chorale while Ferdinand was conducting, but he also added his own singing--in falsetto, of course--to the higher voices. Because Ferdinand and his choir were paying close attention to each other, no one discovered the source of these extra sounds--even though Karl's singing was amateurish."

Stan looked at his watch (or his wrist) again, holding his arm up to suggest he had only a few moments left before he would have to leave for his lesson. But Hatter ignored the meaning of his gesture.

"Naturally, it was the King who found out what his court jester was doing. He came into the hall quietly, before being formally announced. He was not," said Hatter, "amused."

Stan thought about his multiple selves in the bathroom: the one actually being shaved, the one looking back in the mirror, the one he imagined in Utopia. He also thought about himself as Buzz on ii/w, exchanging pleasantries and innuendos with a woman who might or might not have three nearly identical sisters. Who was speaking for him? Who was speaking as him?

"Leopold truly loved music and was not amused at the antics of his court jester. He himself had studied with some of the great masters of his time and knew the sounds heard at court must reflect the qualities of

215

a great monarch, one chosen by God to be the center and model of this universe. All voices should blend harmoniously into one hymn of praise for the sovereign. Discord was destructive. Karl was doing nothing less than destroying his kingdom."

Stan recalled himself in Spider-man costume. He remembered the role in which he cast his younger self, opposite Marilyn Monroe/Sugar Kane in *Some Like it Hot*/Pullman Car. A dream version of himself floated over his childhood home listening to a fantasy Felicia, the lion tamer cracking a whip. His voice tried to find its place with Robin's, Chester's, and Linda's.

In the past there had been one family man, a single one-man security firm, an irregular member of Holy Trinity's quiet congregation--all the same person. "*[F]ill me with life anew*," he prayed, "*that I may love what thou dost love, / and do what thou wouldst do*."

"So, the King devised an appropriate punishment for Karl. Because the jester would not submit to authority, the music master or the King, he was put in a solitary cell for one week. The only voice he would hear from Sunday to Sunday would be God's, the supreme ruler's."

Stan remembered his watch tower days. He'd known loneliness. Until Felicia pointed out his isolation, though, he'd been able to deal with it. The octangular space had resembled his attic bedroom, where he'd lived in his projects, listened to distant voices on his short wave radio, imagined playing with The Circle's other children he so often heard outside his window: "*until my heart is pure . . . / until this earthly part of me / glows with thy fire divine.*"

"Karl did not hear the Lord's voice in his isolation. He became obsessed with the slow drip of water from somewhere high above his dungeon cell to the floor

216

beside his bed. Drip, drip, drip, as regular as the moon. He tried to conduct the sound, his hand rising and falling, rising and falling . . . until . . . until he went mad, completely mad."

As he told the final part of his story, Hatter began crossing the den with small but deliberate steps. His face was frozen in its ugly grin, and Stan started to think he was losing his grip just as Karl had. He glanced at the poker in the fireplace. Which man would grab it first and assault the other?

Felicia came into the den with a plate of desserts. "Hi, Professor Hatter, I thought you boys might like something to snack on."

The Professor did not stay for cookies.

Chapter 34: A Green Hill Far Away

The next day Stan picked up *Journal of the Mother Road* to resume the story Fel had given him, "*Jesse James.*" He liked it, but why had she asked him to read it?

Before the Jameses left on their next New Mexico excursion, Martin dropped another roll of film into the night slot, as the store was not open this early. Elizabeth had shot him the day before leaning casually against the suspension bridge railing.

Martin couldn't tell if she was enjoying this vacation. She went willingly on the day trips he'd planned, but she showed few signs of being affected by it all. What occupied her thoughts, looming large on her mental horizon? What had shrunk to insignificance in her gaze?

Valle Grande was in the mountains beyond Los Alamos, a giant meadow nearly two miles above sea level. Mountains on all sides marked the ancient rim of a volcano that had erupted here millions of years ago. Occasional small clumps of trees dotted the valley, perhaps ten miles across, twenty the length.

"Look at the cows," Elizabeth marveled, pointing directly across the valley. "They're tiny." They were black specks at this distance, ants standing in a field.

Martin was glad she was taking an interest, seeing the odd landscape. He pointed to what looked like snow under the pine trees, but it turned out to be hail from last night's thunderstorm.

He was still preoccupied by his pictures back in Santa Fe, worrying again that they were being lost or destroyed in processing. Focusing on the faraway cows, he shaded his eyes with one hand. Were their heads down, cropping grass? Did their tails swish flies, atom-sized in this view? Did one lift its head, bits of chewed photographs dropping from the sides of its mouth?

He put his arm around Elizabeth's shoulder. "It's a beautiful place."

"It is," she agreed, but she said nothing more. Martin felt the absence of communion. They both liked this place, but was it for the same reasons? He had wanted harmony between them on this trip, consensus established by the lawyer's pro-and-con logic he had pursued successfully in court for nearly forty years. Elizabeth seemed to have slipped off the witness stand, however, silently asserting that her testimony was not relevant to the case at hand. Was this true, or did it mean she just didn't care?

Stan replayed Fel's rescue of him from Professor Hatter. Was she acting for him or the whole church? He wondered who *"only could unlock the gate / of heaven and let us in?"*

Martin and Elizabeth took the park service walk at Bandelier, down a narrow canyon whose sides contain natural and man-made caverns. A "primitive" people had come here on foot perhaps a thousand years ago, lived well for several centuries, then disappeared. They farmed the floor of the canyon and the tops of the high cliffs. No one knows what became of them.

Martin asked Elizabeth if she wanted to climb into one of the lower caves, once inhabited.

"Take a picture instead," she suggested, and he did.

Again they were late getting back to Santa Fe. Martin had wanted to stay at Bandelier watching the hummingbirds on the park's snack bar patio. The tiny creatures, with gorgeous colors of green and blue, totally unlike the crows and house sparrows they knew at home, zipped in and out right over visitors' heads. Martin bought a feeder to take home with him and shot the rest of the day's film. Elizabeth purchased a book about desert flowers.

He dropped the third roll of film into the night slot. This time he added a note identifying himself, explaining why he had not been there in time to pick up his other rolls, and promising that he would be there before closing the next day.

The next day, however, was Sunday, and the shop was closed. He began to fear he was losing control of the holiday.

They took highways 84 and 503 to the museum at Los Alamos on Sunday, working computer programmed displays of the laboratory's successes and watching a film about the Manhattan Project, development of the first atomic bomb. It rained, not a day for pictures. Martin kept seeing in his mind's eye *the final scene from the film, total destruction of Nagasaki.*

They came back to Santa Fe and the famous street of shops, Canyon Road. Elizabeth bought a broad-brimmed straw hat, totally unlike her, Martin thought.

"Let's stay in tonight," she suggested. "Maybe watch a movie." She loved Westerns.

"I was thinking of dancing," he returned.

"I'm walked out. All these stores."

She agreed, however, to go for a short ride up toward the Sangria de Cristo mountains and watch the sun set across the desert. Martin gazed at the glowing red ball, seeing instead Ground Zero in August, 1945. He imagined his lost pictures at the heart of the conflagration, negatives and prints shriveled and melted.

Involuntarily, Stan recalled television pictures of the invasion of Afghanistan. Felicia had made him watch. She showed him statistics about the number of civilian deaths, even though she admitted we had to eliminate the terrorist training camps.

On their last day they drove down Interstate 25 to Albuquerque for the tram ride up Sandia Peak. Somehow they got started without picking up the pictures. "We won't forget them when we come back," Elizabeth insisted.

"It would only take us twenty minutes to go back now," he offered.

"No. Let's go on."

The panoramic view at ten thousand feet was spectacular. Reading in a guide book,

Elizabeth explained that taking the train to the observation deck moved you through terrain and climates like those ranging from Mexico to Alaska. Convinced that his pictures were lost, Martin couldn't concentrate on what he was seeing.

In a small gift shot at the tram station, Elizabeth bought post cards for the grandchildren, wrote notes, and dropped them in the box on the sidewalk.

Martin drove directly to the photo shop. He wouldn't stop for lunch until he had his pictures. Driving, he imagined conversations with the clerk:

"Your pictures? We must have confused them with someone else's."

"James? No, nothing here. When did you leave them?"

"You're the man who wrote the notes, aren't you? We have no idea what happened to your film."

Elizabeth sat in the car while he went in. They were there, all the rolls. He gave an OK sign with thumb and forefinger to the parking lot, but she wasn't looking, perhaps listening to the radio. While the clerk totaled his bill, he carried the package out to her. She took them through the window.

Inside the store, he charged the pictures, not even noticing that the price was steep even for fast service. He pushed the store's door open, delighted that he had not lost the pictures, curious about what they showed.

On the sidewalk he felt a burst of elation. He borrowed a gesture from his grandson, one of those arm-pumping, clenched-fist poses sports stars use at big plays. It was totally out of character, but Elizabeth, studying the pictures, didn't notice.

He wanted her to see, though, so he put one foot on the car's bumper, rocked the old station wagon on its suspension, and raised both hands high in a victory salute. Still, her head was down, intent on the photographs.

Martin climbed up the hood of the car on his hands and knees. "Awww right!" he called. She did not look up. He poked his head around the corner of the windshield, peering in the open door window. Elizabeth held one of the pictures by its corners, studying.

"Well?" he asked.

She looked at the picture then beyond it, but she didn't seemed to be focusing on him. He glanced back over his shoulder. Perhaps she saw those mountains high above the city?

This time her gaze found him. She looked back at the picture, still held up before her. Her eyes shifted to his face, then back to the photograph.

"You know?" she asked.

"Yes?"

"You know what? In these pictures . . . . " She was smiling now.

"Hmm?"

She tapped the picture, pinched between her thumb and forefinger, twice on his forehead.

"In these pictures, with the shadows, and the background, you look like one of those outlaws in the Old West. You look just like . . . " She *reached up and kissed him. "* . . . *Jesse James."*

Stan went to find Felicia.

"There was no other good enough / to pay the price of sin.*"*

Chapter 35: Touching Every Place and Time

The visit of the Rev. Wright was so successful that some on the committee wanted to ask him to become the rector without even bringing in the priest couple. Felicia was half of that mind herself, though she suspected she just wanted any one of her many crises resolved.

For once the diocesan consultant was reasonable, arguing that you can't make an invitation to a candidate (or pair or candidates) and then withdraw it. And it's always better to consider, to compare and contrast strengths and weaknesses. Father Tack, of course, reminded them that his friend, Paul Hamm, was still available. So, in the end the committee agreed that the simplest course was to proceed with the Hightower visit.

Stan thought Chester's escalation of the campaign against Hatter might cause a major blowup before this search was completed and was beginning almost to regret his sponsorship of the Route 66 Choir. He was realizing how much strain Felicia was under, not only from her duties at Holy Trinity but also from, apparently, one more new challenge at Over-Due. In the end, his rebel choir did inspire an explosion.

At the same time, Stan had to admit to himself that he was thrilled at his own improved singing. With Robin's coaching and Chester's encouragement, he was starting to hear, not his own voice by itself, but his tenor blending with the soprano, also, bass--a single sound. Even Linda was accepting him as adequate backup when she had the melody.

And now Chester felt the group was ready for its escalation. "Phase II," he announced Sunday after church.

"And that would be?" Linda asked.

"We need to do some dancing while we sing--you know, cool steps in sync with some good hip movement, especially by the ladies."

"Oh, I can *do* that!" Linda said, "ha-HA-ha-ha!"

"I know some basic spins," offered Robin, "clapping, the two-finger wipe."

"Let's pick a signature step: Hand Jive, maybe The Dog, or--I know--the good old Funky Chicken!"

"Okay, okay. We need to choose one, work on it a bit, and then exaggerate the . . . um, suggestive parts." He paused. "Stan, there's a problem?"

Stan's face said there was. "I . . . um . . . I don't dance. Or, at least, I've never danced with anyone but Felicia. And, to tell the truth, not too much with her."

He thought of Fel teaching their children, who insisted he take part in the home lessons. He was stiff even in that privacy, though he could often feel the rhythm. He wanted to match the moves of everyone else, but never relaxed enough to do it.

"I can show you," Linda said. "And I kind of owe your wife."

"You do?"

"I'll explain later. In fact, I'm coming by your house to meet with her this week. You and I can dance then. I bet she'll help."

Some weeks ago he'd had his hand on Robin Shure's belly. What now!

The rebels decided to come Sunday morning in outfits more appropriate for *Dancing with the Stars* than a high-church Anglican service. They would be covered by robes in church, and jackets could be put on for the social hour. Still, Stan wondered if he should warn Felicia.

"We want our new song to make the rest of the choir boogie," said Chester at the end of their rehearsal. "It should be infectious!"

It was infectious. Professor Hatter fled the choir room as if pursued by an epidemic. He went directly to Father Tact.

"I want every one of them removed from the choir, if not the church!" His face, though composed as always, was bright red in places, ashen white in others.

Tack looked at the top of his desk. "I can't do that. In fact, I can't do anything."

Hatter waited for an explanation.

"The bishop has offered me a new position. It's an administrative position at diocesan headquarters. In charge of . . . as I understand it . . . compiling their 'Miscellaneous' files for the last . . . um . . . fifty years. Quite exciting, actually."

Hatter paused. "They're buying you out. You can't accept."

"The cat's in the bag, I'm afraid. They know enough about . . . um, some of my past work . . so that I really shouldn't object to anything. I get to keep my pension."

"Then I'll disband this choir myself." He spun on his heel, but Tack stopped him with a groan loud enough to be heard outside the room.

"You can't do that either. I've been told I must . . . must ask for your resignation."

"My resignation?"

"The vestry met this week. And the bishop has backed their decision. I'm afraid you may have been the kettle tarred by the black brush. It's time for both of us to move on."

"I had nothing to do with any trouble you've had. You know that."

Tack sighed. Hatter noticed that there open boxes by the desk, things taken from the drawers already overflowing the cartons.

"The choir complained to the vestry about you at the same time . . . and the association with me didn't help. You're to be paid through the month, with another month's salary added. Melody Robinson has returned to direct, and Ms. Cooper will sing an anthem this morning."

"That idiot Measure! He must be behind this."

"I've been told that's not so. In fact, he's just the squeaky wheel that greased the plank, if you know what I mean."

The choir learned some months later that Marvin Barnes started the chain of events leading to Tack's and Hatter's removals. The veteran policeman has contacts throughout the state and beyond. And at some point he remembered reading something somewhere about a priest who had been moved on from post to post. And that tickle of memory took him to the vestry.

Marvin had unusual theories about crime, especially the notion of networks. While he acknowledged that groups of criminals--white collar embezzlers as well as regular burglars--band together to stage operations, he resisted seeing a shared profile for every individual. Things aren't so simple, he explained in his closed door presentation to the vestry.

"Movies, like *The Godfather*, perpetuate the notion of 'the family,'" he told the unhappy gathering, notching quotation marks with two fingers on each hand. "Everybody in 'the family' plays by the mob's rules. They're all essentially the same, or that's conventional wisdom. So, when we look for 'who done it,' we work from a stereotype. But we're all different."

The chief warden asked, "Are you telling us we're dealing with distinctive personalities here, highly specialized outlaws?"

"Actually, I'm not telling you they have criminal personalities at all. You have a person who once made some mistakes, maybe not even malicious ones. Perhaps it was just to cover up a basic incompetence. But it's a good time for him to step aside. The search is nearly complete anyway."

"And his choice of music director?"

"There I have to beg you to take action on your own. The man's a horse's ass."

The vestry had heard this from others, in and out of the choir. So, perhaps the Route 66 Choir's performance was a trigger, but it wasn't the cause of change at Holy Trinity.

Stan never admitted who wrote the juvenile lyrics for what turned out to be a farewell salute to his nemesis, but, of course, everyone knew the tune to "Goin' to the Chapel." The rebel choir's version was neither rock and roll nor a hymn, but many in the rest of the choir hummed along as they began: "*Going to the bathroom,/ we're going to the Bach-room.*"

The song did become more personal, though who in the quartet was in on the variations was never acknowledged: "*Haaat-ter get mar-ha-ha-ried, / Haaat-ter get married / to the one I did.*"

Perhaps the interim music director heard these words as he came down the stairs toward the choir room. When he reached the door, he was greeted with the worst: "*The choir is blue / (whoa-whoa-whoa) / Who'd you do? / whoo-whoo-whoo?*" And that's when Linda swung her backside at the mad Hatter to accentuate the point, figuratively knocking him from the room.

Though he might have felt a tiny tinge of remorse, Stan heard another tune and different words as he sang: "*Women and men, in age and youth, / can feel the Spirit, hear the call, / and find the way, the life, the truth.*"

Chapter 36: Not the Labor of My Hands

Stan's deceased father's ancient cousins dropped in the next week out of the blue. Alone at the house, Felicia--stunned because Stan had never told her about them--graciously took the four seniors to the den for tea and cookies. Having just come to terms with the vestry's decision about interim rector and choir director, she was sent reeling again by the existence of these relatives.

Stan, coming in from his bike ride with Chester, realized immediately how old his visitors were and how frail. He was embarrassed that he'd complained about his own aging.

Oscar, the oldest, reached his feet the most quickly to greet him, gathering momentum by tipping back in the high rocking chair and then virtually pitching himself into a standing position. "Woof!" he said, offering a surprised look through his thick, heavy framed glasses.

The two widowed sisters and the one old couple had been on a retirement outing, Stan quickly learned, coming now from Arkansas (visiting other family members) on their way through the Ozarks (several nights at a casino hotel) to Kansas (their home). They wanted to see poor Lars' son. No one had heard from him in such a long time. Felicia had raised her eyebrows and tried, embarrassed, to explain his reclusive ways.

Oscar's wife Olga had been sitting straight in the easy chair beside her husband. But when she stood, holding tightly to Oscar's left arm, Stan discovered that her thin body came in two distinct stages.

Arthritis had put an extra bend in her lower back, now revealed by her tubular pants suit. "So nice to see you," she said, nodding and extending a hand.

Shorter and heavier than Olga, cousin Hulda searched around the sofa for a place to push or pull on. In the end she had to lean out over the rug, maneuvering her rounded body into a position where it could stay forward as her legs unfolded beneath her. And the last cousin, Minna, whose weight was distributed more evenly on a tall frame, waited patiently until Stan came to her. She was the group's hummer, softly accompanying conversation with an undercurrent of tone and accent.

"Thank you, young man," she said, fully aware of his age.

What distracted Stan, beyond the time the old folks took rising and the enormity of their efforts, was the unselfconscious chatter they kept up about their own failing strength. "You'll have to help me to the driveway later," cheerfully announced Minna. "I might tumble across the yard." His lawn was made uneven by some large rocks.

"I've eaten more than my share of cookies, again," said plump Hulda. "One day I'll not be able to get up at all!"

Oscar whistled through his teeth as, at Stan's urging, he resettled himself. A big man, he had shrunk with age; but it was still a long reach from shoulder to toe. Olga, hiking her purse strap up her arm again, said, "I'm not much help for him, what with my hips so bad."

The old ones were all accustomed, Stan realized, to needing and taking time for any move. How they had made the trip to Fairfield from Branson was a mystery. And whether they could drive the three hours it would take to get back before dark, when their weak eyes would have trouble distinguishing form from shadow, was another question he didn't want to consider.

"Oscar," said Minna after they had given an update on the few remaining members of Stan's father's generation. "Oscar, have you shown them your book?" She spoke softly as do so many people who are hard of hearing. Looking around for a place to set her glass, she finally rested it on her knee.

"Oh? My book?" Oscar looked down beside the rocking chair he was sitting in. A paper bag, which Stan had not noticed when he came in, rested on the rug, its top closed and folded over. Oscar's eyes opened at the bag as if in surprise to find anything there, let alone this bag.

"He takes it everywhere," observed Olga, balancing her drink precariously on the arm of her easy chair. Hulda, who could not reach the end table from her place on the sofa, wedged her glass behind a pillow. Must remember it's there, thought Stan.

"Let's see what we have here," said Oscar. He leaned over slowly, trying to get a grip on the paper bag, grunting as if it contained a shelf of books. Finally he swung it up on his lap. Minna hummed in a satisfied way, probably unaware that others could hear her.

Oscar set his drink on a coaster on the end table and pulled a huge looseleaf notebook out of the bag. Several pages had pulled free of the rings and showed outside the blue canvas covers. "Do you know any songs?" he asked, folding open the book on his knees.

This was a hard question to answer other than affirmatively. Felicia saved Stan from silence. "Sure," she said brightly.

"Not as many as Oscar," smiled Hulda from the sofa, surely part of their routine.

"I've been collecting the words to popular songs-- oh, how long, Olga?"

"Must be sixty years, Oscar, nearly as long as we've been married." He opened the notebook, revealing the lyrics of songs handwritten on lined pages. They were arranged alphabetically, with sections for each letter separated by heavier, tabbed pages.

"Here are the A's," he explained. "'All of Me,' 'America the Beautiful,' 'As Time Goes By.'" It was an eclectic collection, whatever he had found over many years. There were hundreds of titles, perhaps thousands. Some pages were yellowed with age, frayed from turning.

"He's got everything," bragged Hulda" 'For All We Know,' 'Forever.' Tell where you get them."

"Not out of any books, let me tell you. I find people who know a song, and I get them to write it out for me, or even sing it. Others, I just listen to the radio and remember."

This collecting method might account for the fact that there was no music in Oscar's book. Of course, Stan didn't expect someone of his generation to use the Internet, but at least the lyrics might have been typed. With a good self-publishing software program and a laser printer, he could show Oscar a real book in half a day!

"Look," said Olga, leaning toward Felicia. "There are no K's." Indeed, when Oscar pulled open the book at the K-tab, there was only a single sheet of notebook paper. The words, "No K. Songs," were handwritten in the middle.

Surely there's some song beginning with a K, thought Stan: "'Keep or 'Kind . . . ' or 'Kiss . . .' Hmm."

"Now, Stan, I have something for you." Oscar reached down for his bag and hoisted it up to his lap. Again, it seemed heavier than expected. He put his leathery hand in and pulled out two rocks, yellowy-brown and the size of small melons, though not so round or smooth. "Here," he said.

Oscar was trying to stand and take the rocks over to Stan, but Felicia stepped over to him. "Thanks," she said. "Thanks very much. This so kind!"

"Those are genuine Ozark rocks," said Oscar, leaning back in his chair with a final gasp from his efforts. "I bought them in a store down at Branson. They'll go nice in your yard here, you bet."

Stan marveled at the politeness of the discussion which followed: how thoughtful this was of Oscar to have brought a gift; where the rocks might be placed; how important it was to have mementos. This is crazy, he thought. The yard already has Ozark rocks. The house is built on them!

After they'd gone, however, pieces of information rose to the surface of Stan's mind, things he must have learned in high school science and college geology courses. He recalled facts long buried under the material of his career, the trivia of small town life, his own retirement obsessions.

Ozark rocks like rhyolite, porphyry, and granite are igneous, that is, once-molten. They belong to the Precambrian era, the oldest geologic unit found on the earth's surface. The prominent rocky knobs, hills, and mountains of southern Missouri were exposed by erosion in the more than one billion years since their fiery formation.

Some peaks east of Fairfield made up a group of islands when seas covered today's Ozarks. After their liquid infancy and unstable adolescence, the area's rocks were washed by water and wind for millennia. Many times plant and animal life changed form and arrangement above them. The underlying rocks stood solid and essentially unchanging.

These tottering cousins--unlike his father, tragically--had survived as well, bending and bowing beneath the weight of years. Rough-hewn, uncomplicated, direct, their experience underlay much that went on in the world's present, perhaps even in Stan's own life. Ozark rocks themselves, they had endured with strengths that lay outside of intellect, sophistication, cleverness.

"Rock of ages, cleft for me," Stan thought, *"let me hide myself in thee."*

Chapter 37: The New Community of Love

"Why in the world haven't you ever told me about these cousins?"

Stan could see she was angry. How could he explain? While it was true he hadn't seen or heard from them in decades, that didn't seem enough of a reason to have pretended they didn't exist.

"I think . . . I think, in those days, when I was growing up, you were supposed to get on with your life after the war, even if you'd lost someone. So many people were without sons or husbands or brothers, my mother said. But the country was growing, everyone was building new houses and new lives. My dad's family, what there was of it, moved on. But Mom stayed where . . . where my father had last been stationed stateside. Fairfield wasn't a family seat."

Felicia frowned. "I know your father was an only child and that his parents had died young. But, obviously, you still had some relatives, on one side at least. I should have been told. Maybe not that they were coming today, if you didn't know . . . "

"I had no idea if they were still alive, or where they were. All through my childhood they lived far away. I guess there were letters or phone calls, but I was so young. They didn't--and we didn't--have much money for travel." He tried to remember what his mother had said about the Measures. "It's as if we'd broken off from the trunk and didn't know the tree was still there."

"Families were more separated in those days, if children moved away for education or jobs. And in the war."

"Well, Mom and I, we were also sort of professional recluses, now that I think about it. In those days, in our neighborhood, you were supposed to be a complete family--mother, father, two and one quarter children. And we weren't that. So, we tended to keep to ourselves."

"You're right: all Smiths and Joneses had one dog, one cat, perhaps a goldfish. Still, my family knew that everyone didn't match the formula."

"You knew and you didn't know. On Halloween, Mom would fill a basket with candy and put it by the front door, like everyone else. Lights were on in the house and on the porch. But most kids passed us by. Maybe they thought it would be painful for her to see brothers and sisters, their lives as full as the bags they carried. And, of course, each family had its two parents benevolently keeping watch from the street. They probably thought they were being kind to the war widow and her only son, the electronics weirdo, by leaving us alone."

"That's not true. We knew what had happened to your father, but we never ignored you. You were the one hiding out. You've told me how falling disillusioned you,.."

He winced. Still, after Stan had taken his trick-or-treating spill that fall--the holiday spirit knocked out of him as completely as his wind--he'd stayed home with his mother on the following Halloweens, ready to refill the basket for her sake. Pussy cats with whiskers, Howdy Doodys and Clarabells, the three nephews of Donald Duck skipped the Measure house as if it were haunted. And, in a sense, it was.

" I remember coming to your house," Felicia insisted. Seeing his faraway look, she tried to lighten

238

the tone. "We stopped at every home. Why miss out on more candy?"

Stan remembered thinking how all those costumed kids on the street had little in common, even though they believed they did. And he shared even less. We were all doomed to our unique personalities, he'd believed, each an item in the journal of unrepeatable results. We don't belong in any category that validates our existence.

He saw Felicia studying him.

Was it possible . . . had he been wrong? "Maybe . . . maybe I'm exaggerating." Could he see a Dorothy skipping up his sidewalk, the young Felicia in search of her scarecrow. "That was a long time ago, and, you must be right, some kids might have been there. I don't remember having to eat *that* many left over oatmeal cookies."

As if that were a signal, Felicia rose to begin clearing the plates and tea cups. But then she paused. "While I'm asking questions, please explain why you call your group the 'Route 66 Choir.' It seems I've been left out of your thought processes recently."

He got up to help, searching for the glass Hulda had wedged behind a pillow. "I don't know that the others agree, but I see Route 66 as the road of adventure, of lighting out for new territories, somewhere better than this."

Stan recalled his watch tower retreat, high on a hill overlooking the landscape of his growing up. He knew he was isolated in there, only a telephone (which he never used) connecting him to the rest of the world. But he'd also been able to see the Mother Road from his tower, Route 66 winding its way east and west. In his conscious mind after his Halloween

239

tumble, he'd been steadfastly cynical. But, deeper in his mind--or his heart--this famous highway had represented freedom, a means of escape.

Felicia understood. "So, you rebels are saying orthodoxy does not contain you. Free voices create new worlds?"

As so often happened, she put into words his own thoughts.

"Well, yes, I guess that's right. Now, I've answered your questions. You tell me why Linda Cooper came by yesterday." Stan had slipped away when he heard Felicia greet the financial consultant at the front doorway. After biking alone on the Oroginee Watkins Trail, he saw that Felicia had seemed happy, though he couldn't guess why.

"The Oval," she explained, "the skating rink egg, revival of 1950s innocence, has imploded, collapsed upon itself."

"Humpty Dumpty?"

"Had a big fall and we got the smell of rotten eggs."

"Hydrogen sulfide, I know that, made some in our basement once. But where is Over-Due in all this? Do you have a contract? Will there be a place for us nostalgia buffs to skate?"

"Not to skate, but the prospects for the Road House have gone up, and the DC is likely to be revived at the same time by a different set of backers."

Stan had never frequented that teenage gathering place. Nursing a vanilla cream root beer at Hillcrest Drugs was as close as he ever came to participating in a high school social scene; and there he was never really in any of the key groups of milk shake drinkers or the sundae eaters at the counter.

"So, you and Meg and Donna have a new contract with Mayle?"

"Oh, no Mayle is out. Linda Cooper found out more about his investors, a somewhat unsavory group, it turns out. We should have known, or at least suspected, from his previous ventures that his idea of 'entertainment' was not a return to pre-1960's amusement."

She went on to explain that Mayle's kaleidoscopes could, with a twist of a hidden, second wheel, move their colored patterns of geometric shapes aside, allowing the viewer to assemble female and male body parts in unusual combinations. His card shuffler contained an extra deck in a secret compartment that soldiers far from home might wear thin in their loneliness.

Reviewing the past investments of The Oval's backers, Linda suspected the female employees, asked to roller skate with patrons for a dollar, were to have rooms at Stony Court. The sculpted figures at the rink's center might be used in suggestive poses for private parties.

"So, you abandoned the project?"

"We did a bit more than that. We assembled what we'd learned from Linda and passed it on to town council. I do believe even that profit-minded assembly has decided to require some additional specifications about the plans. And that will inspire the project to evaporate."

"Or move to another city."

"Maybe, but with the Internet, word about such things can spread quickly. It will be hard for other elected officials to claim they are out of the loop. And in all this scurrying around, Linda found new funding for the Road House and the DC. We'll be busy now on two design projects."

"So, if you could just get a new priest for Holy Trinity, your life might be shaping up."

"I liked the Rev. Wright, but I'm also finding, the more I learn about the Hightowers, the more I like them. Of course, I still have an electronics weirdo husband inciting rebellion."

"Hey, I was just the catalyst. There was going to be an explosion with or without me."

Felicia admitted, "Folks did get on the bandwagon once it became clear they would have support." She recalled the words from a hymn the Hightowers had said was a favorite: "*Together met, together bound, / we'll go our different ways, / and as his people in the world, / we'll live and speak his praise.*"

"You know," Stan offered, "there is a way to bring the electronics weirdo back into the system."

"I hope it involves Catwoman requiring a trick from Robin."

Chapter 38: The Portals of your Heart

At the reception hosted by Larry and Susie (Bell) Thornton, the Reverends Hightower told a story about a couple who had been in Ruth and Bob's first church. Felicia was pleased at how gracefully they traded the role of narrator.

A young husband and wife, Bob explained, had taken on the ambitious project of remodeling an old house in a small Illinois town which lay, like Fairfield, on the path of historic Route 66. Ruth added that their experience was also about *"a temple, set apart / . . adorned with love and joy.* Bob began the account, but they alternated in the telling.

> *Our friend, Helen, finally admitted one day that she'd never fix the old doorbell herself. "Tell Ruth," she told her husband, "I'm ready to go with her to sweet talk her friend with the lathe."*

Felicia made a mental note: Ruth had friends who made things. She liked that. Ruth stepped in to continue the story.

> *Wayne didn't know she was planning a secret party for his 40th birthday (conveniently on February 14th) and wanted the doorbell repaired in time for the event. He just assumed she'd finally conceded help was necessary on some restoration projects. They loved the 150-year-old house on High Street, knowing when they bought it that some things would have to be fixed or replaced. But Helen wanted to do everything herself.*

"I want to feel my own hands have shaped our house," she insisted.

"Ah, yes, 'sweat equity,'" Wayne said. He sometimes saw things in the terms of his profession."

"Well, that's the new term, I guess, but it's an old idea, that your touch has entered the wood, the plaster, the polished metal. Ours will join the Stillwaters,'" They had lived in the two-story frame house for generations. The Evers, amazingly, were the first owners outside the family. "And, as you know," Helen concluded, "I do my own Valentine's Day cards for a reason."

Wayne was stumped. Because their budget was stretched with the purchase, he had agreed to take on any tasks they could do themselves. Handwriting cards meant they were able to afford more small pleasures for Isabel and Benedict, their children.

The doorbell was a small item, but Helen felt it mattered as much as anything. "It announces company," she argued, and entertaining friends and family was their chief social activity in this small town. She also felt Wayne worked too much, so any chore that took him away from spreadsheets, data bases, and small cap/large cap calculations was beneficial."

This particular doorbell was one of the old twist kinds set in a round brass plate with the word "Welcome" embossed around the edge. Rather than push a button or pull a cord, you turned a flat disk on a little shaft that went through the door. It spun a ringer inside a metal hemisphere on the other side. The metal produced a brrrrt sound, like an old bicycle bell, that just might be heard upstairs.

Wayne balked when he saw that the shaft was actually broken, a part missing. "In this one case, why don't we just get a new doorbell? You know, the button you push closes the electrical circuit that sounds the chime in the kitchen?"

She stuck out her lower lip in the faux pout that had made him fall in love with her fifteen years earlier. It meant she truly wanted to fix the doorbell but would sacrifice her desire for him if he insisted. She claimed she ought to be able to find something herself that would work as a substitute part.

He sighed. "Let me ask around. Maybe someone at church or the office knows someone who knows someone who does doorbells."

But several weeks passed, and he'd turned up only one lead: Ruth, who, with two other women, was doing some charity work for the local historical society, told Wayne at church about a retired friend with a lathe. He had worked in St. Louis as a machinist for Chrysler, but retired and kept up a small trade for local hobbyists."

Helen complained, "Lathe Guy would be doing the real work. I'd just be installing the product of his hands."

"He's done lots of things for Res-Cue," explained Wayne.

Bob interrupted the story at this point to explain that Res-Cue was Ruth's redecorating company, currently working on what had been a living church years ago, recently declared a historic building. Felicia's eyes looked like saucers. "This woman and I are soul-mates!" Stan wondered at the coincidence.

Ruth then continued with the account, explaining that she told Helen Res-Cue liked to stay true to original design, historical accuracy.

Wayne insisted, 'People do like to help.'"

"She knew he was right about this, but pouted anyway."

Wayne scoured old stores and antique shops in the area, but the dealers claimed no one kept such mechanical devices any more. He had located antique doorbells just like the one they had for sale on e-Bay. And there were modern replicas of the old style available through specialty dealers. But he found it hard to justify the expense, so he didn't tell Helen about these options. A brand new unit, in a contemporary style, would cost about a fifth of what replacement with an authentic doorbell would run.

She didn't tell him what she'd learned about the Stillwaters. Once a prominent family, the children had moved away to big cities and another way of life. The grandparents held on for years, hiding from the other generations their increasingly restricted lives. Outliving their contemporaries, they stopped going out, had no visitors but one faithful neighbor, withered and faded into the very air of a dusty and neglected house. Helen would bring their home back to life, the way it had been.

Wayne couldn't guess her growing urgency about the doorbell: his birthday was the next Saturday. Fifty friends from church, the neighborhood, and the bank had been told to gather on the expansive front porch at 7:26 p.m for a 'demi-luxe gala.' One was to turn the doorbell. And the doorbell was supposed to ring!

So Helen told him on Wednesday at dinner that she wanted to see Felicia's friend with the lathe immediately.

Benedict, who was five, shared his mother's passion but didn't know how clever his manner of expressing it was. "It's the key to everything in our home, Dad!"

His sister, nine, saw it all as an fanciful adventure. "Remember when Mary Poppins floats down on her umbrella and rings the doorbell at the Banks' house? She'd be standing at our door all day, and we wouldn't know it."

"She could use a cell phone," muttered Wayne, but he saw that he was outnumbered.

"No, Dad. It has to be the old way, a doorbell. It's how it's always been." How could she know, thought Wayne, even as he marveled at her insight.

"She's right, Wayne. It's small town, close community, tradition--mechanical doorbell."

On the night of the party, Wayne, still in the dark about his birthday surprise and unaware that the doorbell had been fixed, heard the ring. "Company?" he wondered out loud. To himself, he added, "At least, the doorbell issue must be closed, thanks to Mr. Tinker." He went back to crunching numbers on his laptop.

Helen had promised him time to work before they got out the dessert, which she claimed was

247

in a cake box in the kitchen. But she looked up briefly from her knitting and pouted. "You get it," she said.

Wayne could hear Benedict and Isabel giggling at the top of the stairs.

"You know, I am the old guy here, and . . . and . . oh well."

"Surprise!" they cheered, the dozens of friends blowing into their hands against the cold.

Bob chuckled, observing that he and Ruth had been among the group, perhaps more pleased than anyone. And Ruth concluded the story.

"Come in, come in!" cried Wayne's family, who had snuck up behind him.Later, when the guests were gone, children in bed, and Helen washing the last of the dishes in the kitchen,Wayne went out on the porch. In the cold and the dark he rang the bell softly and sang, "Happy birthday to me.'"

Felicia knew another song: "*our hearts to thee we open wide; / let us thy inner presence feel; / thy grace and love in us reveal.*" These are the priests for us, she thought, if only we can convince them to come to Holy Trinity.

Stan had stopped listening midway through the story. Where was the security system in that house? A doorbell is good, but a modern, electrical, alarm system keeps out the people you don't want in.

When he imagined Wayne going out on the porch to ring the doorbell, though, Stan recalled seeing himself in the fog-free mirror. Who was in? Who was out? If the doorbell rang in visitors, what was the purpose of a church bell? And could the choir be seen as echoing those church bells, calling in anyone who was alone?

Chapter 39: Men Made Strange

"122 over 84. Not precisely where I'd like it to be, but acceptable," said Dr. Montgomery, pulling her stethoscope from her ears and letting the bell fall to her chest. She smiled. Stan assumed she was claiming the credit for his good check-up.

"I've been much more regular in the biking, three times a week, unless the weather is bad. You should try it yourself," he said, then realized he was not advising her on health matters but wondering just how good she'd look on a bicycle.

"One day, maybe. I'm a runner, at least while my legs will let me."

"Well, yes, that's good. Jogging is popular."

"I got my personal best at the Marine Corps Marathon in D.C. last year, but they say distance runners continue to improve through their thirties. How is your singing?"

He'd forgotten he'd told her about music as a way of reducing tension and lowering his blood pressure. "You know . . . you know, that's worked out better than I thought."

"You have your own group, as I recall."

"No, no, I may have said something about trying to start one, but it turns out the church choir is, really, quite satisfying." He chuckled. "After all, I'm still learning, and I've got some coaches, veterans who are bringing me along."

"So, anxiety is less. That's good." Now she paused, studying his chart. "Um, Mr. Measure, I think we can leave your medication where it is; no change there. But, one of the times you were in, I see here, you talked about . . . about, occasionally, having trouble making love, not always being able . . . "

"I think that was a temporary thing. Reaction to stress. My wife, too, she was doing so much--she has her own business, you know, and was chair of the committee looking for our new rector, and . . . and, well, there was me to look after."

She laughed, "The retired husband who's around the house all the time."

"Right. But now we think we have a new priest. It's not official, but Fel's told me, we're just waiting for the paperwork to make it final. And her business has scaled back its plans for the next year. We're doing . . . pretty good . . . together."

He could tell from her smile that his smile was positively goofy. "Okay then, no medicine change for you. Shall I see you in . . . six months, unless you feel there's a problem?"

"That works for me. I'll stop at the desk."

He made his appointment with Dr. Montgomery, rather than Dr. Heady, not knowing exactly why or what it might mean. But, what the heck, she didn't seem to mind. Maybe, though, he should tell Felicia about the new, young, attractive physician? Still, he was old enough to be her father! What was there to confess?

He'd told Dr. Montgomery the truth about his frame of mind: there was a deeper satisfaction with his life in retirement. Perhaps he should have mentioned that Felicia, on the other hand, had added one more concern to her life. With Larry Thornton, Robin Shure, and a few others she was organizing a grass roots political movement to question the nation's longterm military goals.

Sonja Petersen's Anti-War Womb was too radical for them--demanding a complete dissolution of our armed forces. This new group, Lysistrata (Stan didn't know why it was called that), sought to broaden the public debate, soliciting new voices, especially those who generally stayed out of politics--the young, the poorly educated, the disaffected.

She was, Stan had always known, remarkable for her ability to bring people together, often those who thought they had nothing in common. And each one was somehow better in the group than standing alone. She strove, as the words of the hymn said, to have *"love to the loveless shown / that they might lovely be."* Although he had never understood--and didn't really care to--the theological meaning of the trinity, he felt her magic with people vaguely analogous to the three-in-one, or one-in-three, or whatever it was.

Although Stan was unaware, the Reverends Hightower were already key figures in Lysistrata. Bob a veteran, and Ruth, a spouse who had raised children when he was overseas, understood the costs of war. And they were alarmed at the lack of community awareness of the strain felt by military families in the current conflict. Like Felicia, they feared a war that would not, according to the government, end in this generation's lifetime.

While these folks were set on changing the world, Stan had less lofty ambitions: bringing the Route 66 Choir to the whole church. Actually, the number of rebels had officially doubled since Hatter moved on (rumor had it he was going to train aspiring conductors at a special music camp near Kansas City--poor innocents!). The Perfect Third joined Robin as an alto, and Melody sang soprano with Linda. Marvin Barnes was a second bass, and--surprise, surprise!-- Bill Lynne wanted to sing tenor.

"Tom can't stand it, but I've always admired Ralph Stanley, that high lonesome blues sound. And, frankly," he told Stan, "you could use some help."

When he'd launched the campaign, Stan would have been unhappy at a second voice on his part. But he had gained such confidence that he felt he could sing from that deep place inside, not just try to match Bill's sound. And wasn't this, in the end, not just about him? They were bringing harmony through music to everyone in Holy Trinity.

That would happen the following Sunday when the eight rebel choristers were to sing "Angel Band" as a prelude. In the shower that morning Stan began to think about how he had come, improbably, to found a musical group. He did it, of course, while examining himself in his fog free mirror.

"So, Buzz," he asked his reflection, "I thought you were an actor and a securities system specialist. When did you decided to become the next Nat King Cole, getting your kicks on Route 66?"

"Well, I suppose it was when the country changed, not so much during the 60s but later. Those revolutions had their effect, and my role as archetypal Roadie seemed less relevant, especially as we neared the end of the millennium."

"I know what you mean. That's kind of how I felt when I retired, My kids were grown, Fel had her own interests, I was more in the way than on the way to anywhere."

Buzz rubbed his chin, feeling for whiskers that might have been missed. "I was surprised at how much I enjoyed singing. I'd always been good at it--well, I'd always been good at *everything*--but, when I get into a song now--really get into it--something inside comes free. It feels as good as riding down that open road in a brand new Corvette convertible or on a Harley."

Stan thought about that. "Say, did it affect your love life? I mean, I seem to, ah, to perform much better."

Buzz raised his eyebrows. "You're singing while you . . . while you . . . ?"

Stan laughed. "Oh, no. At least I haven't been. But now that you mention it . . . "

"The woman I'm with now, Samantha, she has three sisters who also sing. Can you believe it? A quartet backup! Of course, I'm not talking about any group stuff."

Stan had not logged into ii/w is a couple of weeks. He'd lost the desire or was just too busy. Nor did he know, by the way, exactly where he'd last put his Spider-man suit.

"Hey, Buzz, in real life, you ever fixed a toilet?"

"Stan, what man hasn't? I even had one start leaking in my trailer when we were doing the show. Somewhere in Missouri, I think it was. I could hear the darn thing all the way in the kitchen!"

"What'd you do to stop it from running?"

"Maybe I shouldn't say. I was pretty desperate. And I'd tried all the old remedies."

"Adjusting the chain, getting a new stopper, bending the float stem?"

"Right! You've been there."

"I think the farthest I ever went . . . have you ever blown eggs for Easter?"

"Sure, as a kid." He paused. "What does that have to do with a toilet's leaking."

"Oh! Oh, nothing, I was suddenly thinking of something else. I mean, this *is* Easter. Say, we're weird people, aren't we? Men."

"I'll say," said Felicia. She'd slipped in to ask if he was ever going to finish in the shower. And hadn't he said he needed to be there early to sing?

"Oh, who am I?" thought Stan. *"Here might I stay and sing, / no story so divine . . . / This is my friend, / in whose sweet praise / I all my days / could gladly spend."*

Chapter 40: Choirs of Jerusalem

Linda began the prelude without accompaniment. The other three members of the original Route 66 Choir joined at the refrain: "*Oh, come, angel band,/ Come and around me stand; / Oh, bear me away on your snowy wings / To my eternal home.*"

Felicia was in the congregation; folded in her bulletin was the text of an announcement that the Revs. Hightower would be their next rector. They had privately convinced Melody to lead the choir for one year. She realized how much she had enjoyed directing, and the middle school seemed to have passed through its difficult phase and settled into a comfortable mode. So Felicia's major goals at Holy Trinity were approaching fulfillment.

Stan felt his voice matching Linda's soprano in "Angel Band," but an octave lower--"*to sweet new strains attune your theme*"--then blending with Robin's at the proper interval.

Robin had begun building an ark on her property in the county. There would be a parade of sculpted animals, she told Felicia, marching out of the woods toward a gangplank.

"It's the big project I've been moving toward-- without knowing it, of course--for years. I had these odd creatures scattered around the place in all sorts of poses--standing, lying down, at full run." And they were strange for this locale: a South American agouti, the siamang from Southeast Asia, a small herd of African duikers. "I wasn't sure why I chose them."

"And now you know?"

"I think I do: each represented a different challenge to my art. It's easier to represent something you've known about or seen all your life. But you find out about these unusual species--well, unusual for small town Midwesterners, I guess--and you have to call on different parts of the imagination to build them. The next thing to do is bring them all together."

Linda sang another verse: "I know I'm near the holy ranks of friends & kindred dear / I've brushed the dew on Jordan's banks, the crossing must be near / I've almost gained my Heavenly home, my spirit loudly sings."

Felicia thought about her first boyfriend, Tom Baettner, who according to Meg, had recently been in touch with one of her husband's friends, a career Army officer. Apparently Tom had been in self-imposed exile from the United States for decades, angered at what he felt was a loss of national will after Vietnam. Now, he thought, as the world's only superpower, we could put that failure behind us. And he was considering reenlisting to be part of major campaigns to demonstrate our right to lead the world.

The double quartet came in for the refrain, and the sound was rich and full of feeling: *"joining heaven and earth again / links to one commonweal the twain."*

Stan looked at Jean Triplet, who stood opposite him in the group's tight semi-circle. She'd become much more outgoing in the choir since her return and, at a recent rehearsal, gave an impressive impromptu explanation of the kind of work she was studying. Chester had noticed the diagram of a semiconductor chip among her papers.

"Are you building a computer?" he asked, pointing to the sheet.

She smiled. "Well, if you can get together enough atoms to store qubits in their ion traps."

"This ought to give you enough atoms," he held up a pencil and tapped the lead. "But I'm out of qubits, and my last ion trap is at the pawn shop."

Again, she laughed, but then became more serious. "Even if we had these things, it's how they all go together that makes engineering fun. Parts are easy; a system that functions with those parts is where genius figures in."

Stan thought about Over-Due and their design projects: the old Fanny's Dairy Delite, a new Road House, the once envisioned but now defunct Oval. His wife and her friends were good at combining things. He'd never understood why Felicia wanted certain pictures in one room, this afghan on the back of that couch, flowers arranged just so in a vase in the middle of the dining room table. Once he'd hammered the nail and straightened the frame, he never saw what was on the wall. When he napped, he was satisfied with whatever settled to the contours of his body. So long as there was enough to eat, it didn't matter what colors shone beyond the plate.

On the other hand, he himself knew the ideal control panel for that set of motion detectors, how big a power supply was needed to serve so much square footage, the best keypad for entering and resetting codes. But those things, he knew, were testable; how did Fel decide that the church supper needed a triangular or a crescent shaped floral arrangement?

"I know I'm near the holy ranks of friends & kindred dear, / I've brushed the dew on Jordan's banks, the crossing must be near / I've almost gained my Heavenly home, my spirit loudly sings."

The bass voices provided a foundation beneath the melody's gentle flight just as Chester's trees provided structures for buildings around the globe. Stan had

258

recently visited the sawmill, impressed by the heavy machinery moving logs four feet in diameter steadily from piles in a field onto conveyor belts through buildings for sawing and out to sorting chutes as lumber.

The veteran sawyer watched a computer screen on which an application analyzed each log, determined how the most pieces could be cut from it, and then-- giant pincers working as extensions of his hands and arms--positioning it this way, then that. The log passed back and forth into the spinning blade, the process repeated so quickly that Stan was dizzy.

In the office Chester and his son surveyed maps of forest tracks for sale in a three state area, reviewed market prices in Europe versus those in Asia, analyzed projections for economic growth or decline. To operate at a profit, the mill had to run eight hours a day, five days a week, fifty weeks a year. A failure in one part of the business could put forty people out of work. At the end of the tour, Stan was grateful to be retired.

After the eight Route 66 choristers sang, "The Holy ones, behold they come, I hear the noise of wings," the rest of the choir, and even some in the congregation, came in with the refrain: "Oh, come, angel band,/ Come and around me stand; / Oh, bear me away on your snowy wings / To my eternal home."

Stan heard Sharon Rich's powerful voice rise up from the congregation and wondered if there was a point where she might yodel. Could Larry Thornton begin another impassioned 9/11 speech, the singers dropping down to double piano as his voice rose above theirs? Would he talk again about the need for patience and love even in times of adversity, James

Fenimore Cooper's characters composing themselves in a cave hidden by a waterfall?

So many gifts in this church, Stan thought. Well, it must be true for the town of Fairfield, America, the world itself. But could they coordinate their efforts? *"And we, as these his deeds we sing, / his suppliant soldiers, pray our King, / that in his palace, bright and vast, / we may keep watch and ward at last."*

Listening to the singing spread into the congregation, Felicia wondered if Stan realized how much had gone on around him that led to this moment. She was thinking not just about what Larry and she had done to focus the church profile, guide others to the selection of the Hightowers, drop hints that brought Melody back. She recalled also talks with Meg and Donna that helped restore her appreciation of her loner husband.

She was grateful she'd never brought the children into a discussion of their marriage, though she knew she could count on them if it were ever necessary. With all the usual friction in a family, those bonds are still the most basic, the most enduring.

Her old alliance with Robin and a surprising new relationship with Linda had also underscored the network of friends in her community, uncovering hidden elements in Mayle's plans for The Oval. On a grander scale she hoped Lysistrata would also link up with community efforts in other places to reexamine the nation's identity after 9/11, a groundswell of healthy self-examination.

She would be pleased to learn in the weeks ahead that Stan had, in fact, come to acknowledge many of the forces around him which had brought harmony to his immediate surroundings. He would, of course, in private talks with Fel, claim far more of the credit than he deserved. But she knew that was only to her, only for effect.

Felicia, who, in fact, sang quite well, added her voice to the growing chorus; "The latest sun is sinking fast, my race is nearly run." She hoped they still had many years together to act on their discoveries. It did seem, perhaps, that the "strongest trials now are past, . . . triumph is begun."

Felicia sought, and found, Stan's eye as the entire church sang one more time, "Oh, come, angel band,/ Come and around me stand; / Oh, bear me away on your snowy wings / To my eternal home."

The End

Epilogue: Every Creature Praiseth

Many of the new rectors' sermons were memorable, especially the one Bob delivered at Christmas that year. The congregation didn't realize it immediately, but he was talking about himself. He referred to the protagonist in the third person, "Bob." As the sermon progressed, however, he gave clues that the "Bob" of his story was his younger self. As she listened, Felicia also began to suspect Ruth had influenced the message. The sermon began:

> For more than forty years, Bob failed to understand how he dropped the ball. I don't mean metaphorically, but literally. At the age of five or six, of course, Bob did not yet think in figurative terms. Seeing symbolically, in fact, is a gift this fellow hasn't developed as much as a minister should (that's what he became when he grew up), since they're always reading and interpreting scripture on many levels.
>
> The dropped ball occurred not long after Bob received his first baseball glove, a hand-me-down, to be sure. His older brother needed a more adult model to participate in Pee-Wee League, so he passed on his old, beginner's, child-size mitt to the runt of the family.
>
> With his father, Bob had learned to catch a tennis ball, not the true baseball, which would almost certainly have caused injuries. And on summer afternoons he practiced his new skill alone by fielding rebounds off the stoop in front of the house and catching balls thrown straight up (or as straight as he could throw them) over his head. There was no reason he should have

missed that young man's easy, under-armed throw.

In the town of Bob's childhood some households let rooms to college students. The single-income families did not necessarily enjoy post-War prosperity in the 1960s and often sought ways to bring in extra income. Bob's next door neighbors, for instance, had student lodgers in the finished room of their basement for many of those years.

On that one day, the current McGregors' lodger was crossing the lawn on his way to campus, two-thirds of a mile away. An errant toss from Bob (well, it was "Bobby" then) bounced in his path. The young man scooped it up one-handed and prepared to flip it back to Bobby, in eager if stumbling pursuit.

"Ready?" he asked, smiling.

"Ready," Bobby responded confidently. He watched the young man's arm go back, then come forward, and the ball arched toward him. He turned the glove on his left hand palm up to trap the ball in the pocket. He would bring his right hand on top to secure it: snap!

Bobby couldn't understand that day--nor could the older Bob for decades--how the ball, instead of settling into his glove as usual, landed more than a yard in front of him and rolled to his feet. He looked up in disbelief. What sort of trick pitch was this? And why did that man, who seemed so friendly, embarrass him with this sort of legerdemain? He was baffled.

That sharp picture of a moment's confusion faded, nearly disappeared, but came back into focus on rare occasions like the day Robert was supposed to meet his new daughter-in-law. As always, he counted on his wife to handle the social amenities.

Robert's wife (Ruth) always had a store of presents she would discover throughout the year on sale in gift shops, curio stores, antique shops. Often she had no idea who would receive her shrewd purchases, but she knew their value and waited for appropriate occasions. Robert admitted he sometimes complained about the time spent shopping, but marveled that she was always ready for the birth of a baby, the graduation of a nephew, a surprise retirement. And her gifts were little things, remarkably inexpensive. Would she have the right item for Richard's bride?

Their oldest son was the rebel in the family, leaving college early to enter the Peace Corps, working summers in Alaskan fisheries so he could make pots all winter, marrying this "Sali" after knowing her only two months. Robert and Ruth had not even seen a picture! But now the couple was coming across the country for Christmas, and everyone was eager to meet her.

"Find a red wine," Ruth told her husband as the doorbell rang. She'd been cooking while others were out searching for the perfect Christmas tree. Robert had been happy to let his daughter, the middle child, lead that party, especially when it was agreed her younger siblings would participate. Robert and Ruth could get the house, the dinner, and themselves ready.

"We can meet this young woman without pandemonium," he said to Ruth, who wouldn't have been rattled in any case.

Opening the cabinet in the pantry, Robert heard the usual joyful sounds of a mother greeting a child she hadn't seen in a year, the more subdued tones of Rich's introduction, a soft greeting from the new family member.

And another voice? A child's voice! What was this?

"Robert, come quickly. We have a grandchild."

The child and her mother were beautiful, Robert thought then, a slim young Asian woman and a smiling toddler bundled in a winter coat at least one size too big. He sees them as even more beautiful now.

In her pew, Felicia thought the words of a hymn: "*All thy creation serveth its Creator, / thee every creature praiseth without ceasing.*" Stan wondered how he would behave when daughter or son brought home someone to meet the parents.

Richard hugged his father, who had always been uncomfortable with physical contact. "Dad, this is Sali. And here is Yao, my son."

Robert remembered taking a young Rich sledding. Back then he found great pleasure in father and son activities. Sometimes, on the fast hills, the boy would ask to ride on his dad's back, both squealing with joy as they flew down the ice. They would compete in telling the tale to Mom when they returned, gloves wet and noses running.

Sali held out her hand, and Robert had to will his to shake it, he was so startled. "So . . . so . . . nice to . . . meet you. Richard told us . . . " He hadn't told them!

Where, for heaven's sake, was Ruth! This wasn't the time to leave him alone just to make sure the ham was baking, a pie cooling, cranberries bubbling.

"Our things are in the rental car," Rich said, "but we can get them later." He took Sali's coat and his own to hang in the hall closet. She was kneeling to extract Yao's arms from his sleeves. Robert looked past them across the snow at a kind of car he didn't recognize. Must be a hybrid.

Then Ruth slipped by him to put an arm around Sali and usher them toward the family room. Yao latched onto one of Richard's fingers, and Robert made sure the front door was firmly closed. He felt positively dizzy.

"This is for you," Ruth was saying and gave Sali a pin decorated with images of bamboo, pine, and plum. "I know it's not your New Year yet, but I found this last summer in St. Louis. I hope you like it."

"It's lovely," smiled Sali and showed it to Rich. Ruth gave her a hug.

"And for you, my newest love, this was my son's favorite when he was your age."

"I thought you'd given that away years ago!" Richard laughed. He slipped down on the carpet with Yao. It was his first book, made of fabrics, each distinctive to touch, presenting a Christmas trip by sleigh to Grandmother's

house. The bright shapes of green tree, white snowman, and many colored houses were cut from wool, felt, silk. While there were no words, Ruth had told the story of the journey in vivid detail, differently every time

"Snap!" said the Reverend Hightower with such vigor half of Holy Trinity's congregation jumped.

Snap, that was it! Bob hadn't, as a five-year-old boy, been catching balls pitched to him at all. Rather, his father had been expertly throwing balls into his mitt. The man's skills were polished, the boy's just forming; but together the ball was passed.

The preacher paused so his listeners could connect the two stories. Stan imagined the ball's flight and its rolling to a boy's foot. Felicia kept the image of Ruth, Richard, and Yao in her mind's eye: "*Three in a wondrous Unity unbroken.*" When he continued, The Rev. Hightower dropped the third person.

My neighbor, the college student, hadn't known he was responsible for the success of a catch, of course. Expecting the five-year-old me to judge his toss, move to the right spot, position my glove--that was too much to ask of such a young man. Maybe you have to be a father yourself--well," he glanced back at Ruth, who sat behind him by the altar. "*Or a mother, of course.*"

The congregation tittered.

"*At that age, I had simply not progressed enough to handle random tosses. No fault, of course, again, of the student. And maybe, now that I think about it so many years later, it was not so much a failure for me, but an experience*

I could learn from, even this many years after the fact and share with you.

Amen.

A surprising number in attendance that day at Holy Trinity concluded that that *is* what parents do: they throw the ball directly into the mitt. Merry Christmas to all!

Route 66 books by Michael Lund

Growing Up on Route 66 — Michael Lund (2000) ISBN 1-888725-31-1 Novel evoking fond memories of what it was like to grow up alongside "America's Highway" in 20th Century Missouri. (Trade paperback) 5x8 260 pp,

Route 66 Kids — Michael Lund (2002) ISBN 1-888725-70-2 Sequel to *Growing Up on Route 66*, continuing memories of what it was like to grow up alongside "America's Highway" in 20th Century Missouri. (Trade paperback) 5x8 270 pp,

A Left-hander on Route 66--Michael Lund (2003) ISBN 1-888725-88-5. Twenty years after the fact, left-hander Hugh Noone appeals a wrongful conviction that detoured him from "America's Main Street" and put him in jail. But revealing the details of the past and effecting a resolution of his case mean a dramatic rearrangement of his world, including troubled relationships with three women: Linda Roy, Patty Simpson, and Karen Murphy. (Trade paperback) 5x8 270 pp,

Route 66 Spring-- Michael Lund (2004) ISBN: 1-888725-98-2. The lives of four young Missourians are changed when a bottle comes to the surface of one of the state's many natural springs. Inside is a letter written by a girl a dozen years after the end of the Civil War. Lucy Rivers Johns ' epistle contains a sad story of family failure and a powerful plea for help. This message from the last century crystallizes the individual frustrations of Janet Masters, Freddy Sills, Louis Clark, and Roberta Green, another group of Route 66 kids. Their response to the past charts a bold path into the future, a path inspired by the Mother Road itself. (Trade paperback) 5x8 270 pp,

Miss Route 66--Michael Lund (2004) ISBN 1-888725-96-6. In the fourth novel of Michael Lund's Route 66 Novel Series, Susan Bell tells the story of her candidacy in Fairfield, Missouri's annual beauty contest. Now married and with teenage children in St. Louis, she recounts her youthful adventure in this small town along "America's Highway." At the same time, she plans a return to Fairfield in order to right injustices she feels were done to some young contestants in the Miss Route 66 Pageant. (Trade paperback) 5½ X8¼, 260 pp,
   Audiobook on 5 CD's ISBN 1-888725-12-5

Route 66 to Vietnam Michael Lund (2004) ISBN 1-59630-000-0 This novel takes characters from earlier works in the Route 66 Novel Series farther west than Los Angeles, official destination of the famous highway, Route 66. Mark Landon and Billy Rhodes find the values they grew up on challenged by America's role in Southeast Asia. But elements of their upbringing represented by the Mother Road also sustain them in ways they could never have anticipated. . (Trade paperback) 5½ X8¼, 270 pp,

AudioBook on CD—Route 66 to Vietnam ISBN: 1-59630-011-6 Michael Lund's fictional commentary from the viewpoint of a draftee. by Michael Lund unabridged 6 CD's --9 hours running time.

Route 66 Chapel Michael Lund (2006) ISBN 1-59630-012-4 Route 66 Chapel, Michael Lund (2006) (Trade paperback) 5½ X8¼, 260 pp, When the forces of progress threaten the foundation of smalltown life—a small church—five senior citizens, a mysterious newcomer, and one young couple band together in an unlikely campaign to save it. The embattled meeting point of old and new is Route 66 Chapel, a building curiously linked to America's "Mother Road."

Route 66 Choir-- A Comedy (2010)

Michael Lund ISBN 9781596300583   284 pp 5" x 8"   In Route 66 Choir Stanley Measure takes early retirement just before September 11, 2001, and his impulsive decisions participate in an unraveling of confidence in the American way of life. His wife Felicia finds that everything she holds dear is in danger of coming apart: her marriage, her church, her business, and even her country. Who or what can orchestrate the recovery of harmony necessary to sustain the spirit of the Mother Road?

Route 66 Bride (Fall 2010)

Educators Discount Policy

To encourage use of our books for education, educators can purchase three or more books (mixed titles) on our standard discount schedule for resellers. See **sciencehumanitiespress.com/** for more detail or call Science & Humanities Press, PO Box 7151, Chesterfield MO 63006-7151636-394-4950

Our books are guaranteed:

If a book has a defect, or doesn't hold up under normal use, or if you are unhappy in any way with one of our books, we are interested to know about it and will replace it and credit reasonable return shipping costs. Products with publisher defects (i.e., books with missing pages, etc.) may be returned at any time without authorization. However, we request that you describe the problem, to help us to continuously improve.

Order Form

Item	Eac	Quantity	Amount
Missouri (only) sales tax .6.925%			
Priority Shipping			$5.00
	Tot		

Name

Address

BeachHouse
Books

www.beachhousebooks.com

an Imprint of
Science & Humanities Press
PO Box 7151
Chesterfield, MO 63006-7151
(636) 394-4950